INFLUENCE

SISTERS OF WRATH

BOOK TWO

SIENNA SNOW

Untitled

INFLUENCE

by

Sienna Snow

Cover Design: Steamy Designs

Editor: Jennifer Haymore

www.siennasnow.com

ISBN - eBook - 979-8-88535-041-9

ISBN - Paperback Print - 979-8-88535-042-6

ISBN - Hardback Print - 979-8-88535-043-3

AI Disclosure

No generative artificial intelligence (AI) was used in the writing of this work. The author expressly prohibits any entity from using this publication for purposes of training AI technologies to generate text, including, without limitation, technologies that are capable of generating works in the same style or genre as this publication.

Tropes List

- Dark Mafia
- Antihero
- Arranged marriage
- Marriage of convenience
- Morally Gray
- Villain romance
- Forbidden love
- Possessive alpha hero
- Virgin heroine
- Obsessive love
- Dark Beauty and the Beast Dynamic
- Found family
- Hero with a tragic past
- Redemption arc
- Forced proximity
- Touch her and die
- Only soft for her

- Powerful heroine
- Dark protector hero
- Power struggle
- Surprise Pregnancy
- Revenge and vendetta
- Hidden identities / secret pasts
- Overthrowing patriarchal
- Rival families
- Fueding families
- Dark secrets
- Alpha male behavior
- Power play dynamic/ bdsm

Author's Note
Content Warning

This book is a dark romance with subject matter
that may trigger some readers.

- Graphic Violence
- Explicit Sexual Content
- Dominance themes
- Kidnapping
- Sexual Assault Trauma
- Morally Gray Characters
- Death & Loss
- Weapons & Violence
- Trauma & PTSD
- Murder & revenge
- Power imbalances
- Emotional Abuse & Manipulation
- Alpha male behavior

- Physical injury and hospitalization
- Character death
- Death of a Parent
- Revenge Killing

ONE

L AYANA

Time to do your part, Laya.

Anticipation twisted in my chest as the car sped through the lush, vibrant hills of the Greek countryside. The blur of colors and shapes outside sent my heart racing, a mix of excitement and apprehension churning in my belly.

Today, I was to meet my new fiancé at his estate.

I inhaled deep, the cool air filling my lungs as I braced myself for what lay ahead. I could do this. I had never shied away from a challenge throughout my life, but this felt different. This decision loomed over me, ready to shape the course of my existence.

Beside me, my sister Avra exuded an unwavering

strength, her presence a comforting balm. She had always stood firm against challenges, a true role model.

"You can still change your mind, Laya," she urged, her brows knitted in concern as her eyes locked onto mine. "You don't have to do this."

I shook my head, my voice steady. "There's no changing my mind. A deal is a deal. I'm committed."

Yet, even as the words echoed in the air, a flutter of unease danced in my stomach. My life had set its course toward reclaiming what had been stolen from our family. This sacrificial path led me to the altar, where I had agreed to marry for a greater purpose.

"That isn't true," Elias Xenos, Avra's husband, interjected from the front seat. "We can turn this car around and go back to my estate if you change your mind."

I couldn't help but smirk at Eli's offer. He was among the deadliest men I'd ever met, yet he showed a softer side only for Avra. Her happiness was everything to him, and consequently, mine was too.

"Don't coddle her," Vik Remes interjected in his straightforward manner.

"Thank you," I replied appreciatively. "At least someone believes I know what I want."

Vik nodded and maintained eye contact with me.

He'd sacrificed his youth to protect us after our parents' murder forced our escape. He arranged for us to settle in Prague under assumed identities and taught us everything we needed to navigate the syndicate world and defend ourselves.

As we transitioned into adulthood, Avra and I formulated a strategy to reclaim control of our family's territories. It involved all three sisters at various stages. Earlier this year, we returned to Greece for the first phase of our plan. Avra had executed it nearly flawlessly, with only minor complications.

Watching Avra negotiate her marriage to the son of our fiercest adversary and transform it into a genuine partnership gave me hope. She demonstrated to the world that the Vitalis family was back in power and that we wouldn't bow to anyone's attempts to control us.

Elias discovered that Avra's fiery spirit and strong temperament were precisely what he had never realized he needed. Together, they formed an unbeatable team, sharing true love and affection for one another.

Technically, no one had forced me into this arranged marriage. I was choosing Nikolas Galanis as my husband, so it seemed illogical for me to feel so uncertain about everything.

It wasn't as if he had plucked me out of a magazine or something and declared, *"That's the girl, get her."*

Honestly, my choice could have been worse.

Nikolas embodied a Greek god, from his chiseled features and custom-tailored suits to his aura of unquestionable authority.

Our brief encounter left an undeniable impression—I couldn't ignore my attraction. However, my interest in him extended beyond his looks. He proved his worth by helping to ensure our little sister, Cali, was safely returned after her abduction. This act greatly enhanced my opinion of him and solidified his place as a valuable ally in our pursuit of power.

Nikolas's Italian mafia ties would help us extend our power further. This was a crucial step in earning recognition and respect from other crime families, which had previously viewed us as inferior.

"Galanis has vineyards spread across the vast landscapes of Europe," Eli stated, sipping his bottle of water. "My recent research indicates that he has exclusive contracts with every five-star hotel and resort on the continent, ensuring his wines are the toast of luxury."

"That is indeed impressive." Vik cast a quick, concerned glance in my direction.

I chose to ignore the worry etched in his eyes, a look that had been a constant presence since we rescued Cali.

My sister dominated my thoughts on most days. Calista was slowly recovering from her traumatic experience. For weeks, our enemies had tortured her. While I felt relief at having her home, anxiety lingered. She shut down about her ordeal, but the haunted expression in her eyes revealed the horrific reality we feared had become an unavoidable part of her life.

I kept a close watch on her, ensuring she knew I was there whenever she was ready to talk. As time passed, I began to doubt that moment would ever come. Unfortunately, it didn't appear to be on the horizon.

Cali moved through her days in a haze, barely acknowledging the trauma she had endured. Yet, the deep impact was unmistakable. She flinched at slight noises, stared silently for hours, and screamed through nightmares.

"It's good wine," Avra said, snapping me from my brooding. "Expensive, but good."

"Good?" Eli replied with a teasing smirk. "You and Laya drank so much of his estate's Xinomavro a few weeks ago, I was sure you'd never stop giggling."

Avra burst into laughter as she leaned against her husband's shoulder. He pulled her close and kissed the top of her head.

Elias was observant and highly intuitive. He clearly sensed my nervousness about my first formal meeting with Nikolas and did his best to put me at ease. I liked him more than I ever thought possible, especially since he was the offspring of our greatest enemy.

However, he was nothing like his father, and I was grateful. When I first met him, I made many assumptions, but he'd proved me wrong on most counts.

He and Avra were perfect complements, resembling two puzzle pieces designed to fit together. Seeing my sister glow with joy, enveloped in the love and attention Elias gave her, was heartwarming. This was what I valued most about him. He would burn the world down for Avra. He had even turned his back on his terrible father for Avra's sake.

Even now, Elias kept a vigilant search for Ozias, one I knew he wouldn't give up until Ozias was six feet under.

In just a short period, everything had changed dramatically. Avra's marriage to Eli and her clever maneuvering against the asshole Ozias had led us to gain control of five territories in the sunlit region of Greece that our father once governed.

Avra had gained one through her marriage to Eli, my future marriage would secure another, and Avra had seized the remaining three after we dealt with three of the men involved in our father's murder.

We had always understood that reclaiming what was rightfully ours would come at the cost of much bloodshed. It was a necessary price to pay to recover what we had lost.

Despite the challenges ahead, nothing could stop us now that our plan was in motion. Like an unstoppable tide, we pressed forward, determined to claim our destiny.

Avra and Eli's marriage marked the beginning. Mine to Nikolas Galanis would bring us even closer to achieving our goals. I would gain his allies, further strengthening the Vitalis family.

We could easily overcome our adversaries with all the strategies we had established. All I had to do was commit myself to a man I barely knew for the rest of my life.

Piece of cake.

As we approached the Galanis estate, my earlier excitement faded, completely replaced by nausea and a churning stomach filled with nerves.

Avra's presence provided a soothing sense of support, filled with optimism and reassurances that a Vitalis woman could face any challenge.

It was clear that, even with our common family traits, Avra and I were entirely different.

Her years of wisdom reflected her vast encounters. Avra

embraced life fully, brimming with adventures and romantic escapades. By the time we returned to Greece and she met Elias, she was sophisticated, mature, and experienced.

That wasn't me—not by any means.

In truth, I'd never taken a lover, never trusted enough while living in Prague. Yet now, I'd soon share a marriage bed with a man I barely knew. It was unrealistic to think that sex wouldn't be a part of life with Nikolas. To what extent, I was unsure. However, to expect a man as mature and attractive as Nikolas not to have desires was beyond naive.

I was a virgin, not stupid.

Our brief, tense encounter during Cali's rescue made a lasting impression on me, and I couldn't help but recognize my attraction to him.

There was an intensity to his gaze, something I had never encountered before when any man looked at me.

My reaction to him prompted me to conduct my own investigation, scouring the internet and consulting several of our soldiers to gather insights about him.

Through this, I discovered that Nikolas was a formidable businessman, known for his ruthless precision in negotiations. He avoided violence until forced to engage, and then he was merciless.

This kind of calculated response commanded my respect. It was akin to provoking a slumbering bear. One could prod it only so much before it unleashed its fury, decimating its adversary. In this regard, Nikolas and I mirrored each other. It took a lot to provoke my anger, but I became fiercely relentless once someone crossed my threshold.

Avra and Cali liked to refer to it as my bubbling caldera. Once I erupted, everyone had to take cover. I wasn't sure I was as bad as they claimed, but whatever.

Another tidbit the soldiers hesitantly shared was Nikolas's infamous reputation with the ladies. I could not comprehend why they assumed I would take issue with a thirty-four-year-old, undeniably handsome man leading an active romantic life.

"What's on your mind?" Avra's question pierced through my daydream, pulling my attention to her expressive eyes.

I met her unwavering gaze and replied, "Umm... just contemplating the future."

Discussing matters of intimacy, let alone the intricacies of sex, while in a moving car and surrounded by the unmistakable presence of Eli and Vik, was the last scenario I had imagined for this conversation. I might have felt more at ease if Avra were alone with me.

Avra seldom shared details about her sex life with Eli. However, every member of the Vitalis and Xenos families was aware of their intimate inclinations, especially the fondness they had developed for the kitchen.

"Everything will be fine," Avra murmured, trying to chase away the swirling doubts in my mind.

Eli flashed a roguish grin, interjecting with playful reassurance. "We can still turn this car around if you change your mind. I'll have you on a jet to the Maldives, and you can rest assured, our soldiers will form an impenetrable shield around you."

Vik's cadence grew more solemn as he cleared his throat.

"Time to get serious. No escapes, no turning back. Laya made her choice."

I nodded, my heart racing as I took a deep breath, the air catching in my throat as my hands trembled slightly in my lap. "You're right, Vik. It's too late now. We have arrived."

The car glided to a stop, the driver easing the wheels onto the gravel of a long, winding driveway that twisted toward a towering, ornate iron gate.

I watched the gate swinging open like a mouth welcoming us into a realm of grandeur. We moved forward along a curved path, the shadows of majestic, deep green cypress trees enveloping us, their slender forms swaying gently in the breeze.

In the distance, the Galanis estate unfurled over rolling hills, its grand mansion standing tall and dominating the landscape. "It's so opulent," Avra whispered in awe.

I took in every detail, my gaze sweeping across the vast estate. The sheer scale of it was beyond impressive. I had clearly underestimated Nikolas's wealth in my earlier research.

On one side, rows of grapevines extended endlessly towards the horizon, meticulously arranged as if in perfect rows. On the opposite side, sprawling gardens erupted in various colors, each flower glistening under the warm sunlight, creating a scene that felt alive.

Eli's words broke my reverie. "This estate must be worth at least a hundred million, if not more. And it's just one of many properties he owns."

"Estates don't matter to Laya," Avra chimed in. "What

impresses her are the state-of-the-art shooting range and a fitness studio that could rival any five-star gym."

The driver guided the car up the steep roadway toward the mansion perched high on the hill.

If anyone outside the vehicle were to see me, I would appear as the calm and unshakeable Vitalis sister, poised to embrace the next stage of my destiny. Yet beneath that shield, my confidence wavered, a sense of unease stirring in my stomach.

Sensing my inner turmoil, Avra reached across and firmly grasped my hand, her warmth seeping into my anxious skin.

"Hey," she said firmly. "You're a fucking Vitalis—unbreakable. Never forget that."

"Right." I nodded, determined, as Avra jolted my anxious mind with a much-needed dose of reality.

I took a deep, calming breath and squared my shoulders as the car rolled to a stop before the imposing flight of limestone steps leading to the mansion's main entrance.

I knew marrying Nikolas was necessary, yet one question haunted me.

Why would someone with his wealth and status marry me?

The answer would reveal itself in time, but my priority was to remain focused and vigilant for now.

A staff member walked over to the sleek black car, and we stepped into the sunlit courtyard. Vik accompanied me, offering his arm while Avra and Elias remained watchful behind us.

As we neared the house's opulent entrance, I looked up

at a vast terrace that gracefully extended along one side of the mansion.

My breath caught. Nikolas stood against the stone railing, his piercing gaze capturing mine with commanding intensity.

My heart skipped a beat, and my feet came to an abrupt stop. All I could do was silently stare up at him, captivated.

He wore simple black slacks and a silk shirt, the top button undone, hinting at tanned skin. His long, dark hair cascaded over his collar, dancing in the breeze, and I couldn't help but wonder if it was as soft and silky as it looked.

His striking muscular frame showcased broad, powerful shoulders that radiated strength. He carried himself with effortless ease and confidence, reminiscent of a trained fighter ready to spring into action.

An image of my fingers tracing the contours of his body flashed into my mind.

An electrifying thrill coursed through me, reminiscent of previous experiences. Yet, this time it felt even stronger, sinking deep into my bones and leaving me restless and gasping for breath.

What was happening to me?

This wasn't what I needed. Nikolas was all about business. I lived in reality and had to keep my feet on the ground, not in the clouds.

This marriage would vastly differ from Avra's, a contrast as stark as night and day.

There was no space for the instant, electrifying attraction that crackled between us like a bolt of lightning splitting the sky. I knew almost nothing about this man, apart from the sparse facts gleaned from reports and whispers of soldiers.

I was unable to comprehend the magnetic attraction I experienced for him, powerful and unmistakable even from afar. Was he aware of it as well?

The desire that burned when our eyes met was as enigmatic and shadowy as his gaze—a profound, unfathomable mystery that captivated me.

Like a storm brewing beneath a tranquil surface, my legs sensed the first tremors ready to unleash.

This was dangerous. I had no choice but to bury these feelings deep within, far beneath the surface of my consciousness.

No matter how these emotions intrigued and tempted me, I had to shield myself, protect my family, and focus on reclaiming everything that had been so heartlessly taken from us.

There was no room for emotions in this marriage. With his dark allure and irresistible intrigue, Nikolas was merely a stepping stone on my life's journey. Entertaining any other expectations would only lead us both astray.

I took a deep breath and stepped forward, determined to face my future.

Two

N IKOLAS

A primal instinct overwhelmed me when Layana exited the car, powerful yet strangely familiar.

Weeks prior, during the tumultuous rescue of her sister Calista, my initial encounter with Layana had left me feeling unsettled. I thought it stemmed from a peculiar reaction to an enchanting woman with witch-like green eyes that seemed to hide mysteries.

But now?

The feeling surged back, stronger than before. It was a scorching heat, an inferno raging inside me, wrapping me in its firm, constricting grasp.

This moment wasn't overshadowed by stress, at least not

in the same way as the high-stakes rescue of the youngest Vitalis sister.

Yet, I couldn't ignore the intense thirst that coursed through me the instant Layana raised her captivating emerald eyes, and our gazes met.

Something primal inside me snapped—hers, mine, inevitable. She was stunning in her white silk sheath, the fabric accentuating every curve and highlighting her radiant emerald eyes. Her chestnut hair was loosely pinned up, showcasing the elegant length of her slender neck, while long tendrils danced lightly around her captivating face. She was breathtaking, a true embodiment of beauty and grace. Very soon, she would be my wife.

From this perspective, I absorbed every detail, realizing that life was on the verge of irreversible change.

Eventually, I'd uncover the truths of her past. However, what I felt now was unlike anything I'd experienced before.

It was both primal and all-consuming, as though the mere fact of Layana's status as my future bride brought out something in me that I never knew existed.

Fuck. What the hell was happening to me?

It should've been a business move. But the way I watched her? That wasn't strategy—it was hunger. I recall the day I accepted her proposal as if it were yesterday. After just one day of reflection, I took a daring and reassuring step. My friends frequently teased me about my years of being single, but I learned that living solo didn't fit my vision for the future. I sought to present a picture of stability, with a partner alongside me to face the challenges of the business world.

Some might have scoffed at the idea of arranged marriages in this age, yet in my circles, it was a common occurrence. I felt the weight of my family's expectations; every choice had implications that rippled through our wealth and influence. As I pondered over the union, I understood the unspoken truth: for the men in the syndicates, securing the right wife often meant safeguarding family legacies.

In that moment of clarity, I realized that selecting a partner was not solely about love. It was a calculated decision in a game where reputation and alliances were more significant than romance.

This situation was no exception.

However, there were additional side benefits.

It freed me from relentless matchmaking attempts by ambitious debutantes and their eager mothers.

Spending time with a woman, or to be blunt, fucking her, wasn't the same as wanting to marry her. Often, this difference in views placed me in the challenging position of having to extricate myself from awkward situations.

An arranged marriage provided the advantage of avoiding the typical emotional challenges associated with intimate relationships. Emotions wouldn't factor in if it were just a business contractual arrangement. I'd witnessed the devastation caused by loving deeply and losing it all.

My father had never recovered from losing my mother, Amara, and my sister, Cora.

Five years ago, they died tragically in a car bombing meant for my father and me. Instead of us, they became the unintended victims of a territorial war they had no part in.

Then I lost my father to a heart attack just three years later. Yet his spirit had already faded with Mama and Cora in that car. Without them, he became a mere shadow of his former self, the brightness in his once-vibrant blue eyes extinguished.

Following his passing, I promised myself to never let another woman into my heart. A cold, arranged marriage was exactly what I needed.

Then there was the ultimate reason for marrying Layana Vitalis.

The future of the Galanis legacy.

The Vitalis family name represented power in Greece and was synonymous with respect and legacy. The Vitalis family presided over the most crucial regions of the nation, earning respect through their actions and character. Tales of their lineage were whispered in shadowy taverns and around firesides, stories passed down through the ages for countless centuries.

Marrying a Vitalis sister meant joining a lineage akin to royalty, bringing numerous advantages. From the moment of their births, the three remaining sisters were regarded as matrimonial prizes. Rejecting the proposal extended to me would have been sheer stupidity.

They didn't choose me by chance—I'd outplayed every contender.

But why had Layana chosen me above all others?

I had a nagging suspicion that the decision wasn't solely hers to make. Everyone was aware of the deep bond she shared with her sisters, and it stood to reason that their guardian, Vik, would have played a significant role in whatever choice was made.

Could it be that he had influenced her decision?

Vik was well acquainted with my father, and as Juno Vitalis's second, he spent considerable time on the estate.

Soon enough, I would uncover the truth behind her choice.

As I headed downstairs, my phone buzzed, interrupting my thoughts. With a sigh of impatience, I pulled it out and answered, "Galanis."

"I have news about your brothers," one of my lieutenants announced, stirring familiar tension within me.

I struggled to suppress the impulse to clench my jaw. It felt like I couldn't get through even an hour without confronting some problem related to my self-involved younger siblings, Stefano and Markos.

"Speak up," I ordered, my patience running thin.

"Our team is watching them. They're on the family yacht near Cyprus." His reply deepened my frustration.

"Why are they there? Who authorized their use of the yacht?" I pressed.

My brothers spent more time vacationing than contributing—utterly useless.

"We are waiting for details from our people mixed in with their men," the soldier replied, a calm contrast to my growing annoyance.

"Report once you receive the details. They're up to something. The last thing we need is for one of them to jeopardize our deals," I instructed, the gravity of the situation weighing on my mind.

"Yes, sir," he affirmed before the line went silent. After hanging up, I tucked my phone back into my pocket and went downstairs. I halted at the bottom, captivated by Layana stepping into the grand foyer.

Her gaze locked onto mine with an intensity that suggested she had anticipated my presence at that exact spot.

What was it about her that drew me so irresistibly?

I had always been drawn to women with fiery spirits, and Layana undoubtedly possessed that quality in abundance. She was no pushover. She exuded focus, determination, and an undeniable aura of fearlessness that was hard to overlook.

I approached her, eager to see how the evening would unfold.

Tearing my gaze from Layana, I briefly greeted Avra, Elias, and Vik before returning to her. I wanted to make her wait, to gauge her reaction.

"It's good to see you," I said, holding her gaze and bringing her hand to my lips.

"You too," she replied as her gaze swept over me.

I couldn't help but comment, "Every time I see you, Layana, you look even more mesmerizing."

Her cheeks flushed, and her sparkling green eyes held me captivated. An intriguing hint of innocence lingered in her coy smile, subtle yet inviting.

I recalled the fierce warrior I had previously encountered,

steadfast in her mission to rescue her sister, and admired her metamorphosis into an embodiment of pure sensuality and femininity.

"You've changed," I murmured. "What's behind this transformation?"

"I embody many things and reveal them only when the moment is right."

Her reply surprised me, and I couldn't help but say, "I look forward to unwrapping every single one, Layana." Then, I turned to the group and said, "I'm delighted you're all here. Shall we tour the estate?"

"We'd love that," Vik agreed, adding, "Your estate is truly remarkable, Nikolas."

"Thank you," I replied. "My family has been building this estate for generations. Right now, it's just me here."

I turned to Layana briefly, then diverted my gaze, noticing her lips parting as if hinting at the possibilities of our future.

Soon, she would roam the grand hallways with me, freely reigning over my sprawling estate.

The idea of someone else living here with me wasn't unpleasant.

As I guided the four of them through the intricately designed tour, I was acutely aware of how it might appear from Layana's perspective, experiencing it all for the first time and knowing that this would be her home as my wife.

"What about your brothers?" Avra asked.

Suppressing my displeasure at their disregard for the land

that provided them with their wealth, I responded, "They prefer city life. The estate doesn't suit them."

"It's stunning," Avra said, awe shining in her eyes. "The vineyards stretch endlessly behind the grand house, like a sea of green waves."

"It does feel that way," I agreed, nodding. "The olive groves on the other side have the same timeless charm. I would lose myself in them for hours as a child, wandering among the ancient trees."

"It must have been amazing to grow up here," Elias remarked, eyes scanning the landscape. "I read that your vineyard produces a significant amount of mavroudi wine."

"It's true," I replied with a hint of pride. "My father had a particular fondness for it, often joking that it was the wine that—"

"—that Odysseus used to get Polyphemus drunk!" Layana interjected with amusement.

I burst out laughing, the sound echoing warmly through the air. "Yes, exactly."

"My father used to make the same joke," she reminisced, her eyes reflecting memories as she looked at me.

I couldn't help but wonder if she was aware of the deep-rooted connection between our fathers. I imagined them sitting together, laughter spilling from their lips as they joked about the popular Greek wine, perhaps clinking glasses in a toast to their enduring friendship. The photographs of the two radiated adventures and camaraderie, showcasing a bond that I rarely saw my father share with anyone else.

As I gazed into Layana's eyes, I felt we would share many glasses of wine, lost in the same amusement.

"You've done an incredible job managing this place, Nikolas," Avra said. "Clearly, overseeing such a large operation demands substantial effort."

"I was lucky to inherit my father's estate," I replied, appreciating her praise. "While I'm proud of it, I'm particularly grateful that my father established such an efficient system and assembled a dedicated team to ensure everything runs smoothly. I cannot take all the credit alone. The daily efforts of many people make this possible. I could never manage everything by myself."

There it was again—alone.

It echoed in my mind, resonating with a certain truth.

Lingering like a shadow.

Technically, I never lacked company, having my days filled with work commitments, various friends, and occasionally a socialite when the need for feminine companionship arose. Additionally, the extensive staff, resembling a small army, meticulously maintained my family's estate in a state of immaculate perfection.

Yet, despite constant company, loneliness haunted me since losing my parents and sister. Stefano and Markos shared my blood, but our connection truly had no meaning. They only reached out when they needed financial support for yet another ill-conceived venture.

"Speaking of the head of the household, let me introduce you to Sotirios, the true genius behind the Galanis estate. We call him Soti," I stated as my trusted oikonomos approached elegantly.

"Good afternoon," Soti welcomed everyone with a graceful bow, exuding a soothing and inviting elegance, much like a fine aged wine. "Welcome to the Galanis estate."

"Soti manages the household. Let him know if you require anything."

"Dinner will be served soon," Soti announced with a firm nod. "I have cocktails ready for you in the living room while you wait."

"Thank you, Soti," I replied. "We're taking a brief tour and will be there shortly."

"Very well, sir," he responded.

Soti disappeared just as mysteriously as he had come, and I led the group around the same curve.

The house opened to a recessed living room, featuring two impressive, floor-to-ceiling windows showcasing a stunning view of the vineyards.

I cherished living here. My parents had constructed this home from the ground up, and living here meant being constantly enveloped by memories of them.

"This view is incredible," Layana remarked as she approached the windows, her tone infused with genuine wonder.

"Every day, it amazes me," I said. "As if it's painted just for us."

She laughed.

"And what do you feel, exactly?" she inquired, her eyes locking onto mine with curiosity.

I smiled and said, "Every moment here seems like a story waiting to unfold. My favorite view is when a storm develops in the east. It's so powerful. I might come across as an old man, reminiscing about my days watching the weather change."

"You hardly look like an old man to me," she teased, with a touch of flirtation, making her eyes sparkle.

I met her gaze with a wink. "Maybe not yet, but sometimes I wish I could anticipate every twist of fate as clearly as the skies change."

A brief silence fell between us as we held each other's gazes.

Her pupils dilated, and she licked her lips before breaking eye contact. Another moment of silence lingered between us, leading me to question who this woman truly was. At that instant, she remained an enigma.

Sure, I knew snippets of her past.

Through my research into her family, I uncovered that she and her sisters endured unimaginable hardships, emerging from a background of violence and power. They escaped to Prague to avoid the grim fate shaped by their father's murder. In this new city and under new identities, they embraced the chance to grow up free from the dark shadow of the Vitalis legacy, leading ordinary lives in a world that once felt so harsh.

"But then it takes away the adventure," Layana said thoughtfully. "I mean, who are we to know the entirety of someone's story before it unfolds? What if knowing causes us to alter it?"

"I concede your point," I acquiesced, then added, "Is adventure what you seek?"

While I awaited her response, I spotted Avra and Vik heading toward the fireplace. Avra's gaze fixed on a photograph on the hearth, her eyes narrowing curiously.

I sensed their impending discovery of the connection between our fathers.

"Look at this, Vik," she said, eyes wide, filled with wonder. "That's Papa."

"This is years before you were born," Vik responded, detached. "Your grandfather was still godfather back then."

Any moment now, the questions would come.

Less than a second later, Avra called, "Layana, come over here."

"Excuse me." Layana briefly glanced my way before joining the small gathering.

Elias then stepped up beside me, giving my back a hearty pat. "Been a while."

"Yes, it has," I replied, nodding. "It's good to see you again, Elias. How's everything?"

Elias and I cultivated a friendly relationship through various business dealings. When I learned he was marrying Avra, I was genuinely happy for both of them, recognizing the significance of their union. All signs indicated their marriage was flourishing.

"Avra and I have found our way together," he answered, gesturing with his chin toward the fireplace. "It looks as if this house has some stories to share."

"Something like that."

Layana picked up a photo of a group of young men posing in front of a soccer field, with Juno and my father at the center, arms around each other.

"Be prepared for an inquisition," Elias warned.

"I'm expecting nothing less. Who wouldn't have questions when they find their father's photographs in a near stranger's house?"

"The Vitalis women are formidable—lethal and beautiful in equal measure."

"I'm well aware of this. I saw them in action a few months ago."

THREE

L AYANA

"Is that Papa?" I gasped, disbelief gripping me as I stared at the photograph. "What the fuck?"

"Laya. Language," Vik chided, reminding me of how he used to scold me when I was a teenager.

I frowned, casting a bewildered look at Avra, and muttered, "I don't understand."

"Me neither," Avra whispered, equally bewildered. She squinted at the sparkling silver frame trembling in my clenched hand, the image of Papa smiling and covered in sweat. Seven other men stood around him, but the one with his arm around Papa's shoulder bore a striking resemblance to a younger version of my soon-to-be husband.

I blinked at the photo, breath catching.

"That's... Papa," I whispered. "And that—" I hesitated, heart thudding. "That has to be Constantine Galanis."

"I believe that's the league Papa played in during his youth," Avra said.

"You're right," I agreed, despite the turmoil in my gut.

I glanced toward Nikolas, who lingered by the window, deep in conversation with Elias, and then looked back at Avra.

"Did you know they knew each other?" I asked, barely above a whisper.

"No," Avra replied, her face a mix of confusion and concern, as if she were piecing together the fragments of a long-forgotten puzzle.

This felt like a betrayal—by my instincts, my research, everything I thought I knew. With all my research, how could I have missed a connection between Papa and Nikolas's family? Had I possibly overlooked a crucial detail?

"Am I wrong about him?" I questioned, shaking my head to cast off the mounting anxiety.

Avra fixed her eyes on me, taking the photo from my shaking hands and setting it back on the mantel like a cherished artifact.

"Perhaps this is a setup," I murmured, striving to avoid attracting attention.

My training had prepared me for danger, but the haunting memories of trauma still threatened to send me fleeing at any sign of trouble.

"We should go," I insisted.

"Laya!" Avra exclaimed, gripping my shoulders tightly and gazing intently into my eyes. "Stop being impulsive. You need to outgrow that habit."

"Something doesn't add up," I replied, nervously skimming the dim hallway that led to a door promising escape from the impending mistake I felt I was about to make.

"How could it be a setup? A setup for what, exactly? Just a reminder, you picked Nikolas. Have you lost sight of that?"

"No," I said, folding my arms defensively. "But maybe..." I paused, forcing myself to calm down.

I shifted my focus from Nikolas to the photograph, then let my eyes wander over the other images resting on the mantel. Each frame held a memory, and my father's soulful gaze stared back at me from two of them. A realization settled in, making it clear that my father had a connection to Constantine, which lingered just beyond our previous searches. How could we have missed such an important link?

Suddenly, a realization struck me like a bolt of lightning.

Vik had been unusually quiet throughout the entire conversation.

I turned abruptly towards him and asked, "Were you aware?"

"Yes, but—" Vik opened his mouth and closed it again.

I grew weary of Vik's constant urge to protect us, not just from physical threats but also from vital truths we had the right to know. Once, I might have sympathized with his wish to shield us, but now it only fueled my bitterness and frustration.

"We're adults, Vik. We can handle the truth."

"Yes," he said. "They were friends. And I didn't tell you because it didn't matter—until now."

I glared, on the verge of hitting him. "We're not girls anymore!"

He glanced up as if asking for divine intervention, a gesture that highlighted our numerous previous interactions.

"Calm down, Laya," he cautioned as he met my fiery glare. "You chose him. I trusted that choice. Nikolas Galanis was merely one of three men on the list compiled by your sister. I gave Avra my opinion on who I favored, but never said anything to you. The final decision was all on you."

"You know exactly what I mean!" I snapped. "You should have told us."

"I figured you'd discover it eventually." He shrugged, treating it as unimportant. "Moreover, it's a harmless detail. You're creating unnecessary drama."

"You're impossible," I retorted, rolling my eyes as irritation boiled over.

"I could say the same about you, dear one," Vik replied with a sarcastic lilt.

I would certainly strangle him if I didn't love him so much.

I looked to Avra, begging her to intervene—but she was lost in the photos, her face shadowed with something I couldn't quite read. As the eldest, Avra bore an unspoken responsibility that grew heavier after our parents' deaths.

Her eyes often revealed a desperate yearning, a silent hope that Papa might somehow come back to lighten her burden.

Viewing these vibrant photographs of Papa felt like encountering a ghost. They prompted me to reflect on Papa's connection with Constantine. Not only were they allies, but they were also friends with a much deeper bond. From the various pictures, they had known each other since childhood.

It made me curious about what Papa was like in his youth. The joyous aura in those photographs suggested shared adventures and a deep, unspoken understanding, a stark contrast to the man I never truly knew.

A sudden prickle of awareness had me glancing at Nikolas.

His intense gaze locked onto mine as he continued his conversation with Elias. I held his stare, trying to interpret the subtle hints in his expression to determine whether I could trust this enigmatic man whose beauty seemed almost unreal.

He had an unsettling charm, suggesting that behind his flawless appearance lay hidden flaws or ominous secrets. His perfection felt as if it served as a meticulously constructed mask, hiding intricate and mysterious motivations.

I couldn't help but wonder if he might have a valid reason for agreeing to marry me. This reason could involve either a hidden motive or a straightforward, practical choice. However, as I noticed his distracted gaze—those fleeting moments when he seemed to reflect on our discussion about the photographs—I felt he had answers too. The idea that I was projecting my hidden intentions onto him was somewhat amusing.

Beneath our polite exchanges and heated glances, I carried my own secrets. With a firm chin lift and a determined set of my shoulders, I silently vowed to remember that essential truth. No matter Nikolas's reasons for this marriage, I stood to gain the most from this union.

I could wait for him to share his secrets when he felt ready. I had no doubt he had considered the pros and cons of partnering with a Vitalis, and the benefits had outweighed any doubts he might have had.

Noticing his distraction during my discussion with Vik and Avra, I became convinced he had the necessary answers, and I was determined to uncover them all.

"I'll find out what's going on," I told myself, leaving Avra and Vik behind as I walked confidently toward Nikolas and Elias.

My determined stride was interrupted when Soti entered the room.

"Dinner is ready," he announced in his distinctly cultured accent.

This added an unexpected air of formality to the statement, enhancing its charm, even though it meant that my search for answers would need to be paused for now.

We entered a magnificent dining room reminiscent of those in ancient castles. A long, elegant table stretched before us, adorned with sparkling place settings. At the center, bowls overflowed with fresh fruit and fragrant flowers, leaving me in awe.

The elegance astounded me. Only yesterday, I'd been lounging in my living room, watching carefree rom-coms while nibbling lukewarm spanakopita. The prospect of luxury like this felt both surreal and overwhelming.

We gathered around the elegant table, and I felt a tingling heat radiate through my skin as Nikolas settled beside me. His proximity stirred something deep within me, igniting a subtle spark of desire. The warmth of his presence sent a shiver down my spine, leaving me both excited and slightly uneasy.

I took a deep breath and reached for the glass of ice water before me. I drank it while maintaining a graceful demeanor, though I doubted I could achieve this.

A small drop of water then fell onto my chest.

Fabulous.

I averted my gaze in embarrassment, attempting to hide the mishap while silently wishing that no one else had seen. My hopes faded when Nikolas's teasing smirk caught my eye.

Avra had persuaded me to wear a low-cut dress, and now my exposed cleavage silently confirmed her choice. Nikolas's gaze fixated on a small, glistening bead of water clinging happily to my bare skin. Embarrassed, I quickly brushed it away, only to see Nikolas raise his eyes toward me and send a wink in my direction.

Despite being a Vitalis, I remembered how my early years were spent in surroundings far more modest than the royal wealth associated with our family name.

Our life in Prague revolved around simplicity rather than luxury. Vik raised us without the extravagant comforts typically associated with our status. He prioritized our safety over indulgence. This modest upbringing fostered an appreciation for simplicity, which sharply contrasted with the opulence surrounding me now.

The present setting, filled with aristocratic splendor, felt alien and somewhat disconcerting. I had always sought refuge in more casual environments, making the prospect of one day managing such extravagance both thrilling and daunting.

How could I convince Nikolas I was ready for a role I'd never prepared for? My lack of experience was an obvious and daunting truth.

Yet, as I took another deep, steadying breath, the way Nikolas made me feel pulsed like an electric current. Every quiver deep within my being, sparked by the charm of his wink, sent a rush of arousal and excitement cascading over me, an intoxicating sensation unlike anything I had ever experienced. Until that moment, my interactions with the opposite sex had been sparse and tentative, making this entirely new and exhilarating chemistry almost overwhelming.

I found everything lively and thrilling, and I realized Nikolas had considerable experience with women.

Questions flooded my mind. How would he react when he discovered that I had never experienced anything in the realm of sex?

I wasn't naïve. I understood that addressing my husband's physical needs was essential to our marriage. I believed men had desires that needed to be satisfied, even as I was still learning to fulfill those needs gradually.

Pleasing a man like Nikolas felt intimidating. I wondered if he possessed the patience to guide me through this unfamiliar territory.

What kind of lover was he truly?

Would his touch be gentle and understanding, or would his desire manifest as an unyielding assertion of will?

Oh my God, I was driving myself crazy with these thoughts.

Maybe I should ask Avra for advice on this?

Ummm, perhaps not. I was embarrassed enough about how clueless I felt about this whole subject.

Amid the subdued hum of conversation and the distant clink of cutlery, my thoughts wandered into forbidden territory. A dark, sensual image unfolded: an illicit night spent entwined with Nikolas, where hunger, passion, and desire eclipsed every polite word. I surveyed the room with intense awareness, convinced that each person present felt the pull of this secret fantasy emerging from within.

Nikolas responded to Avra and Eli's inquiries with calm, enchanting assurance, a presence that deepened the magnetic pull I felt. I watched him intently, studying every subtle nuance of his expressive face, and each flicker of his eyes created a spellbinding trance around me. His articulate words melted into the background, while his gestures spoke a languid, hypnotic language, each movement of his confident, graceful hands punctuating the air like forbidden incantations.

My gaze remained fixed on his full, inviting lips, a silent promise of forbidden pleasures.

I bit the inside of my cheek as a slow-burning desire unfurled deep within, coiling its way from my core. I lost myself in the tantalizing fantasy of sharing a bed with him under the muted twilight glow, where first touches could ignite an electric current of anticipation or drown us in delicious, chaotic yearning. The impending dark magnetism left me suspended in a swirling vortex of longing, with Nikolas at its center.

I shivered as I imagined how his cinnamon-hued eyes might react if they were to learn that no other man had ever touched me.

Would they widen in raw surprise or deepen with a secret, knowing fire?

The idea itself was a dangerous lure, a spark that could ignite his desire or unravel him completely—an intoxicating mystery that only intensified our attraction.

His captivating presence drew me in, and my eyes followed the graceful movements of his hands. I allowed my gaze to trace his sculpted forearms, where his fitted black shirt revealed a hint of olive skin sprinkled with dark hair—an unspoken invitation to discover the texture of his body. I yearned to explore and feel him against my skin.

Then, I felt a firm but subtle pressure that shattered my fantasy. Nikolas's knee pressed against mine beneath the table.

My heart thundered as I met his gaze for a fleeting second before he returned to an animated conversation with Elias about a particularly brooding vineyard wine. His casual demeanor stood in stark contrast to the intimacy of his touch.

My breath quickened when his hand rested on his leg and his fingers brushed against mine, and a flush crept to my cheeks. Instinctively, I averted my gaze to my plate.

What was I experiencing?

The fluttering in my stomach became a silent companion to our hidden desire. Encouraged by his touch, I grazed his thigh with my fingertips, acknowledging our secret connection.

This was ridiculous. What was I doing? And why couldn't I stop?

I never imagined I could be so bold.

The meal unfolded with a secret game playing out between us, and by the time dinner ended, an electric charge filled the space surrounding us. This dark, potent force left me both incredibly intrigued and outrageously aroused, ensnared in the promise of a passion as dangerous as it was irresistible.

It was clear that I'd lost this match.

I couldn't concentrate. I couldn't think clearly.

On the other hand, Nikolas effortlessly charmed my family and engaged them in conversations on various topics while finding ways to touch or brush against me.

Desire and anticipation simmered beneath my skin. I was certain that marrying a man like Nikolas Galanis would plunge my life into an endless world of raw passion, unquenchable need, and a promise of wicked discovery.

"Would you care to join me for a stroll outside?" Nikolas asked as everyone prepared to leave the dining room.

I glanced at Avra, but she gave me no indication of what to do. She merely lifted a brow and smirked.

Thanks for nothing, big sister.

"Yes, that would be nice." I slid my palm over his outstretched hand, and once more, the fiery sizzle I had experienced earlier danced over my skin.

We left the others behind, and Nikolas guided me to a secluded study.

"I love it out here," he murmured, swinging open a pair of doors at the far end of the room, which revealed a vast terrace.

It was the same one I had seen him standing on when we first arrived. Stepping onto the terrace, he stretched out his arms, welcoming the sun's warm rays.

My heart skipped a beat, and I could only stare. Was this man even aware of his sex appeal? It felt like he expected others to accept him as he was and couldn't care less if they didn't.

His dark and magnetic eyes locked onto mine, promising hidden pleasures. Now that we were alone, each breath became a delicious struggle.

The electric bond that had briefly sparked during dinner immediately burst into a blazing fire between us. The depth of our chemistry was almost surreal, reminiscent of the passionate films I watched with my sisters or the enticing novels we secretly enjoyed away from Vik's disapproving stares.

How could something so visceral and suddenly all-encompassing be real? How could I trust a passion that emerged so unpredictably from what was intended to be merely a business arrangement?

Business. Merely a business arrangement—one filled with sultry overtones and the unspoken promise of carnal pleasure. Perhaps I was letting my inexperience blur the lines between fantasy and reality.

With his arm outstretched, he beckoned me to take his hand. "Shall we go for a walk?"

I placed my hand in his, feeling the comforting strength of his palm as we strolled side by side. I absorbed the lush beauty of the expansive gardens on the southern side of the grounds, envisioning countless hours spent among the roses and the intoxicating scent of passion.

"I've waited for this day, Layana," he eventually confided in a low, husky tone.

"Please, call me Laya," I replied.

We were well past formalities.

As the sun began to set, its golden light caressing his sculpted features, my gaze wandered over his perfect jawline and lingered on his full, inviting mouth. Hypnotized, I licked my lips, a silent invitation that made him break into a smoldering smile.

"Very well. Then I want you to call me Niko." He glanced away for a heartbeat before turning back. "There's no need for formalities between us, Laya."

I nodded as he voiced my thoughts.

The pulsing energy between us grew too powerful to ignore.

"Laya... Laya... Laya..." he repeated, each utterance dripping with magnetic allure.

I stared at him, utterly entranced, fighting to calm the burning sensation prickling over my skin and the tremors of desire growing deep inside me.

Could I handle a man like him?

Of course, I could. I was a fucking Vitalis.

What was wrong with me?

Vik and Avra had raised me to be a confident and self-assured woman, not this uncertain dodo, shaking in her stilettos, completely overwhelmed by doubt and vulnerability.

"I'd like to show you something, Laya," he murmured, clasping my hand with a familiarity that felt as instinctive as my heartbeat.

I waited, holding back my questions and savoring the electric tension and mysterious allure that filled the air between us.

He guided me along the ancient terrace, its stone edge smoothed by time. I trailed behind without hesitation, admiring every detail of his sculpted, commanding presence.

The deep, dark greens and intricate shadows of the lush, vibrant foliage enveloped us like a soft velvet cloak.

Tall mulberry trees and brooding Kermes oaks stood like sentinels at the edge of the property, their branches stretching skyward in a silent, watchful embrace over the sprawling gardens below. We halted at the center of the terrace, where Niko paused before a pair of French doors thrown wide open, revealing a dimly lit bedroom beyond.

My breath caught at the sight of the enormous bed, visions of tangled sheets filling my mind. The room's exquisite and strategic placement suggested it was the mansion's primary sanctuary, perhaps Niko's personal lair.

A thrill coursed through me. Could this be the bed I might someday share with him?

It was easy to imagine the two of us, entwined and vulnerable beneath the chaotic covers, a torrent of passion unleashed as Niko's touch ignited every one of my dormant yearnings. Heat pooled between my legs, and the urge to press them together prickled at the back of my mind.

Stop it, Laya.

I chastised myself and averted my gaze from a sight I shouldn't behold. Instead, my attention shifted to Niko as he stared at the grand oak tree that stood out from the open door, like a majestic figure rooted deep in the heart of the garden.

Dense and majestic, its rounded canopy spread like a protective dome over the landscape, while its trunk stood rugged and gnarled from years of enduring nature's whims. This tree seemed carved by time, its roots anchoring it so firmly that not even the fiercest storm could hope to dislodge it.

"Meet Dryad," he said, his hand sweeping toward the tree.

"Dryad?" I repeated, arching an inquisitive brow as I admired the tree's ancient beauty.

"This tree has a story. My parents planted it together during their first year of marriage. I grew up with it as my silent companion, spending countless hours climbing its various branches and even falling out of it a few times."

His sheepish grin added charm to his recollection, and I envisioned him, agile and daring, climbing its limbs like a nimble cat.

"Why is it called Dryad?" I asked, wanting to know the story.

"My mother named it," he explained. "She believed that every tree harbors a spirit, a soul, much like the sacred oak before us. In Greek mythology, the spirit or nymph of an oak tree is called a Dryad."

"That's beautiful, Niko," I murmured, my heart warming as I listened to the tale. "Thank you for sharing it with me."

"Absolutely," he said with a relaxed shrug.

This sensitive side of Niko surprised me.

How was a girl supposed to protect herself if the sexy-assin man she intended to marry possessed the qualities she truly desired in a husband?

"My father wanted to name it Zeus." He chuckled, pushing his long black hair back and revealing his chiseled cheekbones as he gazed affectionately at the tree, his thoughts miles away.

"Why Zeus?" I inquired.

"Zeus believed that the rustling leaves of the sacred oak carried messages from God. Folklore tells us he had priests to interpret these signs." He paused, a faint grin appearing as he turned his gaze back to me, his eyes inviting and kind. "But in the end, my mother prevailed. She always did with him."

I nodded, feeling moved by his candidness.

"You speak so fondly of your parents."

He nodded, his dark eyes deepening. "I loved them dearly."

"I understand," I replied. "I cherished my parents too." He offered a quiet nod. "They were everything a child could wish for in a mother and father."

The photographs of Papa in his living room flashed through my mind. I considered bringing them up, but as if he sensed my thoughts, he quickly changed the subject.

"I also love this estate." He turned away and gestured toward the vineyards and groves. "I grew up here. It's all sacred to me, not just this majestic oak."

"I would feel the same way if I grew up here," I said.

My heart sank at the thought of what had happened to my childhood home. I could almost feel the emptiness where the laughter and love had thrived. Ozias had stripped it of its light, leaving only shadows behind. The pain of knowing it would never return to the beauty I once relished struck me harder than I wanted to admit.

Before that fateful night, the Vitalis estate had been a sanctuary of joy, where moments felt timeless. I clung tightly to those memories as if they were all I had left.

Niko shifted, his gaze steady. "Shall we address the elephant in the room, Laya?"

I met his eyes with a smile, sensing the tension in the air. "Absolutely. You're referring to our agreement to marry."

His expression grew serious. "Yes. Now that I've accepted your offer, I assume you'll live here on this property with me."

I nodded, feeling a warmth wash over me. "I've assumed that as well, Niko. I'd be honored. It's an enchanting place."

A shadow of concern flickered across his face. "I'm very glad you feel that way. How will you feel about giving up your current lifestyle?"

"Exactly what lifestyle are you referring to?"

His brows furrowed slightly. "You've lived in the city for most of your life, haven't you?"

"Yes, that's true," I acknowledged, recalling the bustling streets. "I considered that. Ultimately, though, I craved peace and quiet. Prague pulsated with vibrancy, but at times, it felt suffocating. Patras buzzed too. Busy cities drain me. If I ever wanted to relive that energy, I could easily take a short trip."

"I can relate. Life in the city isn't for everyone," he said with a brighter expression. "You'll thrive here."

A thought struck me, and I leaned in, fixing him with my gaze. "I have one condition, Niko. It's essential."

He locked onto me, his eyes searching, deep and penetrating. They seemed to peel back layers, seeking any hint of hesitation within me.

"Name it," he urged, his voice low but unwavering. "And I'll ensure you get it."

"No one restricts my training."

He raised an eyebrow, curiosity piqued. "Your training? You mean your martial arts? I thought that was just a rumor."

I lifted my chin, meeting his gaze with conviction. "It is a fact, not a rumor. I won't give it up."

My passion for the sport blazed within me, fierce and unyielding. I wouldn't let anyone extinguish it.

"You'll have no issues from my side, I assure you," he began, looking at me as if he could see into my soul. "I was impressed by your skills during our first encounter. I'd heard that Vik ensured you three could fend for yourselves, but seeing you in action..." He paused, shaking his head. "Wow. You and Avra moved like a coordinated team of assassins."

I laughed and shook my head. "No, we simply trained incredibly hard. Vik wouldn't have allowed us to be any other way."

I briefly thought of Cali, aware she had fought tooth and nail with those same skills. But the odds were against her from the moment of her kidnapping—one small woman facing a group of men.

"It was truly incredible. I wanted to share that with you," he responded.

"Thank you." I felt my cheeks flush once more. "I could say the same about you."

He looked at me, allowing silence to surround us. The powerful connection crackled between us, expressing everything we felt without saying anything.

"Since we're being so open, Laya, I'd like to take this

opportunity to clarify something important with you. I hope you don't mind my being frank?"

"Of course not. Please do," I responded, waiting breathlessly.

His eyes transfixed me, as if he had me in a firm hold. He made me feel like I was on the edge of my seat, eagerly anticipating his next word, his next graceful gesture, and the subsequent spark of desire in his gaze. I could still feel his knee pressed against mine under the table.

"I understand that you proposed this marriage as a business arrangement." The dark look in his eyes, sharp and piercing, reflected a tempest of emotions beneath the surface.

"To unite the strength of our family names," he went on, his gaze unwavering and almost intimidating, "I need you to understand that I fully intend to honor this marriage. I never do anything halfway. You will discover this about me soon. When I commit, I follow through. This will be a genuine marriage for me. I will be entirely devoted to you and expect the same from you. In every way."

He glanced behind me, and I knew he was looking at his bed, envisioning the same thoughts I had earlier.

"Does that include love?" I asked, barely above a whisper.

His eyes widened, flashing across his features. Instantly, I regretted the question and wished to heaven I could take it back.

"That remains to be seen."

I nodded. Deep down, his response sliced through me like a knife, making me realize I wanted what Avra and Eli had. But it wasn't something I could expect or hope for.

"However," he continued, "we will share a bed. I want you to be prepared for that. Otherwise, this won't work."

I peered up at him, my heart pounding out of control. I understood what he was saying, what he expected.

And I was anything but prepared for this, not in any genuine way.

I could project a powerful, fearsome demeanor, stand tall, and elevate my chin, speaking words tinged with insincere confidence. However, that was a well-practiced act, a fragile guise concealing the turmoil inside.

No amount of time spent on online research could prepare me for the overwhelming and immediate assault on my senses that I was feeling at this moment.

My mind whirled in confusion while my body burned with a jumbled mix of desire and apprehension.

I had no idea what to do next. This was all new to me.

He expected me to be prepared? Prepared, like how?

Panic rose. Maybe this was when I should confess I'd never even kissed a man.

My emotions roiled like a storm at sea, and my body wrestled with the desire and arousal that Niko seemed to ignite, alongside the anxiety of my ignorance churning in my belly.

No, I was stronger than my doubts and insecurities. I wouldn't waver in my commitment to my family because of them.

We had come too far for me to let this moment crumble into weakness. I suppressed the torrent of my inner turmoil, allowing a small, defiant voice of confidence to rise above the clamor, shouting over my anxiety until it silenced every lingering doubt.

I wasn't going to let my carefully crafted mask fall.

Fuck that.

I squared my shoulders, lifted my chin, and nodded, masking my trembling nerves. "I guarantee you, I'm fully ready for this entire experience, Niko," I stated with a surety I didn't truly possess.

Whether he believed me or not, I wasn't sure. He gave no indication either way.

Though it seemed that the false bravado blared at us like a neon sign etched on my forehead.

"Excellent," he replied with a firm nod. "As long as we're clear."

His piercing gaze shifted from my eyes to my lips, making them tingle from sheer anticipation.

"We're clear," I said, desire a throbbing ache growing deep in my belly.

"I'll be honored to have a wife like you," he murmured.

How was I expected to respond to that?

Was he always this open, this admiring, this direct? Would I ever get used to it?

"Thank you," I mumbled, unable to tear my gaze away from his burning dark eyes.

"May I kiss you, Laya? I've been staring at your beautiful lips since you arrived."

My God, the sheer directness of his request startled and thrilled me. There was no beating around the bush with him.

It both unsettled and intoxicated me in a way that sent shivers racing through my veins.

"Yes, I'd like that," I managed to say barely through a whisper.

His eyes darkened with fierce intensity, as if I'd awakened a feral creature, he said, "I was hoping you'd say that."

As he leaned toward me, his movements deliberately slow and measured, I felt a surge of anticipation so powerful that it threatened to overwhelm me.

The heat radiating from his body mingled with the growing storm in his eyes, deepening with each inch that closed the gap between us. When his lips finally brushed against mine, the tender caress took my breath away.

I braced myself for a strong, assertive kiss, but instead, I encountered a sweetness that was so patient and tender it felt unreal.

My stomach flipped with excitement, and I found myself breathless, caught in a swirl of surprise and desire.

That light, airy sensation made me crave more, my lips silently begging for another taste.

A brief pause hung in the air. He withdrew, eyes glimmering with triumph that contrasted with the deep, unrelenting craving spiraling within me. I barely opened my mouth, yearning in silence for his touch once more.

He traced my lower lip with his thumb, a sultry grin creeping across his features. "There will be more when you're truly mine, Laya," he said, his voice laced with an enticing promise.

His thumb lingered a moment longer before it disappeared too quickly, leaving me to stifle a whimper, the emptiness amplifying my desire.

Before I could fully recover, he took my hand and pulled me along, guiding me across the terrace as if nothing had disturbed the serenity of our evening. As he led me through the property, it felt as though he was casually threading our fate together. All the while, my mind wandered in a blissful fog of burning desire and sweet trepidation.

FOUR

NIKOLAS

ONE WEEK LATER

I stood by the window, the soft light filtering in, as Soti asked, "Is everything to your satisfaction, Kyrios?"

I took a moment to appreciate the serene charm of the guest room. The fresh scent of linens and lilies hung in the air, wrapping around me like a comforting embrace.

"Absolutely, it looks wonderful, Soti. Thank you for your meticulous care," I responded, warmth blooming in my chest as I noticed the little details he had arranged with the house staff to enhance the room's allure.

He nodded, a hint of pride in his eyes. "I want your future wife to feel completely at ease."

I smiled back at him, grateful for his thoughtfulness. I imagined her walking into the room, seeing the flowers, and feeling the warmth of his considerate touch.

"With your extraordinary attention to detail, I'm sure she'll be very well cared for. The lilies are such a delightful touch."

Soti was more of a trusted friend than simply my house manager.

I found it amusing that, despite my repeated requests to stop referring to me as "kyrios," which means "boss," he persisted in using the term, just as he had with my father throughout the years. With me now in charge of the estate, his continued use of the title showed his recognition of me as our family's rightful heir and godfather.

However, my brothers would surely contest that.

They distanced themselves from the daily operations of our empire, yet they never missed an opportunity to stake their claim. Fortunately, Stefano and Markos were too busy globe-trotting and partying to pay attention to the intricate details that kept everything running smoothly, leaving me to handle most of the work without their superficial complaints.

I needed to focus. This was about respect, about doing things the right way. And yet, after that kiss on the terrace, I wanted nothing more than to take her upstairs and taste her again.

Afterward, I intended to explore every sin she awakened

in me. I planned to revel in her body over and over, as much as she allowed.

Laya had consented to move in early and settle before the wedding, streamlining everything and ensuring the estate was properly organized for our eagerly awaited honeymoon.

We had decided to marry as soon as we could arrange it logistically, and neither of us felt the need to delay. After all, this was a contracted marriage, so there wasn't a necessity for a lengthy period to get acquainted. It would naturally happen over time anyway.

For now, she'd have privacy in the adjoining room, with a lock if she wished, though she needn't know how easily I could breach it. To ensure everything was ready for her arrival, I consulted with Eli and Avra about Laya's preferences, from her preferred coffee style to her favorite shampoo brand. I made sure everything would be prepared upon her arrival. It was important to me that she felt thoroughly cared for and at ease.

After all, she would be my wife, and it was my duty to attend to her needs.

First on my agenda was a private appointment with my jeweler, who would showcase his finest engagement rings for her to select from. Laya deserved nothing less than the very best that money could buy, beginning with the unique symbol of my commitment adorning her finger.

I planned to invest a significant amount in her, expecting her to hesitate and shy away from the larger gemstones. After her visit last week, I was eager to uncover everything I could about her. Her shy, hesitant, and almost naive flirtation entranced me. She blushed like someone inexperienced, leaving me with many questions regarding her past.

My investigator revealed her modest life in Prague, which was far from luxurious, explaining her unease at my dinner. However, that still left the question of her shyness open.

I pressed my investigator to look into any previous romantic relationships she may have had, but he came back empty-handed. Laya's time in Prague was devoted to training at Vik's facility and caring for her younger sister.

She either seldom socialized or understood the importance of keeping her personal life private.

Could Laya be as innocent as she seemed? Surely, someone as stunning as her must have had previous lovers. Something felt amiss. Eventually, I'd uncover the truths of her past. The Vitalis sisters skillfully maintained a low-profile life, encompassing every aspect of their history.

"I'm going to work in my office until Laya arrives, Soti."

"Of course, Kyrios," he replied. With a respectful nod, he turned and disappeared down the lit corridor, leaving me alone with my numerous thoughts.

I walked past my room and paused to glance inside. The bed was meticulously made, and the room was serene, a stark contrast to the house staff's usual morning bustle.

Sometimes, I treated myself to extra time in bed, but on most days I woke up before dawn and worked until sunset. I couldn't help but smirk as I remembered how Laya had looked at the bed during her visit. I understood precisely what was on her mind.

I, too, had imagined the two of us sharing that bed, just as I found myself doing now.

However, since it was the dead of night, I envisioned her bathed in moonlight with her skin enveloped in a glowing light. She would scream her pleasure, head tilted back as I lost myself between her legs, savoring her sweetness.

"Jesus," I muttered, reaching down to adjust my growing erection.

These days, it felt like a hard cock was a permanent fixture in my pants, a constant, throbbing reminder of my obsession with her. She was under my skin already, and I hadn't even touched her yet.

I sighed and turned my eyes from the neatly arranged bed, my imagination racing with unending dreams of Laya. Striding down the corridor, I clenched my fists to suppress the storm of emotions swirling inside me, resolved to focus on the pending tasks in my quiet office.

I focused intently on my work for the next hour, stopping briefly to get a hot cup of rich, dark coffee before returning to my messy desk. The distribution deal papers lay scattered, demanding my full attention as they detailed the final steps of agreements with my cousins in Italy, when suddenly, the sound of heavy footsteps echoed down the hallway.

I barely glanced up before the door exploded open, and there they stood—my brothers, their faces twisted with rage.

"Hello, dear brothers," I drawled, one eyebrow arched as I steeled myself for what was coming. "Did you forget to knock?"

Stefano let out an exasperated grunt, while Markos shrugged, both emanating an air of shameless entitlement.

"What a surprise to see you both," I continued, injecting sarcasm into my tone. "I might have called it a pleasant surprise, but I know you'd see right through that, wouldn't you?"

My irritation with their reckless arrogance pulsed under my skin. They moved in perfect sync, always defending and enabling each other in their worst moments, like the archetypal rich kids spoon-fed their entire lives, taking every luxury for granted.

Resentment bubbled beneath the surface, ignited by the bond I had formed with our father. He had pinned his hopes on Stefano and Markos embracing the family business, but they rejected the idea of hard work.

Instead, they pranced around Europe, chasing extravagant parties and spending money like it was water, never satisfied and always seeking more.

It drained me just contemplating their endless indulgence.

They were lucky that my father had secured their inheritance; otherwise, I would have cut ties with them long ago. His foresight was exceptional. He barred them from claiming any interest in the family enterprise, insisting they should remain permanently excluded from its legacy since they refused to learn its complexities while he was alive.

This decision infuriated both of them, fueling their deep resentment stemming from their lack of genuine influence despite their vast wealth. Although their bank accounts held millions, it never felt like enough—a constant longing that would never be satisfied.

Watching them continue to vie for a position at a table they had never earned through effort or sacrifice was downright laughable.

Today, whatever minor grievance had upset them was clearly evident in the scowls on their faces.

"Is it true?" Stefano suddenly demanded, his eyes blazing with anger as he pointed a finger at me.

"And what rumor have you heard this time?" I replied, remaining unbothered by his childish display.

Years of dealing with their theatrics had shown me that silence was the most powerful response to their explosive outbursts; the less I stoked their flames, the less power their anger held.

"You plan to marry a Vitalis," he sneered, the name bitter like poison on his tongue.

I leaned back in my chair, crossed my arms over my chest, and asked, half-amused and half-exasperated, "Why do you care about my personal life?"

"Personal life!" Markos bellowed, his voice echoing off the walls. "It's hardly personal, Nikolas! Did you forget that we're discussing our family here? Our bloodline!"

"I promise you," I said, "this won't impact either of you, so spare me your theatrics. You're acting like a couple of spoiled teenagers. Grow up."

"Is it true, then?" Stefano accused.

I merely shrugged with indifference.

The atmosphere grew tense until Markos, in annoyance, threw up his hands. "This is unbelievable!"

"If it were so unbelievable, you wouldn't be standing here before me, would you?" I countered coolly.

"You blindsided us. This marriage affects the entire family legacy—ours included." Stefano insisted.

"My marriage is none of your concern. I hardly need permission from either of you." They were mistaken if they believed I would seek their approval before making any life-changing decision, especially concerning whom I would marry. I never trusted their advice, and I never would.

"Ever since our father died, you've claimed the title of godfather of the family!" Markos roared now, his anger seeping into every syllable as I fought the urge to cover my ears.

It was a familiar, tired argument we'd gone over countless times before, and I was not in the mood to debate who truly held the family's reins.

Everyone knew the truth.

"You both drain my very existence." I sighed, rolling my eyes. "Don't you have a party to attend in Ibiza or something? Or perhaps you should return to the yacht you took without consulting the proper channels."

Although I understood the source of their frustrations, I refused to take the bait and escalate into a needless battle. Their jealousy was clear. Everyone knew that aligning with the Vitalis sisters enhanced power. The two of them simmered with envy at the fact that my new union would empower me, not them.

"Don't overlook us," they insisted together.

"We play a role in our family's decisions, Niko, whether you acknowledge it or not," Stefano added.

"I'm not interested in arguing right now, Stefano," I warned, the threat palpable in the air.

Markos's thin lips twisted into a sneer as he shot back, "Let's discuss your true role, Niko. If you're planning to marry, it's your responsibility to ensure the Galanis family name isn't stained by the tainted blood of a fucking Vitalis, of all families."

I sat up and replied, "Are you certain that's what you mean, Markos? Choose your words wisely."

I released a feral growl, rising from my chair, the tension in my body coiling like a spring ready to snap. Luckily for the fucker, the solid wood desk acted as a barrier between us, or I would charge at him and pummel his face in.

I'd learned to endure their jealousy. They could bitch and complain about me and their situation as much as they wanted. However, they crossed the line when they insulted and attacked Laya and her family.

They pushed me too far and edged into dangerous territory.

I protected what was mine.

Laya was mine.

"We're not scared of you." Stefano's chin quivered in a feeble act of defiance.

"Then why does your voice tremble?" I taunted, giving them only a mild taste of the menace I could unleash upon them. "Nothing you say will alter my choice. My mind is set, and I won't change it just because you refuse to accept it. It's in everyone's best interest if you accept this and move on."

"Like you'll do when you're finished with her," Markos sneered.

I tilted my head to the side. "What did you say?"

"Be honest, Niko. You're only doing this to get into that woman's pants. I bet she's nothing more than a slut, just like her little sister," Markos spat as if dripping with venom.

"Her sister?" I repeated, feeling the predator inside me coiling up.

"It's common knowledge that she was whored out during her abduction," Stefano stated. "That's not a secret."

My blood froze instantly, and without hesitation, I rounded the desk. Before they could react, I grabbed their throats, slamming them into the wall. "Say that again!" I shouted, seething with rage.

The urge to kill coursed through my veins.

The loud footsteps of my guards reverberated through the hallway, quickly alerted by my raised voice. They stopped short the moment my brothers and I appeared.

I gripped harder, their frail bodies trembling as my anger turned them into statues of terror.

"You little bastards! If you utter another disparaging word about the Vitalis family, I swear you will regret every beat of your pathetic hearts!" This was a promise of retribution I pledged to my soul. "I am the rightful heir to this family, and you will respect that! You will respect me, my wife, and her sisters. Do you understand me, you disgusting little fuckers?"

Their eyes, once hard and defiant, now gazed at me with a mixture of disdain and broken pride. Under the relentless pressure of my grip, that defiance ultimately gave way to despair.

"Let go," Markos croaked, as he clawed at the unseen barrier between us. "Please."

I shook my head, squeezing just a little harder. "Never doubt I'd enjoy killing you both. Cross me again, and your precious inheritance disappears. You wouldn't want me to cut that off."

"You can't—" Markos began.

"Can't I?" I challenged, raising an eyebrow with cold amusement. "If even a whisper of rumor reaches me that you continue to pour venom from your mouths, I will show just how completely I can ruin your wretched existence. If you're not careful, you'll be begging for scraps on the streets like a pair of destitute peasants."

My men lingered at the doorway, their faces a mixture of readiness and silent approval, waiting for any sign that intervention was needed.

Finally, noticing the eerie blue tint spreading over their skin, I forcefully pushed them out of my office, loosening my tight grip. They staggered away, struggling to breathe as they grasped at their constricted throats.

"Now get out—and don't return uninvited," I snapped. I turned away without a glance, suddenly desperate for a drink.

FIVE

L AYANA

"Laya, are you sure about this?" Cali asked, her anxiety evident as we approached the imposing Galanis estate, and I turned to her with concern.

Cali's worry echoed the unease I hadn't admitted—even to myself—about the impulsive decision to let her move in without telling Niko.

I considered asking for Niko's input, but dismissed it. As his equal, I didn't need permission. And if he objected? That would be the red flag I needed before saying "I do."

"Yes. I want you at the estate. I promise, Niko won't have any objections."

Or at least, I hoped he wouldn't.

From my limited time with him, I suspected that he'd be surprised at first, but he would ultimately welcome her.

"You weren't exaggerating. Damn—it's massive." Cali stated, clearly skeptical.

A smirk tugged at my lips. "Trust me, my description didn't do it justice. You'll see."

Please let this be the start of her healing, I thought.

"My God, is that the house?" Cali froze in place, her voice barely above a whisper.

I grinned, but my pulse quickened—what if she hated it here?

"Part of it," I replied. "As we draw closer, you'll see that what we're looking at now is merely a small section of the entire property."

The Galanis Estate unfolded before us like a grand painting. The massive stone mansion stood in stately solitude, its weathered gray exterior exuding timeless elegance and quiet strength beneath the expansive blue sky.

When we finally came to a stop, Cali's gaze rose toward the magnificent structure in wide-eyed amazement, her mouth agape with disbelief.

"Holy shit, Laya. This is nothing like our place in Prague."

I stared at the mansion, absorbing every detail, the intricate stonework, and the sunlight dancing upon its surface.

"I'm still trying to wrap my mind around it," I admitted, awed and unsettled by the sight.

Though our family wealth outshone Niko's on paper, our

lives told a different story thanks to Papa's trust. Our home, filled with the warmth of laughter and simple joys, was a haven. We felt the comfort of soft, threadbare couches and the aroma of hearty meals simmering on the stove, yet there was never a sparkling chandelier above us or silk curtains fluttering in the breeze. Each day unfolded in a tapestry of shared moments rather than opulence, where the sun lit up our humble garden rather than dazzling jewels. We were surrounded by abundance, rooted in love and connection, but never in excess.

"You deserve this, Laya. We all do. Do you remember what Avra said? It's finally time to spend the money Papa left us," Cali reminded.

If only Cali could fully embrace what she'd said. However, before she could, she had to confront the lingering demons of her abduction, striving to reclaim the innocence and carefree spirit that once defined her.

Though I knew in my heart that the carefree and adventurous Cali of the past might never fully reemerge, I also believed that she would heal and grow even stronger. Beneath her fragile exterior, she harbored the fierce soul of a lioness. She was wounded, perhaps, but with time, she was destined to roar again.

"I believe we both do. Let's go inside."

Soti appeared at the threshold, greeting us with a respectful bow. Cali smiled at him, instantly charmed by his courteous demeanor.

"Ms. Vitalis, I see you've brought a guest," he said, welcoming.

"Soti, this is my sister, Calista. She'll be staying with us," I introduced.

"Welcome, Calista. It's a pleasure to meet you. My name is Soti, and I am here to assist you with anything you need. I will prepare a guest room for you right away. Ms. Layana, your suite is prepared, just as Mr. Galanis instructed," he assured us, his efficiency and kindness putting us both at ease.

I wasn't sure if he meant my room or Niko's. The idea of sharing a bed with Niko caused goosebumps to prickle over my skin.

Nope. Not going there. Not until I knew which room I'd sleep in and why.

Soti motioned for us to come in, and we entered the main foyer, our heels clicking on the white marble floor.

"I'll be back in a moment." He disappeared around the corner, leaving Cali and me alone in the spacious foyer.

Cali's eyes widened as she took in the opulence surrounding us. I hoped we'd swiftly adapt to our lavish new surroundings, yet I couldn't shake the feeling that living here would always resemble residing in a museum. I glanced at a life-sized marble statue of a naked woman at the base of the grand staircase and shook my head. Getting used to this would certainly take some time.

More than anything, I longed for us to feel safe. It had been ages since we experienced that sense of security, not since our parents passed away. Our time in Prague had been anything but secure, as we constantly looked over our shoulders, expecting trouble at any moment. Perhaps we could finally find a little peace amidst all this luxury.

I paused to let Cali take it all in when Niko began descending the grand staircase. His striking face took my breath away, and thoughts of him flooded my mind. The idea that he would soon be my husband thrilled and frightened me, stirring a mix of awe, excitement, and a hint of fear.

Ever since that dinner, I couldn't stop thinking about him, still feeling the lingering echo of his kiss on my lips even hours later.

When Niko saw us, his face lit up with a broad smile as he opened his arms in a welcome, instantly calming my nerves.

"Welcome!" he exclaimed, echoing throughout the marble-clad room.

He descended the stairs with effortless confidence, his gaze fixed on us, making it seem as if he could command the room merely by his presence.

Once at the bottom, he nodded in greeting to Cali first.

"Cali, welcome to the Galanis estate! I'm really glad you could make it," he said as if he had been expecting her all along, making it easy to overlook that I hadn't sought his permission before bringing her.

I couldn't help but appreciate how he kept a respectful distance. That small gesture confirmed my suspicion that he was thoughtful. Cali's past trauma had made her cautious about hugs and unfamiliar men getting too close.

My heart warmed instantly at his effort to make Cali feel comfortable and safe right away, and it paid off. I saw it in her eyes, in the way her shoulders relaxed, and in how she smiled up at him as if he made her feel secure and welcomed.

"Thank you for inviting me," she said politely.

"The pleasure is all mine," he replied, his eyes locking onto hers, their intensity bridging the gap between them. "I hope you feel at ease here. Please, stay as long as you wish."

Then he turned to me, and I sensed the world shift, as if a tide had set a ship adrift. His penetrating gaze made the room subtly spin around me as he took my hands.

"Welcome home, Laya."

Those simple greetings carried profound depth that tugged at my heart.

Home.

This would become my sanctuary, where I could lay down roots and flourish. The thought anchored me while filling me with a hopeful anticipation that stirred deep within.

"Thank you, Niko," I whispered as I looked up at him, my heart fluttering with the thrill of his touch and the sincerity in his gaze. The connection between us crackled like electricity in the air; his hands cradled mine in a cocoon, drawing me ever closer as if by an unseen force.

"Ms. Calista, if you'll follow me, I can show you to your room now," Soti interjected, appearing at our side, silent and almost like a shadow until he spoke.

"Oh, that's wonderful, thank you." She met my eyes briefly before trailing after Soti down a nearby hallway, leaving Niko and me enveloped in the quiet intimacy of the room.

"I'm so glad you brought Cali," he said.

"I hoped you would feel that way," I replied, my cheeks warming under his steady gaze. "I considered asking, but I decided it was easier to seek forgiveness than permission," I teased lightly.

"You don't need to ask, Laya." His matter-of-fact delivery was somewhat disconcerting. "This is as much your home as it is mine. Rest assured that she'll be safe here. If it helps, I can arrange for someone trustworthy to watch over her."

I looked up at him and slowly shook my head, feeling the weight of his offer.

"That's a generous thought. We have our security if necessary. Cali prefers not to have someone with her all the time; it feels constricting, making it hard for her to relax."

"I understand," Niko said thoughtfully. "Still, she deserves protection. I'll make sure someone inconspicuously checks on her. She won't even notice."

"Thank you," I whispered, as I gazed at him. My hands remained safely nestled in his, reflecting my deep sense of belonging.

Everything Niko had shown me so far had been gentle and considerate, contrasting sharply with his ruthless and temperamental business reputation. Perhaps those claims had been exaggerated, I thought. The man in front of me now, smiling down at me as if he would snatch the stars from the sky if I asked, was nothing like what I had prepared myself for. He was someone I could easily fall in love with.

Whether it was dangerous or not, I couldn't tell yet.

"Thank you for making us both feel so welcome," I said.

"Of course!" he replied. "Soti and the staff prepared a wonderful feast for dinner, and—" His sentence was interrupted by three massive Greek shepherds bounding into the room.

As I approached, a wave of surprise washed over me, quickly replaced by delight as I saw the beautiful dogs. Their lush black-and-white coats shimmered in the light, and their sweet eyes seemed to penetrate my heart with warmth.

"Oh, my goodness!" I exclaimed, feeling joy bubble inside me. They instantly sat at my feet, their gaze fixed on me, tails wagging in eager anticipation. "Who are these beauties?"

Niko stepped forward, a grin spreading across his face.

"This is Cerberus," he said, gesturing to the largest of the trio.

The three-headed guardian of the underworld inspired his name, and I chuckled as I reached down to greet him. Cerberus's dark eyes squinted in pleasure as I ruffled his fur.

"And this," Niko continued, his hand moving to the dog beside him, "is Ares, named after the God of War. He only becomes a true warrior when a bloody bone is at stake."

Ares sat perfectly still, his tail wagging vigorously behind him, radiating both energy and calm.

Niko's fingers found the last dog, gently scratching behind her ears. The dog leaned into his hand, her eyes closed in bliss.

"This is Artemis. She takes her name from the goddess of wild animals and hunts. If I let her, she would roam the property day and night, hunting anything that dared cross her path."

Looking at Artemis, I couldn't reconcile Niko's fierce description with the softness in her face. She exuded warmth, her tail wagging happily as she welcomed my touch.

"Well, she certainly looks like a ruthless killer," I said, laughter spilling from my lips as I stroked her fur.

Niko's eyes sparkled with mischief. "Looks can be deceiving, as you well know."

"Do I?" I shot back, standing to meet his gaze.

"If you passed me on the street, Laya, I would never suspect you were a vicious warrior capable of annihilating your opponent in the blink of an eye."

"You give me too much credit," I replied, a playful smile crossing my face.

"Only when it's deserved," he replied, his eyes dancing with wicked, unspoken promises.

"You're so kind, Niko. Are you always like this?" I inquired, intrigued by the effortless ease with which he navigated life.

With a sigh, he admitted, "I must confess, this is the approach to life I favor. Am I always like this? No, but I try to be until life gives me a reason to change."

"I see." I nodded, pausing for a moment before turning my attention to the animals. "Are these dogs always this well-behaved and obedient?"

"Not really. They're highly trained. They only behave like this around me, but they've included you now. I suppose they can sense that you're part of our 'pack' too."

"And you're the pack leader?" I asked with a smirk.

"Absolutely," he replied with a casual shrug and a wink

that suggested much more. "Which means you're mine now, by extension."

I laughed at his joking tone, rolling my eyes while keeping my thoughts to myself. I had never truly belonged to anyone and valued my independence—the idea of being his felt futile. Suddenly, an idea struck me.

"Hey, could we get a dog like this for Cali? She loves animals and having one might bring her a sense of security without overwhelming her."

"Yes, I think that's a wonderful idea. I'll take care of it," he agreed. "You're such a wonderful sister. Cali is lucky to have you."

"We're lucky to have each other," I replied, feeling tears well up in my eyes.

The weight of guilt clung to me, a constant reminder of Cali's kidnapping. As her older sister, I'd felt it was my role to shield her, and the thought that I had failed gnawed at my insides.

Niko lifted my hand, and his warm lips brushed against the back. As he smiled, a silent understanding passed between us, his thumb tracing delicate circles in the softness of my palm. An electric flutter coursed through me, awakening every nerve at the intimacy of his gesture, while the unwavering confidence in his gaze sent my heart racing.

But then, like a shadow creeping in, doubts about our upcoming marriage crashed over me.

What was I getting myself into?

Niko exuded self-assuredness, his touch and kisses flowing so effortlessly that they unsettled me. I felt like a fish out of water, unsure how to mirror his affection. Each moment was an uncharted sea, and my inexperience loomed like a storm, threatening to capsize my heart.

I abruptly pulled my hand back, casting my eyes toward the dogs, longing for some distraction.

"One more thing," he said in a playful lilt. "We have an appointment coming up."

"Where?" I asked, my curiosity piquing.

"I arranged some private time with my favorite jeweler."

"Jeweler?" I echoed, my eyes widening with surprise and anticipation.

"Of course." He shrugged. "I can't make you my wife without giving you a proper ring, don't you think?"

I felt my cheeks heat up. "Niko, I hope you understand that nothing extravagant is necessary. Perhaps just a simple gold band..."

"A simple gold band would be completely unsuitable for my bride."

"Niko, no, I—"

"We'll leave in an hour. I hope that's enough time for you to settle in. If not, I can reschedule the appointment."

His firm stance left no room for debate, so I refrained from arguing. Instead, I expressed my gratitude and decided to find Cali to introduce her to our new furry companions. I discovered her relaxing on the stone patio behind the mansion, just under the terrace. She was lounging on a chair, enjoying the sunshine. In the yard, the leaves of Niko's oak tree, Dryad, danced and created shadows on the grass below.

When Cali saw the dogs, she squealed with delight,

confirming my choice. She buried her face in their fur and hugged them tightly. The dogs, in response, wagged their tails even more vigorously and squirmed with joy, completely taken by her affection just as she was by them. This was the happiest I had seen Cali in a long time. Maybe, just maybe, everything would work out well after all.

———

Two hours later, Niko drove me to a luxurious home nestled several miles away from our estate, its grandeur evident even from the driveway. As we stepped out of the car, I glanced around, unsure.

"I thought we were heading to a jeweler," I remarked, curiosity tinged with confusion.

"We are," he replied, a playful glimmer dancing in his eyes. "I never claimed it was a store."

When the door swung open, an older gentleman appeared, eyes sparkling with delight at the sight of Niko. Without hesitation, he swept Niko into an exuberant embrace, his laughter echoing through the entryway.

"Spiro!" Niko exclaimed, returning the hug with equal warmth.

"My boy, Niko! It's such a joy to see you!" Spiro exclaimed with genuine affection.

I stood close by, a smile breaking across my face as I witnessed the energy of their joyful reunion.

"You too, Spiro." Niko pulled back, his gaze locking onto

Spiro's brilliant azure eyes with an intensity that spoke volumes. "Thank you for having us."

With his wild gray curls framing his beaming face, Spiro wore tailored trousers that complemented his forest-green shirt. A plaid vest added flair, and a jeweler's loupe hung around his neck like a badge of honor.

"Are you kidding? I was overjoyed to receive your call, dear Niko. I've been eagerly anticipating that you'd need my expertise for such an important milestone in your life."

Spiro's vibrant turquoise gaze shifted to me, his grin widening, lighting up his entire face.

"And you, lucky girl, must be the enchanting soul who persuaded this boy to finally become a proper gentleman."

"Now, Spiro..." Niko mock warned.

Spiro took my hands, pressed his lips to each one, then leaned in and brushed kisses against my cheeks.

"I'm Laya," I said, laughing. "It's a pleasure to meet you, Spiro."

"The pleasure is all mine, darling." He shook his head slowly. "Let me rephrase that—Niko is the fortunate one here. You are one of the most beautiful women I've ever seen, Laya."

"Oh, thank you," I managed, irresistibly charmed by him. In that moment, I felt a spark of affection.

"Please, come in! I have so much to show you!"

He hurried inside, and Niko gave me a wink and teased, "I think he likes you."

"I might be falling for him." I laughed.

Niko sighed. "Oh, wonderful, now I've got some competition!"

He left me speechless for a moment. Who could compete with a man like Niko? Perhaps I wasn't in love with him yet, but I couldn't help but wonder if I ever would be. Still, I kept these doubts to myself.

Niko led me farther inside, pausing at the doorway. I stepped into Spiro's home, where the leather furniture bore the marks of many gatherings, and the fire in the stone fireplace created an inviting glow. This space felt familiar and lived-in, a far cry from a typical jewelry shop.

"This way!" Spiro shouted from down the hallway as Niko led me toward him.

"You've been here before," I noted.

"Yes, indeed. Spiro was a close friend of my father. He became one of the most renowned jewelers in Athens during his prime, specializing in the rarest gems. Now, he mostly enjoys retirement, choosing clients based on personal connections."

I raised my eyebrows in admiration.

"He adores you," I remarked.

"My father often took me along when he visited Spiro during my childhood," Niko explained. "The man is delightfully eccentric and can charm anyone. So, when I needed a ring for you, he was the very first and only person I trusted with the task."

I was touched to learn that he had such a personal connection to the person from whom we would purchase the ring. As we turned a corner and entered a different wing of the house, my eyes widened in surprise at my surroundings.

Though not a typical retail space, this area of the home displayed a stunning array of jewels, elegantly enriching every surface. Spiro's collection of necklaces, earrings, and bracelets draped in black velvet, was arranged in artistic displays. A complete set of shimmering tiaras was showcased on one wall, illuminated by display lights.

"This is magical," I murmured, taking in the scene. "It feels like a dream."

Stepping behind a glass case, Spiro lifted a black velvet drape to reveal a tray of shimmering engagement rings.

"I took the liberty of selecting a few pieces for you. Once I understand your taste better, I have more to show as well."

My heart raced as I approached, the sparkling rings enticing me like a radiant tunnel. I scrutinized each one, my eyes growing wider with each piece. Slowly, I shook my head.

"They're incredible," I murmured as Niko approached from behind and placed his hand on the small of my back.

A shiver raced up my spine, and despite my reaction to the spectacular jewels before me, I realized it was his touch that had triggered the shiver.

These extravagant jewels only made me feel nervous.

"Do you like them?" Niko asked.

"Well, how could I not?" I laughed. "But..."

"But what?" he prodded.

"They're just so... I just don't think..." I stammered.

"Yes, they're beautiful," Niko acknowledged. "But none are as beautiful as you, Laya."

"Niko," I murmured, shaking my head. "I truly don't need any of this, I promise..."

Spiro remained in the periphery, observant and quiet.

Niko's unyielding gaze made me uncomfortable. He ignored my objections and continued his attempts to console me.

"You don't need them. Remember what you are worth," he said, guiding my chin up to connect our gazes. "You'll be my bride. You're a Vitalis and soon to be a Galanis. You deserve the best, always."

I took a deep breath, trying to find the courage to stop worrying about the cost of such an expensive item and allow Niko to do as he wished. Perhaps in time, I would adjust to this. Ultimately, wearing luxurious jewelry and embracing a lavish lifestyle might become instinctive, allowing me to navigate my new life as effortlessly as everyone believed the Vitalis sisters always did.

But I had so much to learn first.

How could I wear something so priceless daily without damaging or losing it?

They all seemed so heavy. They could easily slip off my finger. The thought of that made me feel nauseous.

"Which one do you prefer?" I finally asked Niko as I turned to face Spiro and relaxed my shoulders.

He glanced over my shoulder, examined the collection, and then shook his head dismissively.

"No, these aren't right," he commented. "Spiro, show us something better, something larger..."

"What the hell? Larger?" I couldn't hide my shock. "You must be joking."

"These don't fit your personality," he said with a casual shrug.

"That might be true," I countered. "But something larger doesn't fit either."

"Why don't you describe the style you're looking for?" Spiro proposed.

I tilted my head, waiting for Niko's input.

His dark eyes met mine. "There's a subtle elegance about you. You're classy, not flashy or over the top. I'm sure Spiro has something that suits you."

"I think I have the ideal choice," Spiro interjected, his eyes shining with joy. "I will return soon."

He sprinted away, his curls bouncing behind him, his oxfords clicking against the wooden floor.

Niko wrapped his arms around my waist, drawing me closer as we waited. My heart raced, and the scent of his cologne enveloped me.

I asked, "Is this necessary?"

"Yes," he replied firmly.

"I don't need this," I protested.

He turned me to face him. "I need it."

"Why?"

He leaned closer. "It signifies you as mine."

"Mine?" I raised an eyebrow. "A ring that says, 'property of Niko'?"

He smirked. "If that's your interpretation."

"I belong to no one, Niko. I am my own person."

"That will always hold true," he comforted me, squeezing me closer. "Marriage binds us to each other equally."

I felt my throat tighten. "Are you saying—"

Before I could finish, Spiro returned with a new tray of rings. "Ta-da! Understated and classy!"

Niko maintained eye contact. "We'll discuss this later. For now, it's time to choose your ring."

I turned to the selection and instinctively picked up a three-diamond circlet ring, lifting it from its velvet cushion to inspect it closely. Tears welled up at its beauty and the memories it evoked.

"Do you like that one?" Niko asked.

I nodded, briefly speechless.

My heart raced, tears forming. "It's just like Mama's engagement ring. After fleeing to Prague, we never learned what became of her belongings."

Niko caressed my back. "It's beautiful."

"I always loved it," I whispered. "There were times she'd let me wear it, and we'd giggle at how oversized it looked on my small finger."

"Give me your hand," Niko instructed.

"What?" I replied, meeting his gaze.

He took the ring from me and placed it on my finger.

"It fits perfectly," Spiro declared. "It was meant for you." The diamonds glimmered through my tears as I looked at my hand, and the emotions I had suppressed finally spilled over.

Niko wiped away the wetness trailing down my cheeks

and drew me in, kissing my forehead. "We'll take this one, Spiro," he said, glancing over my shoulder.

Six

N ikolas

Walking back to the house, I noticed the olive grove leaves rustling, creating a soothing melody. My mother had always reminded me to pause and appreciate nature's music.

Listening revived my memories of her, much like the moments spent by the Dryad near my bedroom. Unlike my brothers, this place meant more to me than mere profit. The estate was filled with emotions; every stone and shadow held the love our parents once surrounded us with.

A scarf fluttered on the chair, and I immediately recognized it as the one Cali had worn this morning to cover her hair. She must have forgotten it.

Laya and Cali had been here for almost a week, and I had comfortably settled into a routine of days spent working on the estate and evenings enjoying Soti's delicious dinners with them.

Having them around was an easy transition, except for one thing.

The craving to slip into Laya's room at night became nearly unbearable and a relentless obsession. She remained completely unaware of the magnetic pull she exerted.

As soon as we parted each night and I sensed her just a door away, my resolve crumbled. I already knew I wouldn't last. I tormented myself with thoughts of whether I could hold back until our wedding night before succumbing to the primal hunger to consume her completely.

Her attraction was evident, despite her efforts to conceal it. I frequently noticed her glancing in my direction. I understood how a woman's body responded to my presence, and my soon-to-be wife was more than intrigued. Her intense gaze burned, leaving me painfully on edge, aching to claim her.

However, I had to tread carefully.

It was evident she was jittery about her own reactions.

Soon, I'd finally have her, indulging in every wicked fantasy she inspired.

I scrubbed a hand down my face. It was time to pull myself together.

I approached the house as Laya and Cali drove up the steep driveway in one of my sports cars.

Correction, one of *our* cars.

The windows were down, and Laya was behind the wheel of the Roma Spider.

They'd just gotten back from scouting wedding venues.

I smirked, recalling my discussion with Laya about our wedding plans. She had admitted she initially wanted to elope but knew her sisters would never forgive her for skipping a proper wedding.

If she'd mentioned it earlier, we could've skipped the circus and spared me a week of walking with a constant erection.

When I rounded the corner of the house, I anticipated seeing Laya's convertible; however, I found two other cars next to hers.

My jaw clenched. "Fucking hell."

Why were Markos and Stefano here? They still saw my instructions as mere suggestions. I hurried into the house, concerned about what I might find. If they'd said one harsh thing to Laya or Cali, I'd make sure they regretted it.

As soon as I entered, I realized my worst fears had come true. I rushed down the hallway toward the living room.

I could distinctly hear Laya's rising anger cutting through the murmurs of Stefano and Markos as they unsuccessfully tried to calm her. I paused in the shadows just before the corner, straining to catch every nuance of the intense argument.

"Am I supposed to care what the two of you idiots think?" Laya snapped. "I'm not marrying either of you. What the hell do your opinions have to do with it?"

On the defensive, Stefano muttered, "Laya, come on—this isn't the time for theatrics."

But Laya shot him a fierce look. "Theatrics? Please, Stefano, tell me that's the best you can do? I didn't tie the knot with a pair of buffoons!" she thundered.

Well, well, well, my fiancée certainly had a temper.

Arousal surged through me, and my cock grew thick and hard like a lead pipe in my pants, desire and admiration blending into a heady mix.

Damn, that fiery, unyielding side of hers was hot as fuck.

Pushing that thought aside, I focused on my idiot brothers. The urge to step in needled me, but she was clearly handling them.

I'd wait and see how it played out.

"Yes, you should consider our perspective," Stefano insisted. "We share the Galanis name. It doesn't belong solely to Nikolas, despite his beliefs."

"From what I understand, neither of you has a legal claim to this estate. Am I correct?"

A heavy silence fell between them until Laya resumed, unleashing brutal sarcasm. "Honestly, I've heard you two are nothing but insignificant losers who couldn't tell Assyrtiko from Agiorgitiko."

I almost laughed aloud at her cutting wit, but restrained myself, enthralled by how she effortlessly took down the jerks.

"How dare you speak to us with such disrespect!" Markos shouted, his face flushed with anger.

With a light chuckle, Laya replied, "In my culture,

respect is not something you can demand. It's something you must earn."

"You and your whole family are nothing but failures," Stefano said, full of malice, igniting a desire to strangle him. "You've squandered all the power your father amassed."

"Maybe we did, but in the end, we proved we were our father's daughters," Laya said, calm and even, yet laced with pure hatred. "We returned, reclaimed what was rightfully ours, and even expanded our territory."

"Good luck holding onto that," Stefano retorted, but his crossed arms and tight jaw betrayed his doubt.

I cautiously edged closer, curious about how my fiancée navigated the tension.

Laya approached them confidently, stepping into Stefano's personal space without a moment's pause.

She tilted her head, her perfectly manicured finger gliding along her jawline. "Let me guess, you're the second child, Stefano? Is that right?"

"Yes," he answered, irritation clear.

"So am I." She raised an eyebrow. "Look at us: completely different beings, wouldn't you say? I returned, reclaimed what belonged to me, and created a life. And you? What have you accomplished? Snorted cocaine? Overdosed on ecstasy? Squandered cash on drugs and fleeting pleasures until you've become just a shadow of your older brother? Or have you genuinely achieved something?"

Every one of her retorts struck like a dagger, and I couldn't believe he hadn't collapsed into a heap of shattered ego. Instead, his glare darkened as he stepped forward in a weak attempt to intimidate her.

"Oh, come on, Stefano," Laya said lightly, almost with a chuckle. "Do you think you can scare me?"

My adrenaline surged alongside my heartbeat. Here was my fiancée, standing her ground like a warrior.

She got into a fighting stance. I was certain that if Stefano attempted to make another move, she would take care of it before I could even consider stepping in.

Stefano growled, but his show of aggression was feeble and unconvincing. Laya just laughed, exuding confidence, unconcerned and completely unfazed.

Just when the tension seemed unbearable, Cali swung open the door to the terrace, accompanied by my three guard dogs. Immediately on high alert, Artemis escaped Cali's hold and lunged at Stefano, sinking her teeth into his leg.

Stefano's scream pierced the air, high-pitched and filled with terror, causing him to crumple to the ground in a heap of pure agony.

The other dogs barked and growled furiously, their leashes tugging as Cali desperately tried to regain control. Amid all the chaos, Laya's commanding presence remained steadfast, leaving no doubt that while words could wound, actions had their own brutal way of settling scores.

I burst into the room, and immediately, chaos engulfed me. The dogs barked and snapped; Cali shouted at Artemis to calm down, while Markos yelled at the top of his lungs. Yet, nothing compared to Stefano's furious screams. "Hey, what the hell?" I shouted as I noticed Markos reaching into his jacket.

The sunlight glinted off the barrel of his handgun, reflecting ominously as he swiftly aimed it at Artemis and clicked off the safety.

"Markos, no!" I ordered, instantly cursing myself for having hesitated for far too long. Everything spiraled out of control in an instant.

I was rounding the massive sofa when Laya, deadly calm, drew a gun and pressed it firmly against Markos's temple.

The room fell silent except for the ongoing scuffle between Stefano and Artemis on the floor.

Laya sneered, her gaze sharp and piercing, chilling the air around her. "Go ahead, asshole. Keep giving me reasons to shoot your ugly fucking face off."

Markos, his eyes blazing with anger, spat back, "Get your fucking woman off me, Niko!"

"His what?" Laya released the safety on her pistol and pressed the barrel deeper against his flesh.

Then, as if on cue, my men charged down the hallway like a small army.

"What do you want us to do?" one of them asked as they closed in, weapons ready.

"Remove these buffoons from my property!" I demanded. "Artemis, heel!"

Artemis quickly released Stefano and rushed to my side, sitting down. Stefano screamed in agony while clutching his leg, blood pouring from the wound.

My men surged forward to subdue both of them. Realizing he was in over his head, Markos reluctantly released his grip on the gun and allowed my men to escort him out.

As he was led away, he shouted back, "We'll be back, you prick! How dare you choose a Vitalis over your flesh and blood, your brothers!"

I glared at him and retorted, "Think twice about returning—my guards won't allow you back!"

I turned back to the women and shook my head in disbelief and exasperation. "Ladies, I apologize for the deeply offensive behavior of those two imbeciles. I'm ashamed to be related to them."

Laya shrugged coolly. "It's not your fault, Niko. Besides, I can handle myself."

"Clearly."

Cali, still trying to catch her breath, knelt beside Artemis, who had tiny droplets of blood trailing from her mouth but sat obediently.

"It was these beautiful babies who saved the day." Cali reached down to pet Artemis, who happily wagged her tail. "You're such a good girl, Artemis. Let's go get you a treat."

Cali stood up, and immediately all three dogs perked up, moving to her side and following her out of the room.

Laya stood there, the cold steel of the gun still clutched in her hand, her presence a shadowy force in the dimly lit room. I approached her, prying her fingers from their viselike grip. The gun clinked against the table, the sound sharp and final.

"You didn't flinch."

Her eyes gleamed with fierce, unyielding intensity. "When it comes to protecting myself and my family, yes."

The tension between us crackled—visible, electric, and alive. Her boldness sparked a primal instinct in me—a dark, simmering urge that tugged at my self-control, threatening to break the promise I'd sworn to uphold: to keep my hands to myself until marriage's sacred bond.

In that instant, she became a goddess of fury and allure, a powerful force poised to destroy anyone threatening her haven. The doubt I once felt was shattered, giving way to a fierce warrior spirit rising from the depths of her past.

In a quick movement, she seized my shirt collar and drew me near, her resolve unmistakable. Her emerald gaze locked onto mine with a force that reflected the storm inside, poised to engulf us both. Our breaths intertwined, each pulse amplifying the undeniable attraction between us. Chaos thickened in the air—a fierce energy igniting between us that embodied our unsaid feelings until nothing else existed but us.

SEVEN

L AYANA

I was amazed by my own boldness. Grabbing him with fierce urgency, I couldn't hold back the desire and need that had been simmering between us for the entire week.

Our close proximity, separated only by a thin wall, left me drowning in overwhelming desire. Every fiber of me burned to feel him—his heat, his scent, his mouth. Every stolen glance and lingering touch heightened my craving for him, electrifying the air around us. I yearned to close the distance, bridging the gap that felt both intimate and maddeningly far. I needed his skin against mine, his scent in my lungs. I tried to respect his desire to wait, yet every second apart felt like pure torture.

One kiss—just one—and I'd combust. At the very least, it would light up the night, and I knew I could no longer resist. My heart raced at the thought of finally surrendering to my feelings.

The moment I made my move, time halted. This visceral need overwhelmed my senses. However, just as our lips drew near, I hesitated.

Fear surged. What if this was a mistake?

Nonetheless, our chemistry crackled with an electrifying intensity, propelling me beyond my fears. One glance at the longing in his eyes melted away any uncertainty I felt. With the flavor of his breath so near, I realized I had to take the leap. Our lips hovered, breath mingling—heat coiled tight between us, ready to snap.

But Niko was anything but frozen. He responded as if I had ignited a fierce inferno within him.

His dark eyes momentarily widened before transforming into a deep, primal hunger. A low, guttural growl escaped, and in an instant, he seized control.

His hand crashed against the front of my shoulder as he violently shoved me backward until I slammed into the wall. I whimpered as the shock of impact coursed through me. With a swift, authoritative motion, he pinned both my wrists against the wall, his strong grip leaving me completely immobilized.

And I found myself loving its demand.

He captured my lips, sealing my momentary gasp. Gone was the tender, lingering kiss from before. In its place was an urgent, blistering conquering—hot, hard, and impatient.

I pulled back, gasping for air as I whispered, "I thought... you wanted...to wait."

"I did." His reply came out in a near growl that echoed inside. "But when you entered my world, you became mine, Laya. Marriage is just a formality."

All of a sudden, my heart raced as if ready to jump from my chest, and my skin felt as if it were on fire.

His piercing gaze turned to me again, and with a fierce, possessive growl, he captured my mouth again. His tongue slipped between my lips, searching, probing, and battling with mine in a teasing, seductive dance.

Instantly, my nipples hardened, and my clit throbbed in a way I'd never experienced before. My core clenched, and a rushing flood of need overflowed like a tidal wave deep inside me.

He pressed on, deepening the kiss and awakening every one of my nerve endings.

I never anticipated such an unrestrained, voracious surge of sensation, but I lost myself and surrendered completely. The raw, mesmerizing, primal dance of his tongue stirred something deep within me, unveiling a depth of desire I had yet to uncover. It was not merely a kiss but a passionate embrace that pulled me into an abyss of need.

This was a seduction in itself.

I arched, needing more contact, but with my hands still pinned above my head, the best I could do was graze my breast against him.

This haze of lust pushed me to the edge of desperation.

"Niko," I whimpered as he moved forward, pressing his hot, hard, throbbing cock against my thigh.

The sensation of it, so thick and long, caused my eyes to snap open. This man wasn't small by any means, and my inexperience wasn't clouding my judgment.

How the hell was he going to fit inside me?

A sudden wave of panic washed over me as he withdrew his lips, his intense gaze fixed on mine. His primal desire sent my heartbeat racing, creating an undeniable attraction between us. At that moment, I felt like a coveted prey held captive, poised for his relentless pursuit as his desire crackled around us. My breaths quickened, the world fading into a blur as all that mattered was the tantalizing thrill of his presence, a fierce storm waiting to break.

Niko's desire for me pulsed like a heartbeat, penetrating deep into my core and stirring every fiber of my being.

A shiver raced down my spine as if our connection sparked a wildfire within. A magnetic pull tethered us, and every moment together heightened my senses, awakening something primal inside.

I ached. There was no other way to describe it.

But I also felt so alive.

How was that even possible?

My reasons for choosing him now seemed insignificant.

A rush of emotions enveloped me, each stripping away barriers around my heart, as if they were a powerful tide of feelings, caught off guard by the depth of our connection.

My heart pounded in my ears, and my skin burned for more of whatever this man could reveal to me.

"Your mouth tastes like the sweetest nectar, Laya," he murmured, trailing fiery kisses down my neck.

I threw my head back, relishing the feathery touch of his kisses. He kissed me with light passes, yet his mouth felt sizzling hot, his kisses searing my skin as he trailed down toward my chest.

Niko released my arms and tugged the straps of my dress over my shoulders, letting them slip halfway down my arms. The fabric flowed down, exposing my cleavage as his desperate kisses moved lower, teasing my hardened nipples and leaving me deliciously bare.

Throughout my life, I frequently envisioned being kissed and touched with intense passion. However, nothing could have readied me for the deep sensation that coursed electrifyingly through every part of my existence.

A heat raged inside me, my fingers trembled, my stomach fluttered, and each brush of his lips ignited a whirlwind of need so intense that I felt drunk and lightheaded.

And I wanted, needed, craved more and more.

When his fingertips added to the assault, gliding seductively along my bare arms, each caress sent shivers of delight over my body.

"Oh," I gasped and moaned, grasping onto his forearms, unable to do anything else. "This feels so good."

I pressed against him, pleading for something bolder, something stronger.

This was a new experience, unfamiliar territory that I was eager to explore. A hunger clawed at me from the inside out. I had to find a way to express my desires.

But how?

I focused on his movements, letting him lead, trying not to think too much.

He growled in response and delivered, making me cry out as he pinched my nipples through my dress. The sensations he brought forth shot straight to my pussy, and a flood of desire pooled between my legs.

I had explored my own body before, but it had been nothing compared to the way his fingers moved. Having Niko awaken parts of me that I hadn't known existed was utterly overwhelming.

He guided my arms to my sides and lowered my dress. However, it caught at my waist.

"You're a masterpiece, Laya," he growled. "I'm the luckiest man alive."

He reached forward, caressing my left breast before cupping it fully in his palm. His thumb traced slowly over the sensitive bud through the lace of my bra, pleasure-filled pain shooting through me.

My core clenched, and my clit throbbed with need as he repeated the same sensual treatment on my right breast. His intentional touches sparked electric currents over my skin, making me feel delightfully mischievous under his unabashed admiration.

Heat surged through my cheeks, a reaction I rarely experienced. His gaze swept over me, absorbing every inch, leaving me exposed.

Goosebumps prickled my skin, and the ache between my

legs intensified, a mix of painful need and vulnerability that was almost overwhelming.

Suddenly, he leaned in again and captured my lips with his kiss. It was deep and commanding until he pulled back, resting his hands on my hips. He lifted me into his arms with effortless strength and took a few steps before setting me down on a desk in the corner.

"Lift up." Niko's palms rested on my hips as he peeled the dress past my hips and flung it aside, leaving me bare except for the red lace panties and the matching bra I had hastily chosen this morning.

His mouth traced a path along the curve of my neck. He left teasing kisses across my throat and shoulder, hinting at hidden pleasures yet to be explored.

I struggled with the buttons on his black pinstriped shirt, eager to reveal the skin beneath. Matching his energy, I slid the fabric from his shoulders, my hands brushing against him as a sense of urgency enveloped us.

My fingers traced his sculpted body, his bare skin feeling like velvet beneath my fingertips. I gripped his biceps, his rippling muscles bunching and flexing beneath my touch. My palms roamed over his arms and down his back, appreciating every ridge and contour. He radiated strength, an embodiment of pure masculinity.

Summoning my courage, I let my hand drift between his legs. My fingers quivered as they brushed against the rigid length of his pulsing cock, straining through the denim of his jeans.

A growl rumbled from his throat as he lifted his head to lock his gaze with mine. His midnight eyes seethed with a fierce, almost savage promise of a storm ready to unleash lust and violence.

This should have frightened me. I was treading into dangerous territory. Yet, my body shivered with exhilaration and anticipation.

There was no turning back. Niko intended to claim me completely, and I wanted every part of that. I craved everything he offered, desperate to reciprocate every ounce of that passion.

In that charged moment, I nearly confessed my inexperience, a truth that perhaps should have been shared earlier.

But experiencing his hunger for me and wanting this ache deep inside of me satisfied, I couldn't afford the risk of him stopping. His cock still throbbed fiercely in my hold, and the raw, intoxicated blaze in his eyes made it clear he wanted me with the same intensity that I craved him.

My heart pounded as I recognized that Niko was leading us into a deep and wild rendezvous, and the thrill of uncertainty sent a jolt of fear straight to my gut.

"Are you okay?" he demanded, low and rough as he searched my eyes for any sign of hesitation.

I knew this was the moment when I could withdraw, confess everything, and have a candid conversation about boundaries.

Yet, wasn't this uncontrolled, fervent longing exactly what we sought? Gathering all my strength, I raised my chin to meet his questioning gaze directly.

Fuck it.

I could no longer hold back.

"I've never felt more alive," I whispered, surrendering the truth and the heated passion of our encounter.

He radiated primal satisfaction as he pressed his lips to mine once more, slow and deliberate this time, yet infused with an unmistakable lust.

He savored my mouth with sensual precision, making me feel as if I might completely lose myself.

"Please, Niko," I pleaded between gasps, pulling away just a bit. "More..."

"I want more- too, Laya. More of you," he replied huskily.

He reached behind me and unclasped my bra, letting it fall away and drop with a confident, tantalizing grin. I bit my lower lip in anticipation as his fingers caressed my exposed skin, his touch both possessive and gentle.

He sank to his knees before me, his gaze slow and measured.

My breath caught as he took hold of my panties, inching them down over my hips with agonizing slowness until they joined my bra, leaving me adorned only with my engagement ring and an ever-growing need.

His attention lingered between my thighs, and I couldn't help but feel a surge of vulnerability bubble up.

He placed his hands on my knees, easing them apart with a firm insistence. My heart pounded in my chest, a wild drumbeat in the silence, as his gaze threatened to unravel me completely. "Lie back, darling Laya," he crooned, his voice thick with lust. "I've been dying to find out what you taste like."

He coasted his breath over my swollen labia, eliciting a shudder from my body. Then he planted a series of enticing kisses along my inner thighs, slowly trailing up towards my pussy. However, just as he neared my center, he withdrew once more. It was a tease, a wicked torment.

The quivering in my aching core grew stronger with each pass.

His smooth hair brushed against the sensitized skin of my trembling thighs, leaving me breathless. By the time he brought the wicked molten pleasure of his mouth to my aching pussy, I felt like I might faint from holding my breath in anticipation.

His tongue darted out, licking over my swollen clit.

"Niko," I shouted, my head thrashing as pleasure cascaded throughout my body in exhilarating waves.

This experience was completely different from what I had envisioned. Instead, it was indulgent, heated, sensual, and delicious.

His tongue flicked out repeatedly. I was unable to breathe or think.

I opened my thighs wider, wanting more, needing more. This teasing had to stop.

I whimpered. "Oh, Niko, please..."

Giving me a small mercy, this time he pressed the tip of his tongue directly on my clit, leaving it there for a brief moment before gradually shifting it slightly circles. The wet heat of his tongue against my most sensitive spot unleashed a wave of sensations.

I'd never felt anything so good, so sweet, so fucking right in my life.

"Yes, God! Oh, my God! Oh, my God, Niko!" I cried out as he delved deeper, slipping around the folds of my pussy lips, exploring every part of me with long, slow, lingering strokes. "Holy fuck!"

Tears filled my eyes as vibrations flowed through my body like waves of white-hot pleasure. The sensations his tongue produced reached every inch of my flesh, leaving me unable to think of anything except the feeling of his hot mouth working against me.

"Niko!" I shouted.

The room.

My eyes flew open as I looked around.

All the interior doors were wide open. Anyone could walk in.

I hoped like hell that nobody did.

Just as I was about to speak to Niko, he suddenly thrust his tongue deep into the entrance of my pussy. My back arched, and every worry I had floated away into pure pleasure. I could think of absolutely nothing with his tongue on me like that. My thighs widened even more, and I pressed my lips up towards his mouth.

"Niko, God yes, Niko!" I cried out, my body writhing under the blissful feeling of his tongue deep inside my pussy.

He fucked into me, then scraped up towards my clit, capturing my swollen pearl in his teeth, and sucked.

"Ooooooh!" I moaned, fireworks exploding in my head. I pressed my hips up again, my body begging for more. "Please don't stop. My God, that's so good."

But the wicked man paused, making me cry out.

His gaze locked with mine. "I want you to come for me, darling. Let me taste your pleasure, Laya."

He lowered his head, returning to his ministrations. He lifted me higher and higher, my muscles tightening and my core quivering. I bucked my hips as immense pressure built up like rolling waves within my undulating body.

He reached up, his thumb landing on my clit and pressing hard, moving in large, rhythmic circles as his mouth fucked into me. He pushed harder and harder, holding onto my flailing hips with his other hand to keep me in place.

"Niko! Niko! Niko!" I cried, his name tumbling uncontrollably from my lips.

The pressure within me built up as if a volcano built hot and molten until it finally erupted in a euphoric explosion of bliss that resonated through every inch of my trembling body.

I crashed over the edge, shaking and shuddering.

Niko continued his delicious torture, working me through the waves of ecstasy as they slowly faded away and left me limp on the desk below him, whimpering in bliss.

He pulled away, leaving my pussy empty, wet, and swollen. He brought his body up against mine and grazed his lips over the shell of my ear.

"Maurodaphne," he murmured.

I could barely hear him through the fog of pleasure still coursing through me.

"What?" I whispered.

"The sweetest grape in all of Greece. That's what your pussy tastes like, darling," he explained, his lips moving hotly against my ear.

I moaned, pushing my breasts against his bare chest. I was exhausted from the pleasure of his mouth, yet I was far from finished with him. My gesture elicited a growl from deep within him, and I smiled with satisfaction.

"Shall we move this to another room, Niko?" I asked. "Anyone could walk in."

"Let them see me make love to my wife. What do I care?"

"But they can probably hear us," I said.

"So? What do I care? In fact, scream louder. I want the entire staff to hear you scream my name. I want them to know I understand how to please my wife."

The way he spoke stirred something deep within me. I wasn't his wife—at least, not yet. But clearly, he regarded me as solidly his. And was that what we were doing? Making love? Here, at this desk? Was this where I was meant to lose my virginity?

Apparently so.

He positioned himself between my thighs, standing over me as he reached for the button of his jeans. In seconds, he was shoving them down his legs with his boxers, standing up and revealing his breathtakingly gorgeous naked body to my virgin eyes.

"Wow! It's so...beautiful!" I exclaimed, my gaze scanning

his chiseled, muscular body and fixating on the impressive shaft swaying between his thighs.

I immediately wished I could take back what I just uttered. I clearly sounded like someone who had never encountered a penis in real life before.

Niko chuckled, moving closer to me. I reached up, gripping his velvety shaft, fascinated with the way it throbbed in my palm. My eyes widened as he placed his hand over mine, guiding it and making me stroke him up and down.

"Laya." His cock swelled and twitched under my fingers as he growled my name.

I lifted my gaze to meet his, and the darkness I discovered there left me speechless.

"I can't wait any longer, babe," he said. "Fuck everything I said before. I was a fool to think I could wait. I need your cunt around my cock. Now."

My mouth fell open at his crude words. Perhaps I should have preferred him to say something more elegant, but coupled with the look in his eye of pure, raw desire, he left me yearning to throw my thighs open wide and invite him deep inside of me.

I followed through as planned. Gradually, I reclined once more, my exposed body laid out for him, my soul unguarded and ready to surrender completely.

"Take me, Niko," I pleaded.

His eyes widened with darkness and desire as he stepped forward, his cock nudging at my entrance.

My heart raced with anticipation as I tried to quell my fear.

I had envisioned this very moment countless times since meeting Niko. Now that it had finally arrived, each breath felt as if it were stolen from my lungs.

I stared up at him, bracing for his invasion, knowing it would likely hurt. I was ready for it. Having endured much pain in my life, I knew I would emerge on the other side. I always did.

This time, however, I would emerge as a different woman.

His cock pressed forward. "You're so damn tight."

"That's because—" I tried to breathe, knowing the moment was here. "I've never done this before."

His eyes darted up, crashing into mine. "What do you mean by that?"

I lifted my hips, urging him to push deeper. I was dying.

"Laya?" he asked, cocking his head to the side.

"Exactly what I said." I shifted again, but his grip on my hips tightened.

His eyes narrowed. "This—as in sex, you mean?"

"Yes," I murmured, looking up at him and awaiting his response while studying him intently.

His gaze searched through mine. "You should have told me."

"Now you know."

"This explains a lot," he said, shaking his head as if everything were falling into place. "It makes sense why you acted the way you did."

I raised my chin. What could he possibly mean by that?

He spoke through clenched teeth. "If you want to—"

"Don't you dare, Nikolas Galanis! I didn't wait this long for you to change your mind."

"You must think I'm stronger than I really am. I lack that kind of willpower." He smirked, looking down at me with dark amusement in his eyes. "I was going to suggest we proceed more slowly, not stop."

"Oh," I breathed.

"I meant what I said. I was a fool to believe I could wait with you in my house, sleeping in the room next to mine."

I smiled up at him, wrapping my legs around his hips and pulling him closer.

"I'm ready, Niko," I declared. "Fuck me. Please."

"Oh, Laya," he growled, pushing his cock in deeper.

He leaned down, grasped the back of my neck, and pulled me close for a kiss before gazing back into my eyes.

"Laya, lovely Laya. You belong to me now. Forever. Do not forget it, not even for a moment." And with that, he surged his hips forward, his cock driving deep into my pussy.

"Niko!" I called out, my arms wrapping around him, my thighs pulling him closer.

I expected pain, but it was more of a sharp discomfort, a hot sensation that morphed into an exquisite sting.

I craved more of it. It was a delicious kind of pain.

"Shh, I've got you, sweetheart." He rocked into me, his cock thick and hard.

He wrapped his arms around me, his hips creating a slow, hypnotic trance.

"You're much bigger than a toy," I muttered, then realized what I'd said.

He chuckled. "Good to know."

"Forget I said that."

"Not a chance."

Ever so slowly, he started transitioning from pushing in and then pulling out to harder, deliberate thrusts.

My body reacted immediately, my pussy quivering and gripping his cock with each pass.

"My God, Niko, it's amazing," I exclaimed, clinging to him, my eyes shut tightly as I allowed the sensation to wash over me. Goosebumps prickled my skin, and desire blossomed deep in my belly.

Soon, my hips met his thrust for thrust, and my core flooded his pistoning shaft with arousal.

Every part of me tingled. The sensations were so different from when Niko had his mouth on me. This was deeper. There was a delicious pain to it that I craved more of.

"More, please. I need more." I raked my nails over Niko's shoulders, desperate to find whatever he could give me.

"What do you need, Laya?"

"I don't know. Just give it to me. I'm dying." I thrashed against him, the ache building to an unbearable level. "I need it harder."

"Harder. Like this?" He pounded into me.

"Yes, more."

Our bodies slammed into each other, our need violent and savage and shared. Niko's thumb grazed over my clit, and I screamed, my pussy clenching.

"Oh, Laya, Laya, you love my cock, don't you, darling?

Tell me, sweetheart. I want to hear it drip from your lips like your pussy is dripping your juices all over me."

His words intensified the onslaught of sensations, propelling me over the cliff I desperately craved.

Spasms surged through my body, radiating from my belly and core to every muscle. "Niko, I'm coming."

"Oh, yes," he hissed. "My God, Laya, look at you, milking my cock."

My mind whirled in a torrent of bliss.

"Do it again, baby. I love the way you feel squeezing me with your tight, wet pussy."

"Niko, God! Is that possible?"

"You're about to find out."

He pummeled my pussy, unrelenting, like a madman, and before I realized what was happening, I was crashing over the edge into another orgasm.

It was mind-blowing and exhilarating.

"That's it, baby," he cooed, his mouth against my ear, his cock sliding out of my pussy slowly, before slamming back in. "You're so beautiful when you come, sweet Laya. So pretty. Look at the pretty little blush on your cheeks."

He pulled himself up and grabbed my hips, his fingers digging into my flesh. His eyes raked over my naked body, fully on display and writhing on the end of his hard, throbbing cock.

I stared at him in awe. He looked like a sex god, fully in control, hard and possessive and determined to take me until he was fully satisfied.

He leaned forward and cupped my throat, applying pressure.

My pussy clenched and I gasped, "Niko."

"I'm going to show you what it truly feels like for me to claim you."

"What have you been doing until now?"

His hold tightened. "Prepping you."

My heart drummed in my ears as I saw the savage hunger in his dark eyes.

"You're mine now, is that clear?"

This was more than him saying it. He wanted me to admit it.

My mouth dried up, so all I could do was nod.

"Say it," he demanded, sliding his cock inside of my quivering pussy once more, as deep as he could go.

I'd come twice already, my lips swollen and throbbing around his shaft.

I swallowed to soothe my parched throat, knowing there was no holding back, telling him what he longed to hear.

"I'm yours, Nikolas Galanis. I'm all yours."

"That's fucking right." He jerked me forward and sealed our mouths together.

The storm brewing since our first kiss had now turned wild and violent. He pulled back, gripped my hips, and began fucking into me as hard and fast as he could, his cock sliding in easily and smoothly, his body searching for release.

"You're mine, Laya! Mine!"

He grunted and growled, thrusting faster and harder, smashing into my pussy with all his strength.

His mouth fell open as he shouted out in pleasure, coming hard and hot deep inside me. The thickness of his cock and the wet heat of his release sent me over the edge crashing into another release, and I clamped onto his shaft.

As our bodies gradually relaxed, we panted, his form leaning against mine, his lips sensuously gliding over my own.

"You belong to me, Laya. I will kill anyone who dares touch you, even my brothers."

Eight

L AYANA

"Niko is incredibly generous," I remarked, feeling both awe and amusement as we lounged in the stylish black limo.

Avra and Cali flanked me, their faces illuminated by the soft interior glow, while we flipped through a glossy wedding magazine—every page brimmed with vibrant designs and promising ideas.

"So, he has no opinions on the decor at all?" Avra tilted her head as she scanned our favorite designs.

I shrugged, feeling the plush fabric of my seat against me. "Not really. He just said that nothing else matters as long as I'm there."

Avra raised an eyebrow skeptically. "Sounds too good to be true. Elias had a million opinions on everything."

I smiled, letting the memory comfort me. "Clearly, they are two different men."

Cali flipped through pages, entranced, then suddenly pointed at a vibrant pink and turquoise spread.

"What about this color scheme?" she suggested, bubbling with excitement.

I wrinkled my nose in disgust. "That's awful—it's far too loud for my taste. I prefer something a bit more understated, something classic and elegant."

"When I get married, I want it to be bold and extravagant," Cali stated.

I raised my brows and nodded. "This definitely suits you more than me. Remember your pink hair phase?"

She flashed a mischievous grin. "How could I forget? It was amazing."

I could still clearly recall that night: the astonishment on Vik's face when she took that daring step.

"I thought Vik was going to have a heart attack." Avra's laughter mingled with the hum of the limousine.

"He nearly did," I added.

Cali shrugged. "He survived. We're all good."

As she turned the page, my gaze landed on a design that called to me.

"Hey, wait a minute," I said. "Let me see that."

"This one?" she asked, stopping on the spread that showcased a stunning cream-colored gown that had caught my eye.

"Yeah, that's the one," I murmured, absorbing every detail of the dress.

It embodied classic Hollywood glamour—sleek and silky, with a fitted bodice and a low-cut neckline crafted from exquisite silk. The fabric gracefully flared at the hips, creating a flowing, swinging skirt that draped elegantly to the floor.

I looked up in Avra's direction. "What do you think? Isn't it perfect?"

Avra leaned in, speaking in a low, admiring whisper. "Wow, it's amazing. I can see you in that."

My heart skipped a beat at the thought. "I love it. It's just as I imagined. Like a dream woven in fabric."

"So, how do we find it?" Cali asked, her eyes shifted to the adjacent page as she read the tiny credits. "Let's see... Oh, here's the designer's name."

With a flourish, she set the magazine aside and pulled out her phone, her fingers flying over the screen until a sharp whistle broke the quiet.

"Holy crap!" she exclaimed.

I leaned closer, curious. "What? Did you find it?"

Cali nodded, her face a mix of hesitation and excitement. "Yeah. Niko did say you could have anything you want—no matter the cost?"

I felt a sudden pang of guilt. "I wouldn't want to take advantage of that."

What she said next struck me like a blow. "That dress costs nearly a hundred thousand Euros, Laya."

I gasped, instinctively pushing the magazine away as if it were a bomb.

"Oh my God!" I exclaimed. "Forget it! What is it made of? Diamonds?"

Avra's sharp gaze met mine, a mix of amusement and frustration on her face. "Have you forgotten who you are, little sister?"

I blinked in confusion. "What do you mean?"

"You're Layana Vitalis. Soon, you'll be a Galanis too. With our combined fortunes, you'll become one of the richest women in Greece. And here you are, hesitating over the price on the most important day of your life? I say you should buy the dress!"

"That's ridiculous!" I shot back in disbelief.

Avra laughed. "Really? How much do you think that ring costs?"

I glanced down at my finger and shrugged. "I don't know. I never asked."

"Exactly," she said. "If you knew your fiancé spent double on that bauble on your hand, you'd be shocked. Forget about the dress's price. If you love it, tell him, but make sure he doesn't see it first!"

I gazed at the ring, feeling a mix of wonder and guilt. "You can't be serious, can you?"

"Only half," Avra replied smoothly. "When you sent me the photo, I asked my jeweler to check it. If you want the truth, it's worth a million Euros."

I gasped and pulled the ring closer as if its cool metal could steady me. The thought of Niko spending so extravagantly unsettled me, and the fear of losing it now caused fresh unease and anxiety.

"Oh, stop clutching your pearls." Avra shot me her big-sister glare. "Buy the damn dress—you're worth it."

I sighed, shaking my head as the weight of our conversation sank in. "Will I ever get used to all this?" I asked as I fought back tears.

"Probably not," Avra replied with a lighthearted shrug, her hand patting my leg in consolation. "But that's part of your charm, sweetheart."

A small chuckle escaped me as I wiped away a tear. "It really is a great dress, isn't it?"

"It's perfect. It's yours." With a decisive snap of her fingers, she added, "Now that it's settled, can we please grab a snack before you run me over with another floral arrangement?"

The tension eased as our conversation took a new turn. "Sure," I said, ready to dive into the next chapter of our lavish adventure.

Soon, we arrived at a charming downtown bistro, its warm lights inviting us in. We settled into a cozy booth and ordered every appetizer on the menu, each one a little masterpiece, along with a chilled bottle of champagne that glittered like gold across the table. Before we knew it, the room was filled with our delighted giggles and happy chatter as we devoured the sweet, syrupy loukoumades like precious treats in just fifteen minutes.

"Your wedding will be absolutely beautiful, Laya," Cali said, gazing at me with hope. "Leave everything to me."

"Gladly," I replied, "but remember—"

"Classy and understated. Got it," she interrupted, nodding.

"You're so thoughtful, Cali. I'm truly glad you came—it wouldn't be the same without you."

In the weeks that followed our arrival, Cali and I had roamed freely around Niko's sprawling property, our steps echoing through ancient groves and the dense, whispering forest that bordered the estate. We joyfully lost ourselves among the lush trees, uncovered hidden spots in the garden for picnics, and savored leisurely breakfasts on the sun-dappled terrace. With each passing day, our bond grew stronger, weaving our sisterhood into a comforting tapestry that nurtured her journey toward healing.

The dogs had immediately bonded with her, trailing her every step. Watching them wander the mansion's hallways together looked like a scene from a mystery novel.

"I enjoy being there," she admitted. She sipped her champagne, looking happier than I had seen her in a long time. "I appreciate that there aren't any old memories there. I'm unsure why, but it makes me feel safer in a new place."

"That makes sense," I murmured, letting her sentiments blend with hope for the future and the weight of the past.

"Everywhere else is soaked with painful memories—the old estate, the gloomy streets of Prague, that depressing apartment in the city. That place still haunts me. Leaving that part of my life behind changed everything."

"I bet." I shared a knowing glance with Avra, and we both hoped Cali would reveal more.

I rubbed my hands together, feeling the warmth fade as I looked at her.

"It wasn't just that," she began. "The city itself—every street and every shadowy corner felt like a ghost of them, haunting me."

"So, who were they?" I asked, preparing myself for her answer.

"The men who took me," she whispered, her eyes filled with anguish. The gravity of her words settled in the space between us, an unspoken truth that hovered, reminding us of those nightmares we all feared to voice.

At that moment, Avra and I reached out to Cali, enveloping her in a tight embrace and providing what little solace we could.

"I love you, Cali. I'm so sorry you endured that. No one should ever experience such horror," I whispered, holding her close.

Her lips trembled as she looked up. "I love you both."

With tears brimming in her eyes, Avra stepped back, her gaze locking with Cali's, silently communicating everything her trembling lips couldn't. "I'm sorry too. I should have protected you, and I failed. I'll never forgive myself for what you went through, Cali."

"I hope someday you can forgive yourself, Avra," Cali whispered. "None of this was your fault. The blame lies solely with those monsters. You did nothing wrong. Neither did you, Laya. And I'm not blaming either of you."

"They'll pay," Avra growled, sorrow and fury mingling in her eyes.

"You don't have to swear it to me," Cali insisted, firm with resolve and determination shining in her gaze.

"We'll get our vengeance," Cali said, solemn and resolute. "But please, don't worry about me too much. I promise I'll find a good therapist soon. And the dogs truly help too. Honestly, since moving to the Galanis estate, I feel like I've made a significant step forward."

My heart swelled with relief and pride, and I shed tears of joy as we celebrated this fragile yet essential progress.

"My only complaint now," she said, "is that my muscles are killing me. You and Vik have been pushing me so hard lately that I can hardly walk."

Indeed, we'd resumed our rigorous training routines shortly after settling in, as I insisted on a strict schedule to ensure our skills never faded. Just because we were now safe within Niko's estate didn't mean danger had disappeared from our lives.

After all, we were still the Vitalis sisters—undaunted, fierce, and ready for any threat lurking in the shadows.

Our enemies were still out there, waiting for us to slip up.

"Well, it's good for you," I said, forcing a smile despite the tightness in my muscles that protested with every movement. "Though I must admit, I'm a bit sore myself. Vik's workouts push you to your limits."

Cali's brow furrowed, her expression shifting from lighthearted to serious in an instant. "Speaking of things that are good for you, there's something important I need to discuss."

My heart quickened, curiosity mingled with dread. "What is it?" I asked, trying to keep my tone steady.

She hesitated, glancing away as if weighing her words. "The other day, I caught some staff whispering about you."

A wave of unease washed over me, cold and heavy.

"Oh no," I whispered, the knot in my stomach tightening. "I'm not sure I want to know."

Images of judgmental glances and hushed confessions flashed in my mind, making my stomach churn with anxiety. The thought of being at the center of gossip was suffocating, a weight I wasn't sure I could bear.

I let out a deep, weary sigh as uncertainty weighed heavily on me.

"Tell me, what did they say?" I asked.

A playful spark lit up Cali's eyes as she leaned in close.

"Well, it actually got me wondering about something," she hummed.

I squinted at her, my heart pounding with a mix of suspicion and apprehension.

"And what exactly is that?" I asked, knowing her answer would embarrass me.

"Is it true, dear sister, that Niko expects everyone in the house to hear you scream his name while he's fucking you?"

And I was right.

"Cali!" I exclaimed, mortified, my cheeks burning, and crawling under the table seemed like a great option. Cali and Avra erupted into laughter, their amusement echoing loudly around me. "Stop making fun of me!" I retorted, giving them a mock scowl and a lifted fist as if I were going to punch them. "Don't make me beat you up."

"Give it your best shot," Avra retorted between snickering. "Isn't that what sisters are for—teasing each other?"

That comment made Cali laugh even louder, and despite the sting of humiliation, I felt a joyous rush of gratitude that she could laugh so freely, even if it was at my expense.

I gazed at them, my heart swelling with fierce love and deep affection for my family. I would have been consumed by loneliness if it weren't for Avra and Cali. I released a deep sigh, shaking my head as I felt the haunting absence of those who couldn't be here today.

I missed our mother, the kind and loving soul whose laughter brightened every memory.

I missed our father, a steady presence who had always been our rock.

I knew, even in my loneliness, that they missed us too.

I often wished they were here to share the moment as I walked down the aisle and exchanged vows with Niko, to see him as the man he had finally become.

But that remained nothing more than a wistful dream.

The ruthless syndicate godfathers ensured we'd never reclaim these lost moments, mercilessly stealing irreplaceable pieces of who we were. They robbed Cali of things she could never recover, vanishing like shadows in the night.

Yet, they dared to protest as we reclaimed the lands they'd stolen, conveniently forgetting they'd ripped away the most precious parts of our lives. In our eyes, what we had lost was sacred and irreplaceable: our beloved ones. They had stolen the only treasures that truly mattered to us.

My marriage to Niko would be more than just a union—

it was a crucial step toward reclaiming what was rightfully ours. Yet, deep down, I understood that no amount of territory could ever replace what we had lost.

A deep, smoldering thirst for revenge consumed me, like a spider, patient and prepared, weaving its web and spotting its prey, allowing it to crawl to the perfect point before striking with its poisonous blow.

Cali's kidnapping had merely stoked those coals into a roaring blaze. In that fervent instant, I promised that the three of us would seize the vengeance we had yearned for. Together, nothing could stand in our way.

Nine

Nikolas

Laya owned me. She was in my thoughts, my blood, under my skin, in every fucking breath. Instead of focusing on the upcoming confrontation with Stefano and Markos, my mind lingered on visions of Laya, flushed and thoroughly satisfied from this morning. She had intoxicated me from the first taste. Every kiss, every touch of her skin deepened my addiction.

Days later, I still couldn't get enough. Good thing I'd moved her into my bedroom that evening; this way, I could turn some of my urges into reality.

Why feign modesty? The entire household had heard her

cries. They knew she was mine. I had no intention of hiding it.

I had stopped caring about others' opinions, gossip, or judgmental looks, especially those of my brothers. Their obsession with bloodlines only highlighted their ignorance.

If Laya and I were blessed with a child, continuing the Galanis-Vitalis legacy would solidify our family's power. That was a concept Stefano and Markos failed to understand.

My idiot brothers were plotting—details unclear, but retaliation was coming.

I'd warned them—Laya was off-limits. Mine. I had warned them. Now they'd face the consequences.

I navigated the narrow, winding roads of a small village I had chosen as our meeting spot. According to the clock on my dashboard, I would arrive early, so I was prepared for this confrontation.

If they continued this campaign against Laya, they were as good as done.

I didn't expect to care this much again after Mama and Cora. There was a spark in her, blending with innocence, not just the fact that she was a virgin until me.

I smirked. I had no regrets about being her first and last lover ever.

However, if I'd known sooner, I could have made the experience less savage.

Then again, Laya preferred things to be unguarded and without pretense. Her order, during that first time, telling me not to stop, had me shaking my head.

Laya knew what she wanted and had no qualms about asking for it.

The timid woman I first met was merely a mask, concealing the bold, fiery passion underneath.

Even this morning she held nothing back, riding my cock with complete abandon, writhing as she rolled her hips until she drove me to the point of losing control and I tossed her onto her back and fucked her senseless.

Laya's previous hesitation and lack of experience had disappeared.

Dammit.

I shifted, adjusting my dick as it grew uncomfortably down the leg of my pants.

I wondered if she would be waiting when I returned home—if that familiar, enticing eagerness would greet me, if her mouth would whisper my name in that breathless, teasing way. I could hardly wait to bend her over and sink myself into her again, to have her lips wrapped around my cock as I fucked her mouth.

I gritted my teeth.

Focus, asshole. It was time to meet with some dumb-asses and knock their heads together, not get lost in fantasies.

The faster I put my brothers in their place, the sooner I could return to her.

I pulled up to a small restaurant in a corner of the quaint village outside Messolonghi.

In the distance, the lights from the boats docked at the nearby marina reflected and danced on the water. It was quiet and peaceful here, providing the necessary privacy for our talk.

I stepped from the car, striding down the brick path to the small restaurant my father's old friend owned. The number of people still in my life who had known my father was comforting. I did my best to keep them close, frequent their businesses when I could, stay updated on their families, and maintain our friendships, no matter how distant.

It helped me feel connected to Papa, even after all this time since his death.

Georgio greeted me at the door, wearing a sharply pressed chef's coat that gleamed. His long black hair was neatly tied back in a ponytail, and his light green eyes conveyed a welcoming presence. His sincere smile helped relieve some of the tension from my drive.

"Niko! Wonderful to see you!" Georgio greeted.

He had a rough edge that made him notorious for barking orders at his small kitchen staff during the busy dinner service. Georgio was renowned as one of the finest traditional Greek chefs in the village, and it was common knowledge that securing a position under his tutelage meant you truly knew your way around a kitchen.

"You too, Georgio. I've been eagerly awaiting your spanakopita for days," I replied, my eyes drifting past him to see that my brothers had not yet arrived.

The aroma of freshly baked pastries and savory herbs filled the air, a testament to Georgio's culinary skills.

"Your table is ready, Niko." He gestured toward my usual spot. "I even opened a bottle of your favorite vintage for you." His eyes twinkled with the shared amusement of our inside joke.

"Thanks for keeping my little secret safe." I winked.

It was our ongoing joke: Georgio was the only one I trusted to order a bottle of wine that wasn't from my family's vineyards. The wine he selected for me was a rare vintage crafted by one of my competitors. While I prided myself on loyalty to my brand, I also enjoyed the occasional discreet indulgence in a peer's creation.

I settled into my usual seat, strategically positioned with my back against the wall. The rich, dark wood of the chair creaked slightly as I leaned back, ensuring I never allowed myself the vulnerability of facing away from the door. I always needed to see who was coming in, as each new arrival could be a potential threat or ally.

The rich red wine swirled smoothly within it as Georgio filled the glass while he chatted cheerfully. I scanned every room detail, noting the flickering candlelight that cast shadows on the rustic stone walls and the soft murmur of conversations blending with the clinking of cutlery.

"Your upcoming nuptials are the talk of the town," he remarked.

"You mean the gossip from the ladies at the hair salon?" I replied, my gaze catching sight of my men gradually arriving.

Their presence was subtle yet purposeful as they attempted to blend in with the evening crowd.

They traveled in a separate vehicle while I arrived early, fully aware that Stefano and Markos would be late. This gave me the necessary time to position my security, who discreetly dispersed around the restaurant, their watchful eyes indistinguishable from those of genuine patrons.

My brothers wouldn't distinguish these men from other diners. That extra layer of protection had been essential, especially after discovering they had met with our rivals to assess how far they would go in betraying me. I didn't trust either of them, not even for a second.

Therefore, enhanced security was not just an option. It was essential.

I wouldn't hesitate for a second. Drawing my weapon and firing a bullet into their heads felt as natural as breathing. As I braced myself for my task, I couldn't shake the thought of the trouble they might be in now. Perhaps they had hired bodyguards or were under constant surveillance. With so many factions involved, nothing ever felt certain.

They were such short-sighted fools. Didn't they realize that any attempt to hurt me would eventually come back to haunt them?

My anger simmered beneath the surface as I waited for them to arrive, each minute stretching like a fine wine savored, warming me from within.

As they finally arrived twenty minutes late, I had already poured myself a second glass, and my patience was wearing thin. They stormed into the restaurant, their inflated egos evident in every gesture. With a loud entrance bordering on rudeness, they settled in, completely oblivious to how their behavior sharply contrasted with the sophisticated ambiance surrounding the other diners.

"Niko!" Stefano shouted, his smile resembling a strained expression one might see in a low-quality theater production.

"Brothers," I said, my voice cool and devoid of any warmth or welcome.

Markos shot me a cautious, calculating glance. I could tell he and Stefano were both bracing for the moment when I might turn against them. Our shared history was intricate, resembling a tangled rope. They remained unaware that I had been silently observing their every action, and I wasn't ready to show my cards just yet. The true aim of this meeting was to decipher their next move.

"So, our last meeting wasn't exactly pleasant. I was hoping another sit-down might clear the air. I'd like to hear what you have to say," I began.

"Our thoughts?" Markos echoed back, incredulous. "Are you referring to your poor choice of companions?"

"Whatever's been bothering you, it's time to share," I said, opening my palms to show my willingness to listen.

Stefano scoffed, shaking his head in clear disgust at the suggestion. "Jesus, brother, where do we begin?" he muttered.

My fists clenched at my sides, heat rising in my chest as I struggled to keep my voice steady. Losing control would only push them further away.

I met Stefano's gaze, his eyes wide with mock concern. "Listen, Niko. We're only looking out for your best interests," he said, his tone syrupy with insincerity. "Layana Vitalis is trouble, plain and simple. She isn't right for you, and frankly, we believe you should cut her loose immediately."

"Is that so?" I asked, each word sliding out more slowly than the last, my mind racing to unpack their motives. "I'd like to understand the reasoning behind such a firm stance. Surely there's something about Layana that I don't know yet."

I leaned forward, curiosity gnawing at me as Markos's smooth words flowed around us.

"Quite clear," he reiterated, a slight smirk playing at the corners of his mouth. I could feel the tension rising within the room, and I held my breath, knowing I didn't want to hear what was coming.

"Despite her Vitalis name," he continued, his tone dangerously calm, "she comes from a family no more illustrious than commoners. Picture it clearly—the Galanis reputation dragged through the mud."

As Markos detailed his list of grievances, each complaint landed like a hammer blow on my chest. My throat tightened as I thought of my next steps.

"She's uneducated, Niko. No proper upbringing, there isn't even a nurturing mother to speak of. And her family's scandalous history?" He sighed, shaking his head in disbelief while his eyes subtly flicked towards Stefano.

"What? Just say it, then!" I urged, my fists clenching beneath the table, envisioning the satisfaction of hurling a bottle of wine at Markos, the red liquid bursting like my chaotic thoughts.

"We mean no offense," Markos offered, his voice a smooth cloak over the storm brewing inside me. "But her reputation in Prague? It leaves much to be desired."

A knot formed in my stomach, and I pressed on, "And what exactly do you mean by 'her reputation'?"

Stefano shook his head, pity oozing from every pore, and I felt my blood heat.

"Your men must have kept this from you. Someone has to tell you," he said, the implication heavy in the air.

"Tell me what?" I shot back, a whirlwind of confusion and anger swirling within me. Was it possible they had information that eluded me? My men had been diligent—I'd even sent them back for more intelligence.

"Your fiancée is somewhat of a..." Stefano hesitated.

There was a charged silence, and I could almost taste the betrayal in the air, a bitter aftertaste I hadn't anticipated for my future.

"A whore, Niko! Layana is a whore!" Markos exclaimed. "They all are."

What did he call her? The urge to kill him intensified. He would not tarnish Laya's or her sisters' names. I knew all too well the truth.

"Are you saying she's merely promiscuous, or are you directly labeling her a whore?" I asked, raising an eyebrow and relying on my training to maintain my composure.

"Precisely that," Stefano affirmed, his gaze locked onto mine with a serious intensity.

That accusation against my soon-to-be wife ignited a murderous rage so violent, it surprised me I hadn't already torn him apart with my bare hands.

"But that's just a rumor, isn't it?" I stated.

"Yes," Markos conceded, "but we're determined to find solid proof."

"Really? Proof? And how exactly do you plan to obtain that?" I challenged.

"We have some men investigating it," Stefano admitted, leaving his explanation lingering.

Those sneaky bastards. What were they expecting to uncover? Torn condoms? Evidence of a fling? It all sounded absurd, and my inner fury threatened to burst over as I struggled to keep my cool.

I crossed my arms and asked, "Is there anything else?"

"Isn't that enough?" Markos snapped. "It's obvious she needs to go. You're better than this, Nikolas."

"Well then, if there's nothing else," I began, drawing in a deep breath. "I appreciate your so-called honesty, and I'll respond with equal frankness. Nothing you've said has made me reconsider my plan to marry Layana Vitalis. The wedding will proceed as scheduled."

"What?" Stefano shouted, slamming his hand on the table so hard that the wine bottle and glasses rattled, attracting the surprised attention of everyone in the restaurant. "You never pay attention to us, Niko! Why did we even have this meeting if you were just going to embarrass our family?"

"That's right," Markos fumed. "You believe you're the only one capable of leading this family, but you're wrong. You're fucking wrong, Niko."

I stifled a yawn at their predictable, worn-out argument. Couldn't they think of something fresh, for fuck's sake?

"I have a question for both of you," I said, barely above a whisper, forcing them to lean in to hear me. "How do you think our father would react to what you just mentioned if he were here with us now?"

They opened their mouths simultaneously to respond, but I raised a finger to my lips, silencing them right away.

They exchanged a nervous glance, not that it was obvious they had annoyed me. They were rather stupid, but they were smart enough to understand I would strike at any moment now.

"I will answer my own question." I gave them my coldest glare. "He would be completely ashamed of both of you, embarrassed by your childish outbursts. Now, regarding my marriage, our father always valued the Vitalis name. Should I remind you of the numerous photos in our home featuring him with Juno Vitalis? Isn't that evidence of his respect for the Vitalises and the legacy they represent?"

"The Vitalises are snakes!" Stefano exclaimed, his face a play of fury. "And if you're not careful, Niko, you'll share the same fate as our beloved father!"

"What, do you mean death? We're all on that path, each in our own way," I replied, leaning forward with a dismissive gesture.

"If you don't cut ties with that filthy family, Niko, your fate will catch up with you sooner than you think."

I raised an eyebrow at Stefano's thinly veiled threat, allowing the tension to linger heavily in the room.

"Don't make an enemy of me, Stefano," I warned. "Trust me, you'll regret it."

"We're only trying to tell you the truth, Niko," Markos insisted.

"It all sounds a lot like a threat to me." I slowly stood up, looming over them with a predatory glare. "Don't even think about messing with me or my family. And let me make it clear that this includes the Vitalis family. If either of you slimy little shits dares to touch them, I promise the revenge will be excruciatingly painful, bloody, and well beyond your wildest nightmares."

Their faces fell as they grasped that they'd crossed a line from which they couldn't return. They'd pushed me too far.

They understood that playing with fire involved the risk of being consumed by the flames and reduced to dust.

Their silence conveyed everything.

With one final, measured step, I exited the restaurant, the weight of my anger palpable in the air. I left them to stew in their well-deserved mix of shame and fear.

TEN

L AYANA

"Are you serious?" Cali exclaimed, furrowing her brow. She placed her hands on her hips and struck a pose that felt almost comically theatrical. "Can't you choose someone else? Is this some punishment for making you buy that expensive dress? It's not like we couldn't afford it."

I smirked as I meticulously wrote Cali's name in elegant script on the soles of my shiny stilettos, justifying my decision with a firm nod.

"No one makes me do anything. I chose this dress because it was ideal and spared me from more hours searching for the right one," I told her, trying to sound resolute.

"Then why are you being so cruel?"

"How's this cruel? You're being overly dramatic. Since relocating to the estate, I haven't had the chance to interact with any other women," I clarified, feeling the pressure in my chest ease slightly. "That means you're my sole option. Avra is already married and off-limits."

"It's a ridiculous tradition anyway," she grumbled, crossing her arms tightly over her chest as I noticed her frustration.

Avra, lounging comfortably on my bed, laughed at our exchange. It was a light, musical sound that resonated throughout the room.

"I seem to recall you weren't complaining when I wrote Laya's name on the bottom of my shoes," she teased, glancing at Cali.

"That's because it was Laya's name and not mine," Cali replied, feigning indignation as she rolled her eyes. "I'll say it again, this is dumb."

"You're absolutely right," I conceded, placing my pen on the polished vanity. "But I'm not about to break tradition. It's bad luck."

"This isn't a real marriage!" Cali protested, cocking a hand on her hip, her challenge clear in her stance.

"Cali! Please don't say that!" I exclaimed, feeling a pang in my heart at her words. "While my marriage to Niko may have been arranged, it is truly real. Could you please humor me for just one day?"

The tradition of writing single girlfriends' names on the

bottom of the bride's shoe might seem outdated, but I was determined to uphold it, whether Cali liked it or not.

"The name that gets scraped off by the end of the night is the one who will wed next. I'm the only one on that list. Why are you sentencing me to marriage next?"

I arched an eyebrow at her as if the reason were as clear as day.

Cali crossed her arms, her lips pursed in stubborn resolve. "Why are you looking at me like that?"

"It was always part of the plan for you to get married eventually, Cali," Avra reminded her in a calm but firm tone.

"Yes, but this means next," Cali exclaimed, throwing her hands up in a dramatic gesture, mirroring our mother's whenever she was exasperated with Papa. "You two are quite annoying right now. I'm going to check on how Vik is doing."

With an exaggerated sigh, Cali turned on her heel and left. Avra and I exchanged amused smirks as the door clicked shut behind her. It was undeniably a silly tradition, a relic from a bygone era. But the Greek customs handed down through our family held a special place in my heart. I could still hear Mama's voice, so strong and melodic, recounting this particular tradition during my childhood, her stories etched in my memory like an old, cherished photograph.

Our wedding would be a tapestry of these Greek traditions, each thread carefully woven in. We couldn't imagine the ceremony without including the Stefana.

Niko and I would wear two ornate crowns, crafted with intricate designs and linked by a slender satin ribbon. This connection represented God's blessing upon our union. During the ceremony, Avra, our Koumbara, would exchange the crowns three times, a ceremonial dance that sealed our bond in the eyes of tradition and love.

However, we set boundaries around certain customs, such as having our bed showered with rice and coins, and the idea of placing a baby on it to symbolize fertility. The mental image of picking stubborn grains of rice from the sheets was far from romantic, so I firmly declined any access to our bedroom for such antics.

Our room.

Ever since that first unforgettable night, I had spent every evening wrapped in the indulgences of Niko's bed. Tonight would be our last night there for a while; starting tomorrow, we would jet off to our honeymoon on a secluded private island in the Mediterranean, a gem belonging to Niko's family. The reality of being with a man who spent his days overseeing vast vineyards, his hands perpetually dusted with earth, yet spoke casually of owning an island off the coast of Greece, was still something I struggled to comprehend.

It was an easy decision when he offered me the choice between three weeks of globe-trotting or seclusion on the island. Nearly a month away from the bustle of family and the demands of daily life would provide us with the rare opportunity to truly understand each other beyond the confines of the bedroom. Not that I had any complaints about our intimate moments so far.

Niko was more than just an incredible lover—he was a master at balancing fiery passion with patience. His dedication to discovering new ways to please me was astounding, as if he found joy in making me reach ecstasy.

And now, the day of our wedding had finally arrived. I'd be lying if I said I wasn't a bundle of nerves, my stomach fluttering with anticipation. We'd chosen to marry on the estate because, despite my efforts, I couldn't find a more stunning location. The ceremony would take place beneath Dryad, Niko's cherished oak tree. The idea struck me like a revelation, the perfect blend of nature and love.

Niko's joy was palpable when I shared my decision with him. He lifted me off my feet and twirled me around with such delight, affirming my choice with every spin.

From our bedroom window, I gazed out at the gathering crowd, elegantly mingling as they awaited the start of the ceremony. Much like Avra's wedding, we had invited many familiar faces, if only for appearances. Niko's family friends and business connections filled the guest list. However, the people who truly mattered to me were my sisters, Vik, and of course, Niko, the man waiting to begin the rest of our lives together.

Over the past six weeks, I had grown increasingly attached to Niko. I had surprisingly become comfortable in his spacious, sunlit home, which was slowly transforming into our own.

After a week of tentative adjustment, I enthusiastically dove into my new life. I felt it was essential to carve out my role as Niko's wife, especially regarding household dynamics.

Although Soti, our diligent housekeeper, expertly handled all the daily tasks, I knew it was up to me to make certain choices that would shape our living environment. With his laid-back demeanor, Niko had given me complete freedom to do as I wished, nodding in quiet approval whenever I suggested a change to the decor or introduced a new routine.

His unwavering trust enveloped me, but it also stirred anxiety. I had only resided here for a few short weeks, and in my experience, trust must be earned rather than freely given without reservation.

I couldn't shake the nagging thought that it might all be some test. Was he waiting for the moment I would inevitably slip up, ready to reel me back in? What would happen when I finally made a mistake, as everyone surely does?

"What are you lost in thought about over there?" Avra asked, her hand shaking my shoulder as if to nudge me out of the frantic whirlwind of my thoughts. "Are you getting cold feet?"

I shook my head. "No, not that at all. I'm just wondering if this dream might be too perfect. Niko has been nothing short of wonderful—he listens, never argues, and grants me the sort of freedom I never knew I craved. He's kind, patient, and incredibly attentive."

Avra smirked and fanned herself dramatically. "Oh yes, I've heard all about his so-called attentiveness. I hear you let it all out with a scream every day, as if you're announcing your presence at the top of your lungs."

"Hush," I murmured, shaking my head and pressing my lips together as if to physically hold back the exaggeration. "That's not what I mean."

"So then, what's really eating at you?" she pressed.

I hesitated and then confessed, "I can't shake this thought—maybe it's all just an act. Before I got to know him, I did my homework on him, as you well remember. Rumors traveled fast about his quick, almost violent temper, swirling around like the liquid ouzo in these parts. So, where is this tempestuous side of him? Is he biding his time until I'm his bride, waiting for the perfect moment to reveal his darker nature?"

Avra burst into hearty laughter, shaking her head in disbelief at the very notion. "Layana, just calm down. Niko is genuinely a kind man. Why can't you relax and accept that? It's obvious, sweetheart—he adores you. And let's not forget, you're strong enough to handle anything. If this supposed 'bad man' ever shows his true colors, I have no doubt you'd swat him on the nose with a newspaper like a mischievous puppy, and he'd obediently fall right back in line."

I found myself bursting into giggles at the absurd image Avra created. Her imagination conjured a scene so surprising that it made me respond with delight. Before long, her laughter blended with mine, enveloping the space in an atmosphere of comfort and joyful energy.

"You're absolutely terrible," I said, shaking my head in amused disapproval.

"But I'm right, and deep down you know it." She winked teasingly.

"Maybe," I murmured with a shrug. As she stepped up behind me, I caught a glimpse of myself in the mirror—my gown flowing gracefully over my anxious hands, each ripple a testament to the butterflies in my stomach.

"You look amazing, sweetheart. I wish Mama and Papa were here to see you. They'd be so proud."

Tears started to well in my eyes. "I miss them so much."

"Don't even think about crying! Not on your wedding day, anyway," Avra warned, just as Cali entered the room.

"Who's crying?" Cali inquired, scanning the room as she made her way over to us.

I replied, "Not me," even as I tried to conceal the quiver in my voice.

Cali tilted her head, regarding me with a mix of concern and practicality. "You look like you're about to march right into your own demise. Are you sure you're okay?"

Avra stepped in to clarify. "She's just a bundle of nerves, like every bride on her wedding day."

Cali's gaze softened as she nodded slowly. "I see. And for what it's worth, I truly believe you've made a good choice. I like Niko a lot. He's also been kind and welcoming to me. I have just one small complaint."

"And that is?" I asked, eyebrows raised.

"He makes you scream loud enough for the whole estate to hear," Cali teased.

"Oh my God." I laughed in relief. "I can't wait for that island getaway—finally some privacy."

"I can't wait either, believe me." Cali gave my arm a firm pat. "So, dear sister, everyone's arriving and seated out there. They're all just waiting for the bride to join them."

I exhaled, my hands trembling and mind racing.

"Fuck," I muttered under my breath, then louder, "Fuck, fuck, fuck! What do I do?"

"Easy," Cali said with a casual shrug. "Just walk outside, say 'I do,' and then, later, fuck your new husband on that deserted island. Simple as that."

"All right, that's enough teasing," Avra interjected, clapping her hands to regain control of the mood. "How about we start this wedding so you can enjoy that island getaway? Are you ready, Laya?"

Steadying myself with a deep, grounding breath, I nodded slowly. "I think so."

"Good," Avra admonished. "Just calm down and breathe, and please avoid hyperventilating. Everything will be all right."

"From your lips to God's ears," I whispered as we stepped out of my room together. Cali followed closely behind, cradling our bouquets in her arms as the sound of approaching guests filled the corridor with anticipation.

Vik stood by the carved wooden terrace doors, his eyes surveying the garden beyond. When he noticed us crossing the threshold into the living room, he stepped forward with slow, deliberate motion. In one fluid gesture, Vik joined us, his gaze immediately searching for me. The moment our eyes met, the contours of his face softened, and tears welled up, glistening under the calm light of the chandelier.

"You're breathtaking, Laya," Vik whispered, his voice thick with emotion. "Niko is one lucky man."

He leaned in and pressed a kiss to my cheek.

I silently conveyed my thanks, feeling reassured by his calm, confident presence. Vik served not only as my confidant but also as a steady presence leading me down the aisle, a role he had taken on with steadfast grace after our Papa's passing.

From the moment he'd entered our lives, he never wandered far from us. His unwavering dedication was clear in every sacrifice he made, putting his dreams aside to care for three daughters who weren't even related to him. His constant presence would always be treasured in my heart, as no one could ever measure up to the one who had taken my father's role.

"How are you feeling?" he asked, affectionately holding my hands.

I admitted, "Nervous."

"That's natural," he murmured, drawing me into a protective and affirming hug. As his arms encircled me, he leaned in, his eyes searching mine with earnest intensity. "Before we proceed, I have something to share with you, sweetheart."

I met his gaze, my eyes wide with anticipation.

Pulling back ever so slightly, Vik's expression deepened as he said, "Laya, your father would have been bursting with pride today. I'm equally proud of you. Watching you grow into this incredible woman has been a true honor, a journey in which I've been blessed to participate."

His sincerity echoed in the quiet hush of the room, and I felt my heart swell with gratitude.

"We wouldn't be who we are without you, Vik," I whispered, trying my best to convey my feelings without crying. "We're incredibly grateful for you."

He hugged me once more, and I felt an overwhelming current of love and reassurance in that embrace.

"No matter what, I'll always be here for you, Laya. Don't ever forget that."

I smiled through a mix of emotions, replying, "How could I? You're the first person I call when I need support."

Then, he added, "Now you have your husband to call first, but remember, I'll always be just a phone call away."

I nodded, my thoughts racing. Every memory and cherished tradition we held onto since our parents passed felt tied to this moment. The burden of change bore down on me as a storm of feelings swirled within, on the verge of spilling over.

"Shall we do this?" Vik asked.

Taking a slow, deep breath, I pushed the nervousness down, allowing a surge of joy to bubble up from within, casting aside the shadows of the past. Today was meant for light—a celebration of life and the budding promise of love. A fleeting thought of Niko flashed before my eyes, igniting a spark of exhilaration.

"Yes, I'm ready!" I declared, alive with newfound excitement that seemed to pulse through every vein of my being.

"Finally," chimed in Cali as she gracefully positioned herself in front of Avra.

A flurry of butterflies danced in my stomach as I peered over Cali's shoulder. At that precise moment, when the soft strains of the wedding march began, my gaze landed on Niko. I caught my breath as his figure came into sharp focus.

Niko stood there, exuding a magnetic allure in his meticulously tailored tuxedo and the gold crown resting atop his head. Everything drew me in from the fierce determination in his eyes, locking onto mine, to the subtle tilt of his head suggesting possessive tenderness.

As Cali began her strut down the aisle, I could barely breathe. Vik's hand covered my trembling one as Avra followed closely behind, the two moving in harmonious sync toward the altar.

Vik and I slowly approached the raised altar when it was finally our turn to advance.

Still, I found myself stealing glances at Niko. His sharp, piercing eyes reflected the turmoil in my heart. The depth of his gaze expressed complex emotions, unvoiced promises, deep passion, and raw, unfiltered determination. It wasn't the first time he'd looked at me that way, but today, it carried a distinct, unfiltered possessiveness that stirred both unease and excitement within me.

A whirlwind of emotions surged across his face. I imagined that mine mirrored his, reflecting the rising wave of anxiety I felt.

Was this chaos inside me love, or merely a strong attraction and infatuation?

I'd chosen him from among many, not because of a fleeting spark encountered in a crowded room, but through logic and reasoning. However, something far more primal and intricate came to life from that initial meeting.

But still. That look in his eyes as I approached...

Primal.

Raw.

Possessive.

Obsessive.

Whatever it was, I wanted to experience it fully. The knowledge that I would soon be the recipient of his uninhibited attention left me trembling with anticipation and arousal.

With a tender kiss on my cheek, Vik placed my hand into Niko's, as if to seal an unspoken promise.

The heat of Niko's palm seeped into my skin, and goosebumps prickled all over my body, adding to the ache growing inside me.

I lifted my gaze to his, something almost cat-like appearing on his face, as if he had captured his prey.

He leaned in, his heated breath brushing close to my ear, and then said in a low, conspiratorial whisper, "You're mine now, Laya. There is no turning back from here."

ELEVEN

NIKOLAS

The island of Galanis emerged on the horizon like a breathtaking painting in gold and amber as our private jet began its smooth descent. Through the oval window, I could see rugged cliffs and a lush, green jungle brushing the turquoise sea—a glimpse of a hidden paradise waiting to be discovered.

Laya slept peacefully beside me, her features relaxed in slumber. Her head rested against my shoulder while the constant hum of the engines and the gentle vibrations of the cabin lulled her into a deeper sleep.

As the sun rose, the clouds glowed with vibrant strokes of gold and crimson, setting the sky ablaze. Sunlight danced across the airplane wing, a gentle morning kiss that stirred my senses, whispering of the day's potential. I could hardly contain my excitement to share the sanctuary nestled in my heart, a place I cherished more than any other.

The weariness from yesterday's whirlwind wedding celebrations clung to us like a second skin. I still felt the echoes of laughter lingering in my ears. I remembered the moment I had lifted Laya from the limousine, her weary frame snuggling into my arms as I carried her toward the plane. A soft yawn escaped her lips, her eyelids drooping heavily from sleep. As soon as she settled beside me, the soothing hum of the engine wrapped around her, coaxing her back into slumber.

I couldn't completely ignore the truth. I was partly to blame. I recalled those early hours when we lost ourselves in each other's company, seizing precious moments until the night slipped away.

In those serene, passionate moments, I cherished every aspect of her. Despite only getting a brief hour of sleep, I became absorbed in the memories of our bond and the lingering guilt of having taken away her precious rest.

I found myself captivated by the curve of her jaw and the steady rhythm of her breathing. The memories of the reception resurfaced in my mind. Laya and her sisters relaxed, their hair flowing free as they engaged with the local villagers, exchanging stories and creating an atmosphere filled with joy and connection. The sound of cheerful conversations and shared moments lingered long after the event had ended.

I recalled how seamlessly they blended in, children raced

about, and elders clapped to the traditional melodies. I had nearly invited everyone from our small town, excluding only a few who could dampen our happiness. By avoiding these negative influences, especially my bitter brothers, I fostered an atmosphere for authentic celebration, highlighted by the lively dances of the Vitalis sisters and toasts that resounded like stars in the night sky.

Yet, underneath all the happiness, a dull ache persisted—the sorrow of absence. I missed my mother and sister, Cora. I could picture them joining in a spontaneous dance or lost in conversations with Laya's sisters, their presence harmonizing effortlessly with the evening's affection. This absence pulled at my heart, reminding me of unfulfilled obligations and prompting me to consider whether I had done enough to protect my brothers from the harsh echoes of our past.

A heavy sigh escaped me as I grappled with a tangle of regret, guilt, and lingering shame. I could almost feel my father's firm hand on my head and hear his deep, stern lectures urging me to set aside my vulnerability as if I were a child sulking in a corner. He had always been as solid and unyielding as a mountain, and his stoicism was something I had once hoped to emulate. But when I saw the soft light in Laya's eyes as I allowed my feelings to show, I realized that strength and tenderness could coexist.

Over the weeks we shared, Laya steadily tore down the barriers encasing my heart. Each lingering gaze and tender touch carved small fissures in my defenses. In her eyes, there was a sense of connection that I had long shielded myself from. As our moments together grew, the walls I had built around my emotions began to crumble, revealing a vulnerability I had kept hidden for so long. Each brief encounter brought forth an increasing recognition of my need for closeness, inviting new feelings that began to take root within me, inviting both the thrill and fear of genuine connection.

Few individuals managed to inflict pain while also providing healing. With part of my family gone, only Laya had opened a door I had tightly shut. This risk coursed through my veins, terrifying me more than any decision I'd ever faced in a boardroom.

As the plane's wheels made contact with the tarmac of my secluded airstrip, my gaze remained fixed on Laya. I recalled the moment she walked down the aisle, each step radiating strength and an enchanting vulnerability that left me speechless.

I recalled the priest's memorable pronouncement during the ceremony, as Avra placed crowns upon us, elevating our union to a higher realm. In that moment, my heart's door creaked open a bit more, and the kiss we exchanged ignited a strong resolve—a silent vow to safeguard her at all costs.

The day marked a fresh start and whispered a bold declaration to the world. With a firm resolve swelling, I vowed to shield Laya from any shadows that threatened her peace. Every flicker of possible danger ignited a fierce instinct, a silent promise echoing in my heart—that I would do anything, even if it meant standing against my own kin.

As the jet slowed and settled into the hangar, Laya stirred awake, her eyes fluttering open like delicate petals. She blinked, absorbing the tranquility enveloping us. The dawn of a new day was upon us, and her sleepy gaze held unspoken secrets and shared dreams—a vow I was committed to fulfilling with every thrum of my renewed heart.

"Are we here?" she asked, her voice still wrapped in the lingering haze of slumber.

I inhaled deep, dislodging the weight of old memories.

Looking down at Laya, I managed a flirtatious grin. "Yes, beauty. Welcome to paradise," I replied warmly. "Ready to explore?"

She leaned in, her movement graceful, and pressed a tender kiss against my lips. The touch sent a surge of electricity racing through me, igniting a raw desire that surged straight to my cock. Just hours earlier, I had lost myself in her arms, yet that primal hunger still gnawed at me, demanding more.

"I can hardly remember boarding the plane," she murmured, crinkling her nose with a touch of bemusement and wonder.

"That's because I fucked you silly, wife." I gave her a mischievous grin.

Her eyes, partially concealed by dark lashes, burned with an alluring intensity as she fixed her gaze on mine.

"Yes, you did," she whispered, her breath warm against my ear. "I can still feel you dripping out of my pussy."

Listening to that sweet mouth use raw, unfiltered things awakened a blaze of desire that roared through every fiber of my being.

The urge to fuck her right here and now grew by the second.

As if seeing my reaction, she pursed her lips and continued, "I still haven't figured out a wedding gift for you. Surely, you want more than just unlimited sex."

I sighed at her challenge, taking a moment to reflect on the underlying significance of her teasing.

I held her hand, met her gaze, and said, "Actually, you're right. I do want something else."

"Tell me," she insisted, her movements a mix of impish flirtation and earnestness.

"I want to spend the next few days on this island with you, enjoying the time of our lives. I want to make love beneath the whispers of ancient trees, indulge in luxurious food and exotic cocktails, laugh until our sides ache, and truly get to know every contour of each other's souls. And I want to share my favorite place on earth with you, a sacred island woven into the fabric of my childhood. My parents brought me here, and I spent my youth wandering through its enchanted woods, exploring every vibrant nook and hidden cranny."

Her hand squeezed mine as she replied, "I can't wait to see it all with you, Niko. I want to hear every story that shaped you."

"Oh, there are so many," I said, immersed in the flicker of memories as the past flashed before my eyes like a montage of cherished photographs. "My mother and sister loved this island, and my father and brothers did as well."

"I can't imagine your brothers loving anything, sorry," she stated with disbelief.

"Yeah." I nodded, capturing the spirited irony. "They

were once innocent, not yet transformed into greedy, insensitive assholes. As young boys, we shared many enjoyable moments. My father once envisioned all four of us running his empire together. Unfortunately, that dream has long since faded away."

"He'd be proud of you today, Niko," she said in a way that somehow seemed to ease the wounds lingering on my soul.

"Thank you," I murmured, each syllable heavy with the hope that perhaps I could make up for the disappointments left in the wake of my brothers' ambitions. "I wish you could have met my mother and sister. They would have adored you, Avra, and Cali."

"You think so?" Her hopeful delight was evident in the question.

"Definitely," I assured her. "They were much like the three of you—fiery, unyielding, and never afraid to speak their minds."

"How so?" she prodded, eagerly anticipating the stories.

"They had sharp tongues and wouldn't take any shit from anyone," I explained, laughing as I recalled the times they'd unleashed their tempers.

Laya let out a bright, heartfelt laugh that echoed in the quiet spaces around us, and in that moment, my heart soared with joy.

"I notice that most in Cali," I said.

A brief shadow flickered across her face, and I knew she was thinking of all Cali had endured and remembering the state she was in when we'd found her.

"Cali is far stronger than you realize, Laya. Never underestimate her. One day, I truly believe she will overcome all her suffering and take powerful action against those who have wronged her."

Laya sighed, nodding in understanding. "It was incredibly hard on her when my parents passed away. Life was upended in the blink of an eye. We had to flee into the darkness without any real warning. If it hadn't been for Vik..."

"He saved your lives, even if you didn't realize it at the time." Admiration and sorrow filled my thoughts. "I remember when my father learned of your father's death. He was utterly furious."

Not long after Laya first entered my life, she asked about the old photographs of our fathers together. I understood that for us to build something lasting, it was essential to share every detail of our histories. So, I'd taken her to a hidden family vault and unveiled documents, old contracts, and heartfelt letters that painted a vibrant picture of the bond our fathers had shared. In the glow of that secret space, we both found comfort in knowing that even amid our turbulent lives, a legacy of deep camaraderie and connection existed.

"Vik did the right thing by faking your deaths and sending you to Prague," I continued. "Keeping your identity hidden was the only way to protect you. That secret is what trapped fate and kept you safe."

She reached up to stroke my cheek.

"Thank you for everything, Niko. You're such a wonderful man," she whispered, her eyes conveying the truth of her compliment.

"I'm your husband now." I took her hand and kissed the inside of her palm, savoring the happiness that lit up her face.

"Yes, and I'm your wife," she affirmed, and as I leaned in to kiss her, our souls embraced in a silent celebration.

"Let's get this honeymoon started, shall we?" I asked.

"I can't wait!" she exclaimed, springing up with bubbling enthusiasm and rushing toward the door. I laughed, thoroughly enchanted by the spirited energy that filled the area around us.

Within twenty minutes, we arrived at the breathtaking estate my father had built for my mother.

"It's like a castle," Laya breathed in wonder as she gazed at the grand mansion.

"Papa went a bit overboard." I laughed. "But wait until you see the view out back. Come on, I'll show you."

I guided her through the elegant corridors, pulling her along as her gaze drifted over the regal decor. Priceless art and carefully chosen antiques adorned each room, with every piece hinting at a life steeped in grandeur and history.

Finally, I brought her to the back of the house and opened the exquisite French doors to reveal an unparalleled landscape. Perched atop a towering cliff, the estate offered a breathtaking view of the expansive, glistening turquoise Ionian Sea, with its waves crashing against the rocks in a constant, soothing rhythm.

"Niko, look at this!" Laya's excitement bubbled over as sunlight danced on the waves. Her wide eyes reflected the brilliance of the scene.

I stood beside her, absorbing the beauty stretching before

us, where the horizon shifted in hues of orange and pink, each brushstroke of color painting a breathtaking picture as daybreak approached.

"I knew you'd love it," I murmured, drawing her closer as we watched the dawn unfold its radiant hues.

This was the very spot where, as a child, I'd seen my parents greet each morning with quiet reverence. Now, every sunrise was ours to cherish.

"This place is all yours now, Laya. Together, we're going to create beautiful memories here," I promised.

"I don't even know what to say," she murmured against my chest. Holding her felt more natural, more right than anything I'd ever known. She lifted her head and whispered, "Thank you for sharing this with me, Niko. I can almost see you as a mischievous little boy, running wild and causing a bit of trouble."

"I sure was a terror," I admitted with a fond chuckle. "The staff's patience was continually tested every time I visited."

"I expected that." Her eyes sparkled with amusement.

In that enchanting moment, our happy expressions intertwined, filling the air with anticipation for a future filled with new adventures and treasured moments to share.

My desire stirred at the sound of her laughter.

The thought of leading her to my luxurious bedroom suite overwhelmed me—a private realm where I planned to let passion flourish, keeping her entwined in desire for days. I was determined to make that fantasy a reality. However, I had an important matter to address first.

"I'm starved, darling," I admitted, hunger and longing rising within me. "Let's grab brunch. Everything should be ready for us in the rose garden."

"That sounds lovely. After our earlier wicked escapade, it's only natural that we're both ravenous."

I took her hand and guided her to the garden, where my attentive staff had meticulously organized everything, just as I anticipated. A lavish display of shimmering fruits and carefully crafted pasta awaited us. Chilled bottles of our vineyard's crisp white wine sparkled in the ice, reflecting the sunlight, while clusters of pink lilies enhanced the table with their faint, sweet fragrance blending into the morning air.

I shook my head, enjoying the sight of Laya devouring pastries and croissants as if they were sent from heaven.

This side of her was beyond amusing.

She plunged her hands into a bowl of ripe strawberries, eating with such enticing abandon that I couldn't resist joining her in that delightful indulgence.

After a few minutes, our pace slowed as intense hunger transformed into a contented fullness from savoring the delightful, homemade fig-filled pastries my chef had prepared just the way I loved.

Sensing the perfect moment for intrigue, I suggested, "Let's play a little game."

"What kind of game?" She lifted an eyebrow.

"Perhaps a little truth or dare?" I proposed with a smirk. "What do you think?"

She laughed, surveying our surroundings and the discreet

flurry of staff moving about. "Something tells me the dares we'd exchange are best kept for the privacy of our bedroom."

"Fair enough. Then tell me the truth. Share something I don't know," I prompted, quirking my brows.

"About what?"

"About you."

She paused, her eyes narrowing as she searched her thoughts. I reached over, letting my fingertip trail seductively along her arm, delighting in the little shivers and goosebumps that followed my touch. "Tell me something you've discovered about yourself during our time together," I encouraged her.

She grinned and replied, "So you want to delve into the realm of sex?"

"Why not?" I countered, letting my touch wander slowly up her shoulder. "When I'm with you, my thoughts are all about you and the art of desire."

She bit her lower lip, an intimate gesture sparking a fierce, undeniable hunger within me and making my cock come to life. I'd never been so drawn to another woman in my life.

"Well," she hummed, "I've learned that when you nibble on my clit, I lose all sense of thought."

"That's incredibly enticing," I murmured, teasingly sliding my fingertip down toward her breasts. "What else have you discovered?"

"When your lips trail along my neck, every touch makes my toes curl." Her lashes fluttered shut in a moment of rapturous recollection.

"That's wonderfully sweet, Laya. Tell me more," I coaxed

as my finger slipped provocatively beneath the collar of her blouse, drawing a delicate gasp from her.

She sighed and then said, "When you do that, it sends my pussy into delightful spasms of pleasure."

I pressed on, sliding my hand deeper and pinching her nipple. "And then?"

"As you keep that up," she confessed, "it makes me want to beg you...to fuck me."

Her admission left us both breathless—my cock throbbing with pure, unadulterated need as the room vibrated with electric anticipation.

"All right," I said, reluctantly withdrawing my hand and standing. "I think we've had enough food for now. There's something I want to show you."

Initially, she gazed at me in confusion, but then I confidently explained, "It's time for a proper tour. The bedroom here is stunning. I have a sense you'll be completely captivated."

"Oh, is that so?" she purred with flirtatious delight.

I took her hand and led her back into the mansion, up the magnificent staircase to my private quarters.

With a flourish, I opened the doors to the main bedroom in the far wing, revealing the space within.

In front of us stood an elegant space featuring a grand four-poster bed enveloped in opulence and illuminated by an iridescent, ambient light. Lush, deep red velvet curtains flowed from the corners, complementing the coordinating bedding to create an atmosphere reminiscent of a scene from a dream.

"Oh my God," she sighed, taking in the lavish bed before her.

She admired the elegant damask wallpaper, a rich tapestry of velvet textures and intricate designs that transformed the space into a secretive Victorian retreat full of character and intrigue. The glow from the wrought-iron sconces enhanced the room's charm, casting faint shadows that suggested hidden delights waiting to be uncovered and explored further.

I could hardly contain my excitement as I envisioned the many ways I would indulge each of my fantasies in this room.

Every detail, from the intentional renovations following my parents' passing to the luxurious elements that echoed my personal style, was crafted with a single intention: to create a backdrop for infinite, pleasure-filled encounters with my new wife.

Yet, before we surrendered to the intimacy of the bed, fate, ever the tease, suggested that our passion begin outside, beneath the shelter of towering cypress trees lining the grounds.

I called, infused with both tenderness and desire, "Come, my beauty. I want to show you the terrace."

Stepping outside, we found ourselves surrounded by abundant colorful blooms arranged in overflowing containers along the edges. Every flower seemed to sing of vitality and secret indulgence, watched over by dedicated gardeners nurturing the lush display.

As I took in the wonder reflected in my bride's eyes, a

swell of emotion surged through me, a potent mix of passion and affection.

The stone terrace, stretching the length of the bedroom, opened seamlessly into the outdoors.

"This place is utterly magical," she whispered in awe, turning to me and gracing me with genuine admiration. "You were right. I love it here."

I watched as she wandered slowly along the terrace, absorbing every scintillating detail. I spotted a pair of large, welcoming couches positioned around a sleek, radiant glass fire pit, and in that instant, I understood exactly what was about to happen.

Drawing her close once more, I enveloped her in my arms, gazing down into my breathtaking wife's eyes and silently thanking fate for placing me in this most cherished place—by her side.

I took a calming breath, soaking in the radiant joy she exuded.

I leaned closer and tucked a loose strand of hair behind her ear, looking deep into her eyes. "Are you prepared for me to make love to you?"

Twelve

L AYANA

My heart raced in my chest as I stood on the sunlit terrace, the echoes of our candid confessions and bold challenges from our meal lingering around me. My body hummed in anticipation of things to come.

Niko's strong presence behind me highlighted all that I still needed to learn. He exuded confidence—an undeniable force echoing within me, pulling me near as if an invisible thread connected us.

"Are you ready to go inside?" he murmured as his breath grazed my ear.

I replied with a quiet nod, letting the growing heat within me convey more than any spoken sentiment.

As the terrace fell silent except for our shared breaths, he added, "I can't wait to see you like this."

He took my hand in a confident grip and led me through the wide-open terrace doors into an elegant primary bedroom. As soon as we crossed the threshold, Niko closed the heavy, carved wooden doors behind us with a decisive click.

He looked into the distance, his breath catching as he spoke. "No turning back now."

The weight of his words hung heavy in the air, a crackle of tension rippling through the silence around us.

Turning, Niko faced me, his dark eyes locking onto mine with an intensity that promised both passion and protection.

"Stay right there," he commanded. "Don't move." The words coursed through me, intensifying the tension with every shallow breath I took, and then I heard him chuckle, adding, "You'll thank me later."

He circled slowly around me, his possessive, smoldering gaze making me feel cherished yet deliciously exposed as if I were his most treasured secret.

Stopping behind me, he pressed his front to my back.

His cool, insistent fingertips trailed over my shoulders and swept languidly down my arms, igniting cascades of goosebumps along my skin.

"You are mesmerizing," he whispered, his lips barely brushing against my neck as he moved closer. "And you belong to me," he declared with such unguarded yearning that I couldn't help but be mesmerized as well. "Do you feel it too?" he inquired as I instinctively leaned in, longing for the profound connection his words suggested.

An undeniable energy crackled in the air between us, highlighting a bond that felt both electric and ancient, as though our souls recognized each other in a fateful dance.

Once again, turning to face me, Niko's hands moved to my waist, pulling me into the reassuring strength of his embrace. My heart raced, each pulse sending electric thrills through my body under his commanding presence.

"Now, strip," he breathed, his lips brushing against the sensitive skin of my ear with deliberate care.

"I want you to take off your clothes," I countered.

A crease formed between his brows. "First, I see all of you. That's how this works. Tell me, are you ready to be completely open with me?"

Meeting his unwavering gaze, I chose not to respond. Instead, I began to unbutton my blouse.

Each released button punctuated the hush of the room as the silky fabric slipped from my shoulders and pooled on the floor.

His eyes darkened with a powerful blend of desire and possessiveness as he murmured, "That's it, don't stop now."

Carefully, I disentangled my skirt from its snug hold and lowered it to reveal lace panties that seemed to awaken a palpable hunger in him.

"Keep going," he urged.

My heart raced as I unhooked my bra, setting it aside among the increasing pile of discarded garments. With each piece removed, my vulnerability deepened—a raw openness merging with the excitement reflected in his unyielding gaze.

Pausing at the waistband of my panties, I felt a wave of exposure mingling with anticipation.

Niko noticed my uncertainty and moved closer, lifting my chin with a touch that made our eyes lock.

His gaze softened as he murmured, "You're perfect, love. Every part of you." He paused, sincerity etched on his face, and added, "If you let me, I want to admire you."

His assurance wrapped around me like an unspoken vow. Our lips met, the kiss beginning with a slow tenderness that quickly transformed into a raging inferno.

I let my panties glide down my legs, leaving me completely exposed under his admiring gaze. He stepped back, taking in every inch of my nakedness, his eyes tracing my form with a reverent hunger.

"Stunning," he praised with a blended admiration and raw desire. "Tell me, do you feel as alive as I do?"

My breath grew shallow as he approached again. His fingers glided softly over the delicate arc of my neck. He placed slow, gentle kisses along my collarbone, each touch igniting faint sparks beneath my skin.

As he gradually descended toward the swell of my breasts, his touch became both teasing and reverent, artfully circling my curves in perfect balance between anticipation and surrender. Each caress elicited a shuddered gasp, and my back arched involuntarily toward the irresistible pull of his desire.

With practiced ease, his fingers found the hem of my

blouse and deftly unbuttoned it further, all while he praised, "You're letting go so beautifully."

Under his steady, possessive gaze, my nipples hardened in response, a testament to the electric intimacy shared between us.

Then, his order emerged as a velvety growl—a low, resonant rumble that coursed through me like distant thunder, infused with both longing and calm authority.

"Come here, kneel, and show me how much you desire this."

I obeyed, lowering my bare knees to the cool marble floor, feeling once again how excitement and longing bubbled inside me like effervescent champagne.

He guided each movement with precision, exhibiting an almost artistic finesse. His fingers moved through my hair with a careful balance of roughness and tenderness. I looked up at him, and his eyes burned with a molten desire that seemed to pull me closer.

"I need you, Niko," I whimpered, desperate and aching.

He responded, "And I want all of you, every part of you."

He slowly unzipped his pants, the metallic rasp echoing in the quiet room as it unveiled his hardened length.

"Are you ready for this?" he asked, half in disbelief at our shared desire and half as a challenge.

Tentatively, I reached out, my fingers wrapping around him, feeling the pulsing veins beneath his smooth, taut skin. He guided my head closer, the musky scent of his arousal enveloping me in an intoxicating embrace.

"Let me see how much you love every moment of this," he whispered, encouraging my exploration.

I extended my tongue and lightly licked a glistening bead of precum from his tip, its saltiness exploding across my taste buds like a forbidden delicacy.

A deep, guttural groan rose from his chest, sending vibrations through me like the resonance of a plucked bass string.

Encouraged by his reaction, I took him into my mouth, my lips stretching to accommodate him as I swirled my tongue along his shaft, exploring every ridge and contour.

Each movement of my mouth elicited murmurs of approval.

"Yes, just like that," he urged, his fingers tightening in my hair to help guide my rhythm.

As I moved up and down, taking him deeper with each tantalizing descent, our shared symphony of wet, primal sounds filled the space—a melody of desire, older than time.

He gasped and murmured, "I love how you make me feel so alive. Keep going, baby."

Our eyes locked in a raw, unguarded connection as his hips began moving in rhythm with my movements, his control slowly unraveling like a spool of thread.

"Just like that," he murmured once more, strained with pleasure—a low rumble reverberating like thunder before a storm.

His body coiled, muscles tensing as his breath came in ragged gasps.

"Show me how much you want every second," he continued, his whispered plea mingling with our shared cadence.

I moved closer, my nose pressed against his skin as his intoxicating scent enveloped me. His grip tightened further, his fingers entwining in my hair as I steadied myself for his imminent release.

Suddenly, with a swift motion, he yanked my head back, pulling away sharply from my mouth. His chest heaved, his breath ragged, and his eyes burned with a fierce, unyielding desire.

"No," he growled in a low, dangerous undercurrent that brooked no argument. "I'm coming inside your cunt. And later—much later—I'll use your mouth for my pleasure."

With that last powerful note, he halted, electrifying the atmosphere, as if challenging me to contribute to this intimate exchange.

"Are you ready for everything I'm going to give you?" he inquired, his gaze steady and assuring, indicating that our quiet exchange of desire was still unfolding.

He lifted me with intent, guiding my trembling body toward a plush mattress promising surrender and sins.

"Lie down," he commanded, and immediately, goosebumps prickled all over my skin.

I stripped bare—nervous, exposed, and aching to be his. Before him, my eyes fixed on his commanding silhouette as he moved with assured allure. A sly, knowing curve touched the corners of his lips as he reached into an ornate, vintage nightstand and withdrew a pair of silky scarves, the cool fabric slipping effortlessly through his confident fingers. My heart thundered with excitement and trembling anticipation as the moment unfolded between us.

"Trust me," he whispered, and our eyes locked in a silent, potent promise that both eased my fluttering apprehension and stirred a deep, all-consuming longing inside me.

"I do," I declared with raw truth and desire.

With intentional care, he secured the scarves around my wrists, the fabric looping gracefully above my head with a sense of firmness that felt both protective and possessively tender.

"Perfect." He leaned in to let his lips trace a slow, intentional path along my jawline, gliding over the smooth surface of my neck and the curves of my chest.

His fingers traced my skin like a whisper, igniting sparks of desire with every gentle caress. Each kiss lingered, warm and intoxicating, drawing sighs from my lips, leaving me breathless and yearning for more as if each moment alone would never satisfy the volatile need building between us.

Every kiss heightened my need, driving up my arousal and quickening my breath. A deep sound escaped my lips, a primal response to the electric energy between us. Our bodies pulled closer, fueling a hunger that demanded satisfaction.

My skin tingled with each interaction, creating a passionate spark that consumed my thoughts and wrapped around my very essence as his tongue teased my hardened nipple.

"Tell me exactly what you want," he said with a steely dominance that challenged me to reveal my secret cravings and dared me to break my silence. "Spill every desire, my Laya."

For a painful moment, humiliation wrestled with a

yearning inside me. His firm yet tender grip on my chin encouraged me to meet his piercing gaze.

"Don't be shy. I want to hear it," he urged. "I promise, there's no judgment here. Trust me."

Trusting him was the one thing I was certain of, especially here.

Swallowing hard and steadying my racing heart, I whispered, "I want you to take complete control. I want you to push me, to make me entirely yours."

A hint of satisfaction appeared in his eyes as he whispered, "Good girl," before redirecting his attention to my breast, showering me with a series of delicious, wicked kisses that sent delightful shivers through every one of my nerves.

"You belong to me," he murmured between nips and licks, his statement resonating as both a promise and an invitation.

With measured intent, his hand drifted lower, exploring the swollen folds between my thighs with slow, seductive strokes. I arched into his touch, my core spasming and flooding with need.

"Tell me, does this meet your expectations?" he asked, his voice revealing a blend of curiosity and enticing authority.

I moaned, my body writhing and begging for him to continue the torment his skilled fingers evoked.

"Yes...it feels so right." I gasped and trembled.

Every feathery touch fanned the flames of my desire, pushing me towards the edge of a cliff I desperately wanted to reach. My gasps and whispered pleas resonated in the room, blending with his deep, commanding timbre.

My pussy clenched and my skin burned. I couldn't think. I couldn't breathe. I was losing my mind. I had to come.

"Niko, please."

"I'm here, Laya. Just let go," he cooed reassuringly.

Then, with a surge of confident grace, he lowered his mouth to my wet, aching pussy. His tongue served as both a seductive invitation and a tantalizing tease. It sought my swollen clit with a desperate hunger.

"Oh, God," I screamed and thrashed.

"Are you ready for me?" The question was more of a husky challenge that made my heart race faster.

My desire soaked his seeking mouth as he explored and teased my most sensitive parts. Every lick became a carefully choreographed dance of power and exquisite agony, his calculated flicks igniting tiny quivers deep in my core and making my thighs shake.

Maintaining mesmerizing control, he kept a relentless, rhythmic pace.

"Tell me if you want it harder," he murmured while his tongue moved in deliberate, pulsing patterns that sent waves of pleasure crashing through me.

With each teasing stroke and nibble, he drew me increasingly near to the brink—only to suddenly withdraw at the last, thrilling instant, leaving me breathless in a state of lingering, exquisite torment.

I cried out, "Don't do this to me. Don't leave me hanging."

"Soon, my love, you will feel everything," he assured, a

hum of approval filling the space between our mingled breaths.

A sound that embodied complete surrender and unwavering control.

My orgasm built within me like a tsunami ready to unleash its powerful force. Everything inside me clenched, my skin tingled, and my body no longer belonged to me.

It was all Niko's.

"Please," I moaned, adding breathlessly, "I need more. Don't stop. I'm begging you."

The sensations were a heady mix of heated passion, the intoxicating taste of desire, the feel of his insistent, wet caresses, and the sound of my moans blending with his low, commanding whispers.

"Now come for me," he ordered, and the hypnotic rhythm of his skillful ministrations sent me spiraling into climax.

My back bowed and my mind clouded as my body trembled and my pussy clenched and flexed. He wouldn't stop. He pushed me from one release to the next, each more overwhelming than the last, until all I could do was take and take.

Between fervent licks and torturous pauses, my skin quivered under his attention, each moment crafted to stretch the limits of pleasure even more.

"Niko," I whispered, my breath uneven as I struggled to contain my need, "I find myself completely lost to you."

His reply was a fierce, possessive growl mixed with tender reassurances.

"I'm just getting started, my sweet Laya." It was a velvety promise meant to scare me and make me beg.

He resumed his artful assault on my senses with measured precision, his tongue dancing expertly along my skin and leaving trails of heat that sent shivers of anticipation through me.

Every lick was intentional, each pause purposeful—a tantalizing performance that tinged my taste buds with the salt of my desire, blending with subtle notes of his musky scent. The sound of his moist explorations mingled with my gasps and whimpers, echoing around us like the steady beat of an ancient drum.

His smooth, strong hands traced deliberate paths over my trembling thighs. He knew every inch, every reaction, every quiver, triggering a series of shuddering, almost overwhelming orgasms, each one more powerful than the last, leaving me on the brink of pure, unfiltered bliss.

"I can't take any more. I need you."

He lifted his head and caught my gaze. The feral light in his stare quickened my heartbeat. It was primal, possessive, and I craved more.

"Do you need me, Laya?"

I nodded.

"You'll have me." With confident grace, he moved between my trembling thighs, his eyes locking onto mine with raw, ferocious need.

He positioned himself at my sopping opening and entered me with a powerful, seismic thrust that sent waves of fierce pleasure through my core.

His desire was unmistakable, each movement igniting waves of ecstatic energy throughout my nerves. Our bodies merged in relentless passion—skin against skin, heat mingling with the heady aroma of sweat and arousal. Each movement deepened our connection, a synchronized dance of lust and control.

"Come for me," he ordered, the cadence of his harsh, commanding authority washing over me. "Now."

Just like that, the dam inside me burst open. A torrent of orgasmic bliss took over, one climax after another—a swirling blend of sharp, pulsating tension and the sweet release of surrender.

"Yes, just like that," he murmured, his voice thick with satisfaction.

My cries and quiet pleas intertwined with the deep, guttural groans of his pleasure, creating a soundscape filled with mutual fulfillment.

The energy in the room hummed with a palpable force whirling around us, pulsing with our combined lust.

"I love hearing you," he added between breaths, the air filled with the sound of his skin slapping against mine, the tender squelch of our merging bodies, and the periodic rush of our ragged breaths.

His mouth covered mine, and his tongue returned to its exploration, this time with renewed urgency, making me savor every mingled taste of salt and desire.

"Do you feel that?" he murmured. "Tell me how much you want it."

"Give me more. I need more," I pleaded.

"Yes, that's it, beg for it."

He pistoned in and out of me, the slick walls of my pussy flexing and contracting around his thick, hard cock. He drove me higher and higher, bringing me right to the edge but leaving me there before dropping me down.

It was cruel, it was wicked, it was evil.

Time and again, my body obeyed his torture, yielding to the addictive rhythm of his mastery. The sounds of his enthusiastic moans and the rhythmic beat of our shared ecstasy formed a raw, intimate symphony—a soundtrack to our carnal surrender that filled every corner of our secluded world.

"I won't stop until you're completely mine," he declared, each ripple of sensation reinforcing his control.

"I'm yours. I swear. I'm yours."

A gleam entered his eyes, and a low guttural rumble resonated from deep in his throat. "That's right. You're mine."

He rolled his hips and pummeled my pussy in the way that hit all the right places. My body reacted, and my mind immediately clouded.

I gasped and bucked, unable to do anything but lose myself in the onslaught of sensations. My orgasm rushed over me like a riptide, so fast and overwhelming.

It was pleasure and pain, agony and ecstasy. I convulsed around his unrelenting shaft as it continued its assault on my tender core.

He groaned and his cock swelled, his rhythm faltered, and in the next second, he exploded, calling out my name.

I wasn't certain if I would ever tire of this, and perhaps that was the point. I never wished to.

"You did so well," he murmured as he untangled the silky restraints from my wrists, his fingers brushing away the remnants of our passionate encounter.

He drew me into an embrace that felt like a comforting cocoon, his lips grazing my forehead while expressions of praise and adoration melted away every trace of tension.

"Rest now. I have plans to pleasure you in more ways than you can ever imagine," he said, his manner soothing.

In the peaceful aftermath, as the echoes of our passion lingered, he kept stroking my back steadily—a silent promise that this raw journey of desire was just beginning.

Thirteen

L AYANA

Returning home proved to be difficult. I had fallen for the island in ways I never expected. From the way the sunlight shimmered on turquoise waters to the salty breeze misting the air, departing felt like I lost a part of myself.

Every day with Niko was a burst of adventure and passion. We embraced the sunlit hours together, exploring the island's hidden coves and secret corners, then winding down on the powdery sands at dusk as the sky shifted to a golden glow. I could have easily stayed there forever, lost in his arms.

But reality called. Niko had commitments that drew him back, and I had Cali waiting for me.

Now, I sat in the backseat of Niko's luxury car with Cali beside me as the city flashed by outside. At least the relaxation from the honeymoon still lingered.

I smiled as I glanced up at Cali. Her skin held a revitalized glow, and that spark, once dimmed by pain, now shone brightly. Watching her, I couldn't help but feel proud and relieved by her transformation. Bringing her to live on Niko's...correction...*our* estate was the best decision possible for her.

"You'll need to join us next time," I stated, my enthusiasm mixing with a sense of longing as I envisioned the island's charm.

I described every aspect: the comforting sway of palm fronds, the rhythmic sound of waves hitting the shore, and the vibrant life around us, all while holding on to the hope of returning one day.

"I can't imagine it being more breathtaking than the Galanis estate."

"I'm really glad you're with us, Cali," I said.

"Me too," she answered. "This was exactly what I needed."

"And what do you need now?" I asked, curious about her thoughts.

Her expression brightened as she said, "Aside from you revealing the big surprise we're about to experience? Hmm, let me think for a moment."

I planned a surprise, a secret that filled me with excitement, and I couldn't wait to see her reaction as it unfolded.

"Well, I still crave revenge," she said thoughtfully. "Maybe someday it'll be more than just a wish."

I knew better than to offer empty words about forgiveness or taking the high road. The past was scarred, and those men who had hurt her owed more than just remorse or accountability.

"I appreciate that you and Avra never told me just to forget and move on as if advancing means erasing the past," she remarked, her voice tinged with a blend of sorrow and strength.

I shook my head resolutely. "Absolutely not. Let's bring them down—I'll stand by you at every step."

A grateful smile illuminated her face. "Thank you."

"Gratitude isn't necessary," I responded. "You're my sister. You're Vitalis, just like me. We don't forget. We make sure they suffer the consequences."

"That's why I love you, Laya." She laughed warmly. "I honestly don't think I've ever mentioned this, but I see so much of Mama in you."

"You do?"

"Absolutely," she replied with a nod. "You are strong and clear-headed, commanding respect in ways no one else can, particularly when you put Niko's brothers in their place that day. It was amazing! And when you and Avra burst in, guns drawn and ready to rescue me, I've never felt prouder."

Tears nearly welled up as I whispered, "It means more to me than you'll ever know. And you've got Mama in you too. Each of us carries a part of her."

"I hope someday I can be as strong as the two of you," she murmured, vulnerability flashing briefly in her eyes.

"Hey," I said as I leaned closer to her, meeting her gaze with intensity. "Remember that your strength has always existed inside you. You have endured challenges many would struggle to overcome, and nothing can strip that resilience from you."

"Thanks, sis," she said, her bright energy filling the car with a shared comfort. "I know this isn't quite the life we envisioned as children. It's not centered around medical school and advanced degrees."

"No," I responded. "But that doesn't mean it's any less filled with opportunities."

"I accept how things are," she continued, exhaling deeply as if finally putting down a burden. "I really can't complain."

"Our life is good," I said, feeling the truth as I spoke. "But remember, Cali, your story is just beginning. Living with me is only one chapter. When you're ready, the world is yours."

"You're the best." She beamed at me.

The car veered off the highway, entering a narrow, dusty driveway that led to an unexpected location. Cali leaned forward, her eyes wide as she observed the surroundings, eager to discover the surprise that lay ahead.

"What is this place?" she inquired, her gaze shifting around the unfamiliar scene, filled with both intrigue and unease.

"You'll see—it's only a matter of waiting a little longer," I replied in a calm, reassuring tone.

"Are we at a farm?" she asked again, wrinkling her nose at the idea, her skepticism almost comical.

"Perhaps," I answered with a shrug, finding her doubt amusing.

Eventually, the car stopped in front of a sprawling white farmhouse that seemed to glow in the afternoon sun. As we stepped out, the distant clamor of chickens clucking and squawking welcomed us, providing a lively soundtrack to the rural scene.

The property was neatly enclosed by a white picket fence, and just beyond the house, a herd of graceful horses grazed in a sunlit pasture.

"What are you up to, Laya?" she asked as we exited the backseat.

I didn't respond right away. Instead, I strode to the front door and knocked, each rap echoing against the old wood.

A chorus of barking dogs erupted almost immediately—a vibrant announcement of their presence. The door swung open to reveal a petite, redheaded woman with bright blue eyes and a mischievous, crooked grin.

At her feet, three large, fluffy dogs bounced happily, their tails wagging in unison.

"You must be Laya and Cali!" Penelope greeted us, her eyes sparkling with enthusiasm. "I'm Penelope. We spoke on the phone earlier."

"Hi!" I replied, feeling a mix of nerves and excitement. "I'm Laya, and this is my sister, Cali."

Penelope's smile widened as she looked at Cali, and soon, a light, infectious laugh filled the air.

"Have you come to any conclusions about what's going on?" she inquired with a friendly, secretive air.

"No!" Cali admitted matter-of-factly. "My sister's kept it all a secret, much to my dismay."

"All right then, come in, and let's unravel the mystery!" Penelope urged.

As we entered, Cali shot a curious glance at me. The house welcomed us with a sense of hospitality, like a cozy hug. The furniture was adorned with handmade quilts featuring intricate patterns, while antique items throughout whispered tales of the past.

Classic oil paintings decorated the walls, seamlessly complementing the home's character, while the delightful scent of freshly baked cookies wafted through the air. A crackling fire in the hearth created shadows over a snug couch that beckoned you to sit down. In that moment, it felt like a serene getaway I never wanted to leave.

Penelope guided us to the back door, swinging it open with a flourish. Another dog, full of energy, dashed inside without hesitation and raced straight for Cali like an old friend.

"Oh, my goodness!" Cali exclaimed, joyfully crouching down to greet the furry visitor.

With her silky fur and exuberant energy, the little dog reminded me of a miniature, fluffy version of Niko's beloved pet. She showered Cali with enthusiastic licks.

Cali's laughter bubbled up. "She's just so adorable."

"Her name is Leo," I explained, knowing it would resonate with her. "It's a shortened form of Leontios."

"That means 'fearless' in Greek," Cali murmured, gazing at me in disbelief. "But how do you know that?"

"Because I named her, sweetheart," I replied tenderly. "And now, she's entirely yours."

"What?" Cali's expression was worth the entire trip.

Leo pranced around her with even more energy, as if she understood all the excitement. Cali wrapped her arms around the dog's neck with unreserved affection, hugging her tightly as tears streamed down her cheeks in pure emotion.

"Really? She's mine?" she gasped, her voice thick with overwhelming joy.

"Absolutely," I assured her. "She's all yours."

"Laya, I can't believe you did this!" she exclaimed, her gratitude evident.

"Why not?" I replied, remembering how effortlessly Cali had connected with Niko's dogs. "It seemed only natural for you to have your own companion."

"Thank you, thank you!" she cried out, as Leo continued to lick the tears from her face.

Before long, joy filled the room, merging with the harmonious dishes clinking and the comforting sounds of home.

"Well, it looks like they're hitting it off, don't you think, Laya?" Penelope mused.

"I'd say so," I responded.

"Seems like a match made in heaven to me," she declared, her excitement contagious.

Just then, my phone vibrated insistently in my pocket. I took it out and noticed a message from Niko.

Niko: I'm dying to know how it all went.

Laya: They're already in love with each other. I can't thank you enough for setting this up.

Niko: I'm so happy to hear that and can't wait to meet Leo!

I could picture him in his office, grinning from ear to ear. My handsome husband, who made all of this happen.

Laya: You're the best, Niko. I love you.

My fingers hesitated for a brief second before sending the message, then I pressed "send."

I slipped the phone back into my pocket as my heart pounded. I had never expressed those words to anyone before, but now they existed in text—an impulsive burst of honesty.

Oh, shit. Oh, shit. Oh, shit.

I waited for a reply, but nothing came, and a lump settled in the pit of my stomach.

Dammit Laya, that was too soon.

As we headed home with Leo trotting happily between us, I couldn't shake the feeling of standing on the edge of an emotional precipice, all because of the reckless need to share my emotions.

FOURTEEN

NIKOLAS

You're the best, Niko. I love you.

Laya's simple declaration echoed in my mind, repeating each syllable like a soothing melody.

I kept repeating them to myself: *I love you.*

Was it real? Had I misinterpreted her confession due to her habit of texting her sisters throughout the day, a potential impulsive mistake?

It seemed so simple, right?

Love was a dangerous, off-limits territory I had tried to avoid, yet her message awakened something that was an exhilarating mix of excitement and deep-seated terror within me.

Three little words, but they carried overwhelming power.

I found myself rereading her text over and over. Each glance at the glowing screen was a desperate attempt to convince myself that my heart wasn't just deceiving me.

But it blared back like a bright neon sign every time, impossible to ignore.

Laya was an unstoppable force in bed, full of passion and wild energy. Yet, we had never allowed anything so emotional to slip into the air between us during our heated physical moments. I exhaled slowly and took a calming breath, attempting to navigate the whirlwind of emotions within me.

Some part of me wanted her to truly mean it.

I wanted her love.

What did that reveal about me?

Was I exposing a weakness—a need for love that undermined the tough persona I'd constructed?

The haunting memory of losing Mama and Cora surged forward, cruelly reminding me of the cost of love. Love meant loss, and the thought of losing Layana was an agony I wasn't ready to face again.

How might my position in the world shift if I desired something more from her than mere physical satisfaction? And did I even love her in return? If I did, it might signal the beginning of my downfall.

Being in love left me exposed, especially around my enemies. Even my brothers might see it as a flaw. Love, with its inherent tenderness and fragility, made me vulnerable to losing something I cherished or having it used against me.

Previously, I'd thrived on the harsh freedom of having

nothing precious to lose. That fierce independence was my greatest advantage, a barrier against adversaries who could never inflict as much pain as someone I loved deeply could. Now, that threat loomed over me like a shadow.

I ran my hand through my hair, feeling its rough strands as I read her message again:

I love you. I love you. I love you...

If there was already love between us, I would be at a disadvantage. That thought terrified me.

Was I ready to give up even a little of my hard-earned control? I had clawed my way through hardship and sacrifice, and everything I had built was now at risk. Moreover, opening myself up to love felt like inviting heartbreak.

If Laya ever left, the pain would be unbearable. I was just starting to heal from the devastating losses of my mother and sister. How could I face another blow of such magnitude?

I reclined on a worn chair on the sunlit terrace, the cool evening breeze brushing against me. Disappointment churned within me as I heard deliberate footsteps approaching.

I turned to see Pavlos Tripi coming over. He was my second-in-command, someone I trusted with my life, and I viewed him more as a brother than those related by blood.

"Pavlos," I called out, noticing the agitation on his face. "Is there an issue?"

"You could say that," he replied, urgency clear in his voice.

Pavlos was a large, imposing man, sharp and strong. With

a mix of educated insight and street smarts, he had stood by my side for years, his loyalty unwavering.

"Sit down and tell me about it." I gestured to the empty space on the worn lounge chair beside me.

Taking the chair across from me, he leaned forward. "I've received some troubling news from Leon Boscos's people."

I raised an eyebrow, intrigued.

As the head of an allied syndicate family, Boscos kept his eyes and ears open for threats. If he reached out, things were about to take a turn for the worse.

"There's a plan in motion against the Vitalis family," Pavlos said.

"A plan?" I echoed, letting it hang in the air like a dark warning. "You mean a hit."

Pavlos nodded, a crease forming between his brows.

My stomach twisted as a cold dread wrapped around me. I had expected treachery, but not so soon—and not so close to our wedding.

"All three sisters, even Avra's husband, Elias, are marked for assassination. The justification is revenge for the recent murders," Pavlos continued.

"Why am I not surprised?" I murmured, sinking farther into the chair with a deep, despairing sigh.

Avra and Elias had exacted their revenge on the three men who caused her father's death. They acted swiftly after the sisters returned, making it clear who was responsible. I believed that retaliation was inevitable, a brutal cycle that affected everyone.

But now, this mess was mine to manage. By marrying

into the Vitalis family, I had intertwined my fate with theirs, just as Laya's had become entangled with the Galanis family. Their battles were now part of my life, and in turn, my struggles were their struggles too.

The news didn't come as a complete surprise, but it added to an already long and deadly list of rivals. Our enemies were ruthless, and the families of those targeted, connected to the brutal acts committed by Avra and Elias, were equally unforgiving. They would stop at nothing to seek revenge.

In that instant, as the sun's last rays vanished beyond the horizon and shadows began to gather, I felt the profound weight of our intertwined destinies, a journey shaped by love, power, and the steep cost of vulnerability.

"Do you know any more details?" I asked, maintaining my composure despite the underlying tension.

"Nothing solid yet, but I've heard rumors that the other family heads are calling for a meeting. It seems our plan has leaked beyond our circle and into other syndicates. None of them appears pleased about the Vitalis sisters returning."

"Of course, they aren't," I murmured, my thoughts racing. "Claiming territory that never rightfully belonged to them and then having the true owners return complicates matters for these families. The presence of the Vitalis sisters undermines the legitimacy of fifteen years of control."

"Exactly," Pavlos agreed, nodding gravely. "The disruption is spreading. Plenty of men are out there simmering with anger, ready to act at any moment."

"Looks like it's time for me to take charge. I will contact Elias and set things in motion to protect our women."

"Is there anything you need me to do?" Pavlos asked, his eyes scanning the darkening terrace as if expecting the shadows to speak.

"Yes, arrange the meeting," I said firmly. "Stay alert. If you notice any unusual movement, let me know right away."

"Will do," he promised, then rose and disappeared into the twilight, leaving me alone with my thoughts. I reached for my phone, its screen casting a faint glow in the deepening dusk, and dialed Elias.

On the second ring, he answered, "This is Xenos."

"Elias, it's Niko," I began.

"I expected to hear from you soon," he replied.

"Yeah, I received some unsettling news," I confessed, subduing my pitch.

"I've heard some whispers too." His clipped response revealed a simmering anger beneath the surface.

I understood him completely.

I felt the slow-burning rage bubbling within me, mirroring Elias's emotions at that moment. Neither of us would ever allow any harm to our brides or their sister. We were committed to protecting them as fiercely as the ancient trees rooted around us, just as Vik had promised.

"There's going to be a meeting between the family heads," I informed him. "My man is organizing it."

"I'll be there," Elias affirmed without hesitation. "Just let me know when and where."

"I'll send you the details as soon as everything is finalized."

After a brief pause, he inquired, "What about Avra and Laya?"

I hesitated before asking. "What do you mean?"

"Are you going to invite them to the meeting?" he pressed.

I drew a firm line. "No—I want to keep the women out of it, at least for now. Their presence would only fan the flames of the already high tensions. I hope to ease the concerns of the other family heads about the Vitalis sisters. If the women are there, they likely won't be able to hold back their emotions, and the last thing we need is another disaster within our ranks."

"I agree, but they certainly have a talent for discovering things," Elias acknowledged. "It won't be long before they hear about this, and once they do, convincing them to stay away will be a struggle."

"I understand," I replied. "But I'm prepared to do whatever it takes to ensure everyone's safety."

"Got it," Elias responded. "I'll remain vigilant and await your update."

"Thanks, Elias," I said. "I truly appreciate your assistance."

"We're family now," he asserted. "Protect my wife, and I'll safeguard yours. That's how we do things."

"Rest assured, no one is getting close to them," I promised with quiet resolve.

"I feel the same way."

After hanging up, I stayed on the terrace, watching the tall trees as their shadows swayed in the evening breeze.

For a long hour, my mind was consumed with strategies and the weighty responsibility of facing the approaching storm. Each idea was as tangled as the roots below the ground.

———

Later that night, I sat at the long, polished dining table across from Laya as we savored a lavish meal of tender lamb and fragrant rice. Each time her silverware clinked against the ceramic plate, the sound felt too sharp, piercing through the heavy, tense air between us.

I couldn't shake the memory of her text.

I love you.

Now, she seemed to withdraw even from sharing the same space at the table.

What was truly happening with her?

I kept wondering if she had somehow caught wind of the dark plot swirling around her and her sisters. But if she had heard anything, I was sure she would have mentioned it. If she had discovered the secret meeting, I would definitely be in trouble.

Perhaps I should bring it up and get it over with. But wouldn't that make things worse? All I wanted was for the tension to disappear.

No, it would be better to remain silent about the meeting. My goal was to protect her, to shield her from the chaos.

Informing her about it would undermine everything I had planned.

Breaking the silence, I attempted to steer the conversation back to normal.

"So, what did you do today?" I inquired, taking a tentative step into dangerous waters.

Her response was curt. "I met with a contractor."

Curious, I probed, "Why?"

"The basement is leaking," she explained. "It needs to be fixed. I also thought we could use the opportunity to make a few changes."

I raised an eyebrow. "Really? Like what exactly?"

"It's very dark, cramped, and musty down there. We could open it up, add some lighting, and make it more inviting." She paused, then added, "And that large, unused space at the end of the hall? I believe it would be perfect for a gym."

"A gym?" I echoed.

"For MMA," she clarified, with a spark of excitement. "Cali and I need a dedicated space to train. We've had to work outside, and when it is cold, an indoor setup will be a lifesaver."

"Oh, right," I said, nodding, thinking for a moment, and then continued, "So, you're indicating you want to spend more time in my dungeon, huh?"

I shot a wink to lighten the atmosphere at the otherwise serious dinner table, but I sensed nothing would ease the tension and invite a more relaxed mood.

"Don't get so excited," she smirked. "I'm not exactly into BDSM."

Her statement felt like a challenge and my cock took notice, growing harder by the second.

"Why not? A little light spanking never hurt anyone, did it?"

She raised an eyebrow.

"Does the idea of me submitting to you excite you?" she taunted, knowing I'd take it more like a challenge.

I moved closer, leaning in as I whispered, "Does the thought of me taking control excite you, Laya?"

My question hung in the charged air. I remembered those distinct moments when she melted into passion. The way she allowed herself to be pinned with her hands raised, the subtle parting of her thighs when I asked for more, the instant hardening of her nipples as I claimed her.

At this unremarkable dining table, even her faintest gasp revealed her true feelings. She tried to brush off my efforts, her objections veiled in subtle disdain.

"Of course not," she said, avoiding a straightforward response as if it didn't matter. "I'm not a woman who needs to be controlled, Niko."

I couldn't suppress the slight curve of my lips. Perhaps she only let her guard down when the doors were closed.

"Controlling someone and being in charge aren't the same thing," I countered, adding to the dark edge she skated on.

"Is that what you think?" she snapped.

"Yes," I admitted, unable to hide my conviction. "I'm the one in charge here, dear wife. Don't you ever forget that."

Her anger boiled over. "I am in charge of myself, dear

husband!" she exploded as she threw her napkin onto the table and stormed toward the door. "I won't let anyone control me. Not you, not anyone."

Before I could say anything else, she was gone.

I called out, "Laya!" but she had already melted away into the night.

Frustration gnawed at me.

"Oh, for fuck's sake," I muttered, exasperated.

What roadblock had she turned into today?

I muttered to myself, "Fuck this," and got up to pursue her.

I spotted her on the terrace outside our bedroom, a slender figure silhouetted against the night sky as she stared out at the lush gardens below.

"Laya!" I demanded, approaching her from behind.

She slowly turned, her gaze locking onto me with a fierce glare before she looked away dismissively.

"Leave me alone," she ordered, unable to hide the hurt and upset.

A wave of disbelief washed over me, stirring an intense annoyance that was difficult to suppress. How could I possibly bring any sense of calm to this chaotic situation? She behaved like a spoiled child, and I was bewildered by her actions, left without understanding the underlying cause.

"I'm not going to leave you alone," I declared, gripping her shoulders firmly and compelling her to face me. "Talk to me!"

"Why?" she retorted, her sarcasm on full display. "Because you're in charge?"

Her mocking only added to my annoyance. The day had been a whirlwind of emotions. One moment, she'd expressed her love for me and the next, I discovered her life might be in danger. Now, inexplicably, she couldn't stand being near me.

"I am in charge here, Laya," I stated, steady and firm, carrying a sense of determination. "I refuse to apologize for that. I am a man. This is my territory, my realm, my household. I will always take the lead."

"And what does that make me?" she shot back bitterly. "Just decoration for your bed?"

Her accusation struck me like a physical punch to the gut. Had I truly diminished my admiration for her to something superficial?

"Is that really how you think I see you?" I demanded, anger growing inside me. "I have always tried to respect you, yet now you say I only see you as a pretty accessory."

"Don't you?" she countered, her eyes blazing with defiant fury.

"No!" I insisted, struggling to regain control of the conversation.

I stared at her, baffled by her blunt defiance.

"And why should I believe you?" she questioned, shaking with emotion.

I paused, my mind scrambling for the right thing to say.

"Why wouldn't you believe me?" I asked, desperately hoping for some understanding.

"Trust is earned, Niko." She spoke with heavy finality and wounded pride.

I gazed into her green eyes, almost desperately trying to decipher the unspoken questions swirling there.

What was she saying? She'd told me she trusted me. Was that a lie?

Did she think I would hurt her? I could never, not in a million lifetimes, betray her or even lay a finger on her. Wasn't it obvious that every part of me existed solely to protect her from life's hardships? And yet, here she was, challenging the fierce devotion that burned within me.

"I don't know what you think," she said, shaking her head and breaking the charged silence.

Then, she stepped aside and moved toward the bedroom. Somehow, the air felt colder.

I thought, "Fair enough," as her graceful figure entered the room. I had always struggled to express my feelings. Words were tangled like threads in a dream, especially now, with each day since she arrived feeling like a jumble of overwhelming emotions.

I had hesitated to share the raw truth with her, not because of anything she had done, but due to the demons of my past.

How could she not know I cared for her? I showed her with my actions.

Dammit. Women were so complicated.

I let my eyes appreciate her form: the strength of her broad shoulders, the curve of her waist, the swell of her hips, and the way her movements hinted at desire.

Every detail stirred something primal within me.

Suddenly, a fierce, pulsing reminder of the storm of passion inside hit me, igniting my growing arousal.

Without hesitation, I stepped forward and blocked her way through the door.

"Get out of my way," she said, her defiance palpable.

I shook my head and said, "We need to talk."

"Niko, move now or I swear I will punch you." Her demand was filled with anger and deep yearning, echoing the turmoil inside us both.

"Why are you so angry, Laya?" I inquired, trying to hide my irritation.

"Because you think you can control me!" she erupted, her fury unmistakable.

"Aren't you overreacting just a bit?" I replied, reminding her, "You're my wife. That means you belong to me, after all."

A flush of outrage crept over her skin, a mix of challenge and desire as she spat, "How dare you say you own me!"

In an instant, her hand swung through the air. I reacted, grabbing her wrist before it could strike my cheek, holding it with both a sense of warning and passion. Her wrist trembled in my grip as I stared at her, a low growl escaping me.

"You're not going to hit me, Laya," I said.

She shook her head, silently daring me further.

"Did you want to make me this angry?" I snarled with promises of things to come and raw desire.

For a long moment, she offered no reply, merely meeting my gaze with smoldering eyes and a bitten lower lip that revealed her inner turmoil. That vulnerability, combined with her determined expression, sent jolts of desire through me.

My cock pulsed hot and hard, driving up my arousal. I envisioned an array of vivid images of experiencing the softness of her skin against my fingers as I traced the curve of her hips, her nipples tightening at my barest touch, and the enticing way her body opened in anticipation.

"Goddammit, woman," I muttered, "you're going to be the death of me!"

Without a second thought, I grasped a handful of her long, raven-black curls, pulling her face close with a mix of possessiveness and obsessive need. Our lips crashed together in a desperate, fierce kiss as if our need and anger demanded it.

A whimper of surprise escaped her as I explored her mouth with my tongue. Our kiss was untamed and a fight for domination, erasing all hesitation.

My anger and annoyance at her doubts transformed into a wild need to fuck that overtook all other urges. Every part of me craved her as I resisted her objections.

Our tongues tangled in a heated contest of dominance and desire, and I let go of her hair to use both hands to cup her ass, lifting her like she was the very embodiment of passion.

I carried her to the bed with determined strength, lowering her in a manner that denied the natural bounce of her body as she landed.

Her wide emerald eyes swirled with a mix of emotions, mirroring the chaotic storm within me.

"Niko, what are you doing?"

"I'm reminding you of something very important, Laya," I replied, unbuckling my belt with determined urgency.

She watched me, observing my intentional actions before meeting my gaze once more. A blend of apprehension and undeniable desire sparkled in her eyes.

"Keep your eyes on me, darling," I said with a commanding firmness, the metallic click of my belt punctuating the stillness in the room.

The atmosphere shifted as my declaration hung in the air, demanding attention and focus. I leaned closer, ensuring my presence was undeniable, as the weight of the moment intensified.

Slowly, I peeled off my slacks, each movement deliberate as our gazes remained locked. In that moment, she lay there, vulnerable yet defiant, a blend of softness and stubborn strength.

"What room are we in, Laya?" I asked, half-teasing, half-urgent.

"What?" she answered, panting.

"No, I mean, which room is this?" I pressed further.

With an exasperated eye roll, she replied, "The bedroom."

"Good girl," I praised, knowing it would prickle at her temper.

She lifted her chin, refusing to back down. "I'm not a girl anymore."

"Oh, right." I nodded slowly. "Because I made you a woman, didn't I?"

She scoffed, and I reached down, letting my fingertips possessively trace the sensitive skin of her throat.

"Tell me, darling, how did I do that?" I asked, my grip gentle yet firm.

Her annoyance very evident, she shot back, "With your cock."

"Where exactly?" I urged.

"In my pussy," she admitted, offering the exact confession I craved, even though I knew her defiance only fueled the fire between us.

A smirk danced on my lips as I released her neck and regained my dominant position.

"That's right," I murmured. "And what did I remind you about our bedroom? When we're in here, to whom do you belong?"

"Niko, is this necessary?" she exclaimed, revealing emotions that were a blend of exasperation and desperate yearning. "Do we need to play these games?"

I let my slacks drop away, stepping out purposefully as every part of me responded to the moment. Her gaze dropped, filled with heated anticipation as she took in every detail of my exposed desire.

Closing the gap between us, I positioned myself above her, our bodies aligned as I leaned in closely, a sultry whisper tinged with authority.

"So I need to remind you of your place in this relationship, Laya? From this position, it appears I do," I said with an underlying threat. "Judging by your behavior, you've lost sight of who holds the power around here."

"You're absurd!" she shot back, pressing against my chest in vigorous protest.

But I remained unmoved.

"Must I keep reminding you who holds the reins in this room?" I pressed, challenging, and unyielding.

Before she could answer, I captured her mouth once again, silencing her protest as my tongue plunged in, hot, wet, and unapologetically fierce, in a passionate dance.

A whimper and the urgency of her kiss only fueled the flames within me.

Then suddenly, in a moment of raw rebellion, she bit down on my tongue, drawing a thin ribbon of blood that mingled with our passion. I recoiled momentarily halted my advance.

She gazed upward, her jeweled irises flared with outrage, ready to scorch me alive. "You don't own me, Niko. You never will."

"You little vixen," I hissed, touching my now-blood-stained mouth, and could only marvel at her challenge.

A flicker of amusement danced over her features, adding to my determination to tame and worship her.

I allowed my gaze to wander slowly over her face and body, absorbing every seductive detail with a hunger so ravenous, I knew it would never be quenched.

Sitting on her hips, I slowly shook my head and warned, "You're going to regret that, Laya."

In a rapid, powerful motion, I grabbed the neckline of her blouse with both hands and ripped it apart. Pearl buttons flew off, clattering to the floor in an unrestrained musical shower, marking the eruption of our passion.

Her mouth formed a small, trembling "o" of pure astonishment. I groaned, overwhelmed by raw desire, the urge to plunge my throbbing shaft deep into her inviting mouth overtaking every thought.

My gaze followed the curve of her heaving breasts, barely covered by the remnants of expensive silk and her vibrant red lace bralette. Eagerly, I reached down and pushed aside that final barrier, revealing her creamy, supple breasts. The beauty of those perfect round mounds sent waves of burning desire straight to my throbbing cock.

I leaned in and captured her right nipple with my lips, biting hard enough that the metallic taste of her blood coated over my tongue.

"Ow, Niko!" she cried, arching her back in a graceful curve as I let my hand wander between her legs, sliding it under her skirt to find her trembling, bare pussy, quivering with anticipation.

Releasing her sensitized nipple from my lips, I gazed up at her in amazed delight.

"I see, no panties." I stroked up and down. "You're so fucking soaked. And yet, you resist, Laya. You're mine. Even your beautiful body knows it. My own personal whore..."

I glided my fingers through the seam of her swollen, damp lips and pushed into her soaking channel.

Without hesitation, I took possession of her other nipple, biting it while simultaneously thrusting deeper into her wet pussy.

Her hands tangled in my hair as she cried out, arching, and her thighs instinctively parting wider. She writhed under my touch, her moans urging me to push even deeper.

I trailed a series of kisses slowly up her chest, stopping near her ear, where my lips brushed against her tender lobe.

"You like that, don't you, you little wildcat?" I whispered, the taste of blood mingling with desire on my lips. "Do you deny it?"

Her response was a husky, "No, I don't," even as she spread her thighs farther, a silent admission of the passion simmering within.

Still, she tilted her head away as if trying to hide the yearning on her skin.

"Liar." I pushed in deeper, curving my finger, rubbing against that bundle of nerves, right before sliding in another finger, and a third.

She gasped and moaned as I stretched her and allowed my thumb to circle her clit.

Then I began to thrust with a hard, quick rhythm that matched the beating of our hearts.

Her eyes flew open in startled ecstasy as she cried out again, her cheeks flushing a deep, vibrant red.

"Tell me again that you don't like it," I murmured, plunging back into her with a controlled ferocity.

"I don't!" she insisted, even as her hips writhed and her body bucked with undeniable need. "You don't control me."

I moved inside her with increasingly harder, faster thrusts, each thrust fueling the whirlwind of our desire.

"Are you saying your drenched pussy is lying to you, darling?" I crooned.

"Yes," she hissed, arching her back as her slick heat gripped my finger, which spasmed in hot, rhythmic pulses. "Fuck! I'm coming!"

I savored the bliss playing over her features as I continued, my hands exploring every inch of her that she so provocatively denied pleasure.

Her pupils dilated, her lashes fluttered with each passionate thrust, and her face flushed with heat, glistening with rising arousal. Her full, wet lips and radiant beauty made her the most captivating woman in the world, igniting in me an overwhelming desire to claim every part of her.

In that moment, any debate about her wetness or resistance faded away.

I pulled my hand from her heated pussy and let my fingertips trace slow, deliberate circles around her sensitive clit until another cry of ecstasy escaped her.

Lifting my body until I hovered between her trembling thighs, I pushed her skirt upward over her hips, unveiling her stunning cunt lined with soft, curly, dark hair. I carefully spread her intimate lips apart, taking in the glistening moisture that shimmered like liquid jewels in the dim light.

"Oh, fuck," I growled, enraptured by the sight of her almost divine pussy and the raw, delicious aroma of her arousal.

I dropped to my knees, unable to resist the overwhelming need to taste that sweet nectar I'd craved for weeks. The flavor of her essence had haunted my thoughts, drawing me irresistibly closer.

My lips met hers in a deep, hungry kiss, and my tongue darted out to explore the tantalizing crevices between her pussy folds with fervent determination.

"Niko, God, yes!" she cried, her hands tangling in my hair as she finally shed her mask of denial. "More, please, deeper. I need your mouth so badly."

I obliged her with unwavering passion, sucking, nibbling, and circling her tender clit with a rhythmic precision that matched the wild, uncontrolled movement of her writhing hips. I gripped her thighs, anchoring her as I devoured every drop of pleasure she offered.

Her skin felt impossibly smooth and warm against my tongue, and the pure, heady essence radiating from her center was intoxicating. Each moan resonated like a melody of sheer joy, confirming that I held the power to bring her to a state of blissful surrender.

I slid a finger inside her again, relishing the cry that burst from her lips as I increased the pressure on her sensitive clit.

My fingers thrust in sync with my tongue as her tight, delicious pussy spasmed around them, drawing me deeper into her desire. She was so hot, so utterly soaked, so insatiably delicious that my cock swelled and pulsed, nearly ready to explode even before contact.

"Niko, please don't stop, please," she pleaded, her cries a sweet harmony to my ears.

In that surrender, the moment she fully accepted that her body, every curve, belonged to me, I felt an absolute certainty. Even if she tried to resist, her shudders and soft expressions of pleasure always confirmed the truth.

I plunged another finger into her, sliding it in and out of her tight, dripping cunt, and her body screamed out its unspoken truth.

Laya desired me. Her entire being yearned for me. As she tumbled over the edge in a flood of spasming ecstasy, her pussy overflowing with sweet, intoxicating arousal, I knew that, despite her protests or any simmering anger between us, as long as we were united in that moment, we could overcome any storm.

The pulse between us was intimate and raw, a palpable, sensual bond that felt both genuine and unbreakable. In that climax, I realized that nothing could ever shake the foundation of our entwined souls.

Her thighs trembled as her pussy exploded in a final, overwhelming burst of pleasure. Seeing her body flush and shudder in ecstasy nearly sent me spiraling toward my own release, but I held back, determined and deliberate.

I needed to be inside my wife. I needed it right then.

I pulled my heated mouth away as she caught her breath, rising between her quivering thighs and positioning myself as I prepared to claim her completely. My cock throbbed, fierce, hungry, and insistent beyond measure.

"I can't wait, Laya. I need to be inside you, now!" I roared my demand with madness that matched the insanity of the lust driving all of my thoughts.

The pressure of my cockhead against her slick, wet entrance suddenly made her cry out.

Her heated, fierce gaze met mine in that instant, and an undeniable charge filled the air. The slight lift of her chin revealed her strong determination, while her stunning face completely took me by surprise.

I had thought that after our wild passion, her defiant nature might have softened; yet here she was, still burning with an unyielding need to tear me apart.

I paused as fragments of the past hours raced through my mind. Just that morning, she had sent a single text that unleashed a storm in my heart and a mind revelation that continued to echo within me. Now, as she looked up at me with a mix of defiance and simmering anger, the moment felt almost overwhelming.

"Tell me!" I demanded, trembling with a raw, desperate need that nearly drove me to thrust into her again.

"What?" she snapped.

"Did you mean it?" I pressed, my emotions bubbling to the surface.

Her face twisted in confusion. "Mean what?"

I growled, shaking my head. "The damn text, Laya! Are you really in love with me?"

A sharp gasp escaped her, and for a fleeting moment, a hint of vulnerability shone through her fierce anger. But that spark was quickly smothered by her resolute defiance.

"And what if I was, Niko?" she replied.

Was that an admission? Why couldn't we be honest?

We were acting like two scared kids.

In many ways, perhaps we were. This marriage thing was uncharted territory for the two of us.

"That's exactly how it should be," I murmured.

She blinked, thinking, absorbing.

At that moment, all I could envision was my wife, exposed and vulnerable, captured in a moment of raw intimacy, with our conversation flowing as freely as our desires.

"And this cock is just as it should be," I declared, delivering one long, smooth, determined thrust deep into my wife's slick, hot center.

Her cry, a blend of pleasure and surrender, filled the room as her thighs spread wide and her head fell back, our eyes silently communicating in perfect rhythm with our bare, entwined bodies.

I continued to push into her relentlessly, long, hard, and rough, with a passion that bordered on the edge of painful desire.

Laya's body was paradise, a realm of exquisite pleasure I never tired of exploring. As I looked at her serene face, eyes closed in blissful surrender, my heart surged with a deep, unexpected emotion. I realized then that my wife was the anchor of my soul.

I kissed her again, our lips meeting with hot, desperate passion as my hips lifted in a frantic search for release deep within her. She clung to me, our limbs merging as I moved in a savage, rhythmic dance.

Her hips lifted with every thrust until we both cried out together, lost in the overwhelming crescendo of our shared ecstasy.

My climax erupted inside her, a blazing burst of heat and desire that transformed her trembling core into a symphony of spasms, driving us over the edge of transcendent bliss.

Afterward, she lay in my arms, breathless and panting, our skin glistening with a fine sheen of sweat, a silent testament to the fierce storm of passion that had just subsided. In that lingering stillness, my thoughts cleared, and a stark realization settled over me.

I was deeply and irrevocably in love with Laya.

Never before had anyone stirred such intense and tumultuous passion within me. That she could ignite such raw, powerful emotions was a revelation—a truth about myself that I could no longer ignore. I had entered this marriage for practical reasons, to unite our families, never truly expecting to find love among it all.

Yet, contrary to all expectations, I discovered it. This realization ought to have brought joy. However, it also bore a chilling, perilous truth.

In a heartbeat, my wife transformed into my greatest and most dangerous vulnerability. She was the sole weakness that could ultimately lead to my downfall.

I loved her, and I'd burn this fucking world down if anything happened to her.

Fifteen

L AYANA

The dull, persistent ache where Niko had bitten me the day before pulsed with each step as I navigated the narrow stone passage of the cellar.

I couldn't stop thinking about watching him disappear down the driveway on his little golf cart, the one he used to zip swiftly between the vineyards, with his security team trailing behind.

Instead of concentrating on the detailed layout plans for the new training studio, waves of irritation and annoyance bombarded me, leaving me no choice but to pace back and forth like a trapped animal.

Yesterday's events still simmered within me. He'd stirred

me up so much, and I now realized with bitter clarity that I hadn't come down to resolve or confront anything.

My husband's cluelessness only aggravated my irritation. He had no idea I had overheard his private conversations that afternoon.

I remembered every detail of what Niko discussed with Pavlos. Then, there was the quiet plotting about how to keep the syndicate meeting a secret from me.

Elias seemed to be winning the battle of wits. As he confidently planned to reveal the secret later, my dear husband was foolishly chatting on that sunny terrace, not even bothering to check if anyone nearby could overhear.

I recalled the moment after a grueling training session with Cali when I had positioned myself just far enough away to catch every syllable ringing out clear as a bell.

One word echoed in my mind: traitor.

The urge to confront him was overwhelming at that moment.

However, I chose not to, reasoning that if he was going to keep secrets, I could do the same.

I intended to take action later that evening once I had developed a clear plan. Yet, the memory of our heated confrontation, his sharp intensity, and his unexpected probing of my emotions made me doubt myself.

This morning, I awoke with my body still aching from yesterday's turmoil, but my mind was clear and resolute. With him now wandering the meticulously maintained grounds, it was the perfect opportunity to make my calls.

I reached for my phone.

First on my mental list was Avra, then Vik.

I had a solid strategy for our next steps but needed to discuss it with the team first. We were united, and betrayal wasn't an option.

I suspected that Vik, who managed operations on the front lines and oversaw one of our main territories, might already be aware of the assassination plot against us. His role kept him closely connected with current intelligence. Reflecting on our progress, I was amazed at how far we had come.

With Avra and Elias overthrowing his father, we had seamlessly united three territories, and my marriage to Niko had added three more to our empire.

Cali's upcoming marriage would further bolster our power. With six regions under the Vitalis name, each was prepared to defend our interests without hesitation.

Even if our rivals protested, it was merely their fear of losing the power they desperately clung to.

We weren't about to back down. We would reclaim what was rightfully ours, and our determination wouldn't waver until we achieved victory.

I pressed the phone to my ear and dialed Avra's number, my heart dancing between excitement and fear. Her voice was clear and confident, with a musical quality that made each word seem perfectly timed.

"Laya, hello," she answered in her usual cheerful way, but I sensed an edge to her greeting that worried me.

And unfortunately, I would be adding to whatever was bothering her.

"I need to tell you something."

"Same to you. But I planned to wait until later this evening for our chat."

"Well then, let me begin."

Over the next five minutes, I recounted the overheard conversation in detail.

The details spilled out, barely keeping pace with the torrent of emotions inside me. Avra sighed, a slow breath that seemed to carry the weight of shared secrets.

"Yes, I heard about it this morning from Elias," she replied.

In that moment, my heart skipped a beat, a mixture of shock and betrayal.

Elias had told Avra, and to my disbelief, my husband had chosen to withhold this crucial information from me.

Anger and jealousy surged through me, leaving me entangled in a blur of emotions I couldn't untangle.

"This is what I planned to discuss in our call," Avra continued.

"I'm shocked Elias went to you," I managed to say with the churning emotions raging inside me.

"Why?" she asked, genuine curiosity woven in her question. "We promised not to keep secrets from each other."

Her reminder struck me like a blow, and another sharp pang of envy stung me. Here was a relationship based on total honesty.

While Niko and I felt adrift, our connection had dwindled to fleeting physical sparks and unspoken arrangements.

He managed his company with an iron fist, leaving little room for me to share the intricacies of his world.

Perhaps he kept me in the dark, believing I couldn't handle his secrets. That thought was infuriating, a raw mix of betrayal and confusion.

Still, amid all the turmoil, I found comfort in Avra's steadiness, recalling how she had once entered a marriage for revenge, only to discover that a true, unwavering love was meant just for her.

"I believe we should go to that meeting ourselves, Avra," I stated, a sense of determination filling my entire body.

I knew it was the right decision to the core of my soul.

"I think that's a wise choice," she responded with conviction. "What about Cali?"

"No, she has endured enough hardship," I replied. "We can handle this without her."

Her agreement provided a small relief.

"I'm calling Vik now to discuss the details," I said, adopting a professional mindset despite the personal hurt I felt beneath the surface.

"Okay, let me know what you find out. I love you, Laya," she said.

I exhaled, a sound heavy with pent-up emotions and unexpressed thoughts about Niko that I couldn't yet disclose.

"Love you too. I'll be in touch soon."

After I hung up, I paced the corridor. Frustration swirled in my thoughts, each heartbeat amplifying the sting of betrayal.

Reluctantly, I set aside my feelings for Niko and called Vik's number.

"Ah, I was expecting your call." His greeting was instantly recognizable and oddly comforting in its straightforwardness.

"Of course you were," I responded dryly. "You have spies everywhere, across every syndicate, feeding you all the rumors. Care to tell me who's watching me right now?"

"I'd never divulge my sources." Vik chuckled.

"Killjoy," I replied, our shared banter lightening the mood for a moment.

Vik always had a way of bringing calm amidst the chaos.

"Let me get right to it," I said. "I'm livid."

"That's clear. I don't need anyone to tell me. I can hear it in your voice. Continue so I can confirm the reason."

"Oh, I'm certain you're aware."

"Just verify it for me."

I gritted my teeth. "My husband is secretly organizing a covert meeting with the syndicates without my knowledge."

"Laya, not everything is so black and white," he said in his firm, parental, chiding way.

I couldn't suppress the agitation that rushed up. The last thing I wanted was a lecture about trust and secrets.

"But keeping secrets from your wife is as black and white as it gets," I shot back.

"You've got much to learn if you believe Niko isn't hiding things from you, sweetheart," Vik warned. "Some things are best left undisclosed."

I sighed, the sound weighed down by mixed emotions.

"I'm not someone who needs protection from the

dangers or consequences of our world. I've dealt with it myself my entire life."

"Remember, Niko has lost every woman he ever loved, including his mother and sister. It makes sense that he's overly protective of you, worried that the past might repeat itself. He doesn't want another tragedy to occur, and I can't blame him for that. He underestimates your strength."

My emotions burned in my throat as Vik's remark about Niko losing every woman he loved stung.

Niko hadn't admitted he loved me in the way I yearned for. It was a truth that always felt just out of reach. I had known his rules from the beginning, as if each step were preordained.

No, this was purely business. Yet, the raw, intense nature of the sex was a major component, so physical and bewildering that I often questioned how such passion could exist without affection.

As I planned my next move, guilt tightened around my chest. Keeping secrets from Niko felt like a betrayal, but his silence left me no choice. The difference between shielding him and deceiving him seemed increasingly blurry.

I cursed myself for sending that foolish text and revealing my vulnerability.

What had I been thinking?

I had left myself wide open to being hurt, and now I felt like nothing more than a puppet tangled in his game.

The memory of him pausing mid-act—a sudden need for reassurance about my emotions—made me shudder. With his longing only half-fulfilled, what was I supposed to say?

I shook my head, trying to clear the chaos in my thoughts. Just because Vik said something didn't make it the ultimate truth. Wouldn't Niko make that clear if he truly cared for and loved me?

Maybe I was mistaken in thinking I understood him.

"Anyway," Vik interjected with a hint of compassion, "take it easy on him, Laya. You're both just trying to find your way through this labyrinth. From what I gather, the meeting is slated for sometime next week. The specifics are still emerging, but I'll keep you posted as soon as I have more information."

"Thank you, Vik," I replied, my mouth curving with a hint of bitterness. "That saves me from having to pry every secret out of my husband's mind."

"That sounds particularly unpleasant. Yeah, wait for my call," he responded.

"Fine, though I'm tempted," I admitted, my irritation mingling with a wry grin.

"Calm down, Athena, Goddess of War," he teased, easing the tension between us.

"I'd rather be Athena, Goddess of Information," I retorted, weariness seeping into my body. "Now hurry up with that call."

"Are you going to tell Niko you plan to attend this soirée?" Vik asked, already knowing my answer.

"My husband seems to love surprises," I mused as a tingling of wicked excitement filled me, easing some of my annoyance with my spouse. "I can always surprise him too."

Sixteen

N IKOLAS

The Domaine Matsa vineyards sloped down the hill, featuring grapevines arranged in neat, symmetrical rows, with vibrant clusters of ripening color. Beyond the fields, a lively valley unfolded as rolling hills merged into the distance, each contour illuminated by the sun's glow, all framed against a sky sprinkled with fluffy clouds.

The syndicates had intentionally targeted my competitor's vineyard as a provocation, delivering a subtle dig to bruise my pride. They sought to unsettle or distract me with their cold, calculated display of strength, hoping to catch me off guard and create the impression that they controlled this intricate power struggle.

However, their plan failed to gain traction.

I was well acquainted with the Matsa brand. While their everyday table wine had a limited audience, it could not compare to the exceptional vintages crafted by my vineyards.

Even their olive oil, though adequate for daily use, did not meet the high standards preferred by master chefs in the top-rated restaurants across Europe and beyond. Some may view my opinions as stemming from ego or family loyalty.

Nevertheless, my company's net profits exceeded theirs for the past decade, indicating consumer preference for my products. No matter how much money or advanced technology my competitors invested in, it never resulted in superior quality. True excellence was born from years of dedicated work, refined expertise, and generations of finely honed knowledge.

They believed they could insult me without repercussions, which marked their first mistake. Deep down, I knew it wouldn't be their last.

My instincts warned of trouble ahead, even with my thorough preparations for every possible outcome. Collaborating closely with Elias, I strategically positioned Galanis and Xenos troops around the city, creating a vigilant network of experienced fighters. Recognizing the need for additional strength, I quickly organized reinforcements.

I even enlisted some of my most trusted relatives, including a group of cousins from Italy, who integrated seamlessly with our local units. Their subtle yet formidable presence ensured our ground surveillance was unmatched. If any ambush was planned against us that day, we would be the first to detect it.

It might have been excessive, but I wasn't willing to take risks.

Alongside all the other dangers was Ozias Xenos.

He kept evading capture, and given that he was the foremost enemy of the Vitalis sisters, I decided to take no chances.

Those who remained loyal to Ozias had assisted him in fleeing from his holding room after the coup at his compound, where he had been captured.

Based on Elias's work and my search, pinpointing every traitor proved nearly impossible.

It wouldn't surprise me if one of the other influential families had helped the old man with his great disappearance.

Too bad they'd chosen the wrong side.

It was clear that today's meeting wasn't focused on avenging the brutal killings of Cristo Caras, Morisi Bella, and Pello Korba. Although the official agenda was to address past grievances, everyone understood, albeit silently, that the real purpose was to confront the audacity of three Vitalis women assuming positions typically held by men.

Our traditions expected women to remain silent and stay in men's shadows, never to outshine them.

Avra and Laya courageously opposed this notion, while Cali had faced significant consequences for her defiance. The recollections of her past resistance continued to haunt her, like a persistent fog that might never entirely dissipate.

Certain individuals would oppose the impact of the

Vitalis women until the very end, fueled by the mistaken belief that their outdated perspectives were the only truth. Their steadfast commitment to these outdated ideas was both baffling and frustrating.

How could they embrace cutting-edge technology while obstinately holding onto antiquated beliefs about women?

In contrast, the women I knew exemplified creativity and innovation. They were diligent, smart, and resourceful, traits that greatly exceeded what the majority of these individuals could achieve.

A few minutes later, with Pavlos trailing just a few steps behind, I reached the heavy, worn door and greeted Elias at the entrance.

"I've been waiting for you." He gestured behind him. "The others are already seated."

"Thanks, I'm ready," I replied, and together we walked down a long, echoing hallway until we entered the tasting room of my competitor's sprawling estate.

Soft, diffused light filled the room, highlighting the polished wood and the lingering aroma of vintage wine and leather, mingling with an undercurrent of tension.

I walked confidently toward the group, shoulders back and chin elevated, determined to convey that I considered their authority inferior to mine. My gaze swept the table, analyzing everyone present like pieces of a dangerous puzzle.

At the far end of the room, Vik sat like an immovable force, flanked by two empty chairs, emphasizing his authority. A group of familiar yet intimidating figures occupied the remaining four seats.

Among them was Leon Boscos. Aside from Elias, I was the only one aware that his people had uncovered the planned hits discussed by the men at today's meeting. We intended to keep this intelligence confidential.

Leon managed one of the three largest sectors in the region, a territory so vast that the others seemed insignificant in comparison. Over the years, I had become well acquainted with him, appreciating his fairness and ruthless demeanor. The public saw him as tough and no-nonsense, though he rarely revealed his softer side.

In our world, survival hinged on a strong exterior; showing weakness invited disaster. This unyielding lifestyle required constant vigilance and ongoing efforts to conceal any signs of frailty.

I paused beside Leon Boscos and inclined my head. "Leon, it's been too long."

He nodded. "Busy. Business waits for no one. And you?"

I smiled slightly. "I'm in the thick of it, as usual. Let's catch up after we get through this."

Next to Leon, Moser Bouras and Franco Dimitri occupied the remaining seats: older godfathers deeply entrenched in this cutthroat game.

"Gentlemen." I greeted them with a curt nod. Elias and I then took our seats beside Vik, maintaining our calm and deliberate demeanor.

I faced the group, ready to withstand any verbal barrage they might unleash.

They wasted no time diving into their grievances.

Moser spoke, toying with the cigar between his lips. "Let

me get straight to the point." A towering, podgy man who rarely handled matters himself, Moser always aroused suspicion. I wouldn't be surprised if a hidden pistol lay beneath his well-tailored jacket. "It's these fucking Vitalis women. The world would have been better off if they'd stayed out of the picture."

The audacity of this asshole to speak this way, especially in front of Eli and me, two men now married to the very women he despised, not to mention Vik, their fierce protector. It took some guts to say it so bluntly.

"They're back," I stated with a calm as unyielding as ice. "And they're not going anywhere anytime soon."

"That would be fine," he retorted, "if they'd mind their own business and stop trying to muscle into our territories!"

"I'm just reminding you, Moser," Vik interrupted, his speech as steady as stone. "Those territories originally belonged to the Vitalis family."

"Yeah, well, times change, don't they?" Moser shot back dismissively. "Just because they've grown up and returned doesn't mean history can simply be rewritten. Those women can't just barge into our territories and claim what isn't theirs! They're power-hungry, and they need to be stopped. Women have their roles in the syndicates, and it isn't at this table or running the show. Who are they to take charge?"

His bitter anger was beyond evident in the flickering motion of his cigar as it hovered near his lips. I fought the urge to stand up, to shake him out of his seat and put an end to this rant, perhaps even to draw my concealed weapon and silence his misogyny once and for all. If he used the word "women" one more time, I silently promised him retribution.

"Do you believe the Vitalis family holds power, Moser?" Elias retorted, tension radiating from him. "And I mean power in the present, not just before Juno Vitalis was brutally murdered, and his family was forced to flee for their lives?"

If I hadn't dealt with Moser at first, it would have been only a matter of time before Elias acted alone.

"Stolen power!" Franco finally exploded, his accusation breaking the thick silence.

"Was Avra leveraging her power when she took down those three bastards?" I inquired, my icy composure covering the fierce resolve inside.

"Yes! Exactly what— Wait, no," Moser stammered, his face flushing deep crimson with anger.

His eyes darted around chaotically as he tried to regain control, the bobbing cigar now a symbol of his unraveling grip.

"Look, these bitches are out of control—that's all I'm saying! Something must be done about them, and that's why we're here. They need to be dealt with, once and for all!"

His undisguised threat had all three of us leaning forward, every muscle tense with anticipation as we focused on him.

"And Juno was voted out! Nobody betrayed him." Franco faltered as he attempted to weave a narrative of misplaced honor. "His death was tragic, yes, but..." His words trailed off, the lie dissolving into the oppressive atmosphere.

Rage surged through me like wildfire. I took a deep, measured breath, steadying myself.

Pavlos, who had been lingering near the entrance, stepped forward but paused, sensing the slight shift of my hand.

My features were impassive to onlookers—a carefully maintained exterior intended to conceal the storm raging within. My father had taught me the art of hiding a tempest behind a placid facade, keeping adversaries off balance until the moment for action was right.

One misstep and I'd unleash destruction on that bastard, though he would never suspect a thing until the time was right.

"Franco," I said, fixing him with an unyielding stare and raising an eyebrow in silent challenge, "stop rewriting history to portray yourself as the hero. Everyone at this table knows exactly what transpired. Juno Vitalis was once a man we all respected—a true leader. He was the godfather of all of you. And you...you killed him! We all share that guilt," I declared, scanning the table before returning my focus to him. "There's Vitalis blood on your hands."

Moser shook his head and let out a mocking laugh, while Franco gazed down at the scarred wood, avoiding eye contact with me.

I felt such hatred for these men, fueled by their actions against Juno, their betrayal of the syndicates, and the suffering they'd caused Cali. The volcanic ire inside me only grew as I clenched my fists, each memory of their wrongdoings stoking the flames. If my sister Cora were still alive, they wouldn't hesitate to use her as a pawn, just as they had with Cali.

"You can't prove we had anything to do with Juno's death." Moser waved his hand as if to brush aside an inconvenient truth.

My mind blazed with a multitude of violent visions of annihilating these despicable people. I was overwhelmed by an unquenchable desire to drag them into the darkest, most hidden parts of my basement, where I could carefully exact my revenge like a hunter skinning his prey.

"The Vitalis sisters have seized what belongs to them, and their campaign is far from over," Elias declared with unwavering conviction, directing a sharp, appraising gaze in my direction, likely gauging when I might erupt with fury. "You'd all do well to accept that."

"Or what?" Moser challenged, the corners of his lips curling into a sneer.

"Or face the consequences," I finished, my tone as cold and unyielding as steel. Moser shook his head in disbelief, his eyes narrowing with disdain as he looked at us.

"The two of you sold out to the pussy, didn't you?" he spat, leaning back in his chair and crossing his arms over his chest. His eyes narrowed into slits, glinting with disdain. "You're like a couple of fucking Vitalis lapdogs now."

I couldn't help but laugh at this man's absurdity.

"They're beautiful women with very comfortable laps," I replied with a casual shrug, the corners of my mouth curling into a smirk. "The perfect place to watch those who betrayed their father cower in fear as the sisters seek their vengeance."

Moser's mouth fell open in shock, his features frozen as the cigar he had clenched between his lips finally slipped and tumbled to the floor.

His face flushed with indignation. He slammed his fist onto the table, the sound echoing like thunder in the tense air.

"How dare you make threats, Nikolas!" he shouted, standing abruptly, his eyes blazing with anger.

All at once, Eli, Vik, and I stood up, ready to confront the escalating tension. When Laya entered the room with authority, her firearm aimed directly at Moser's hideous, bloated face.

"This isn't a threat. It's a promise," she declared, her gaze sharp and unwavering, as if each syllable could cut through the tension in the room like a bullet.

SEVENTEEN

L AYANA

"Go ahead, old man," I muttered in a low, venomous tone, while shaking my head so sharply that the fresh scent of my leather jacket mingled with the bitter tang of disdain. "Pull out that gun. I dare you."

Once an expansive space where hesitant conspiracies could echo, the room now felt like a suffocating cell, every inch pulsed with tension and the grim promise of violence.

My eyes burned as I disregarded the brief flash of shock and concern that crossed Niko's face while I fixed my gaze on Moser. He returned my look with cold, hard eyes, glinting orbs that caught the scant light like shards of broken glass.

In that charged moment, Moser embodied pure evil, a

dark figure whose presence drained the light from the room and left only memories of the heavy, oppressive fear experienced by a little girl fifteen years earlier.

A surge of electric anticipation coursed through me, my heart pounding with a silent vow of retribution.

I gripped my gun with measured calm, muscles tensed and nerves alert, ready to unleash deadly force at the slightest misstep. If anyone deserved a bullet, it was that bastard.

The bastard had twisted Papa's tragic end into a mere demotion instead of the premeditated murder it truly was. I could almost hear those sordid details echoing in my ears, mingling with the quiet, conspiratorial murmurs that filled the air before Avra and I had stormed into the room. His deceit made my skin crawl, each lie a burning sting in my memory.

As if the betrayals weren't enough, he also callously buried his debts to my father as though they had never existed in the first place. A wave of disgust washed over me, my blood boiling at the idea of a man who orchestrated cruelty with a mere flick of his wrist and regarded loyalty as a disposable pawn in his perverse game. In my eyes, he and anyone who aided him were marked for death by the relentless hand of a true Vitalis.

I fought the urge to glance at Niko, though a small, burning part of me yearned to see his reaction, to know if his face revealed even a hint of respect for my merciless resolve or if, beneath his calm exterior, outrage simmered at my directness.

But there was no time for that distraction. I kept my

focus on Moser as my mind raced with a thousand possibilities, while the air itself seemed to vibrate with the threat of imminent danger.

Images of Niko's unwavering defense of the Vitalis name flooded back—he'd spoken with unapologetic loyalty and razor-sharp wit.

I remembered how his clever comebacks dismantled anyone who dismissed him and Eli as mere egomaniacs, revealing them as the petty fools they truly were. In that moment, my heart swelled with deep, tender love, not just for his physical strength but also for his keen, unyielding determination, which always left me in awe.

The rush of shared energy forged an unbreakable bond. Previously, I'd relied heavily on Vik and my sisters, believing they were my only support. However, with Niko's unwavering encouragement, everything clicked into place. My long, solitary journey and the challenging, isolating steps were ultimately about protecting my true sanctuary—my family—while keeping others at arm's length.

With Niko beside me, I remembered how, right from the start of our journey together, his decisive actions had always resonated more than things spoken aloud. I remembered our first day as a couple when he solemnly vowed that our marriage would be built on truth and integrity. Each time he defended me with passionate, righteous fury, my heart overflowed with fierce, tender love that swept away any lingering doubts.

Then, shattering the charged silence, Avra's shout pierced the air like a battle cry.

"Layana," she called, her hand gripping the handle of the cold, gleaming gun.

The polished barrel caught stray beams of light, casting tiny reflections that danced over the skeptical expressions of the men huddled at the far end of the table.

"These men are showing signs of dementia. They're ancient, after all. It seems they've forgotten who built their history. How about we give them a swift, brutal reminder?"

I squinted, furrows of defiance etching my brow as I watched Moser. His fury simmered behind barely restrained eyes, coiled and ready to strike.

"I think you're right," I agreed, each syllable weighed like a soldier's march on the battlefield.

"Juno Vitalis was a good man." Avra's sharp anger gave way to sudden tenderness. "He worked tirelessly, building a life from nothing but sheer will."

Moser paused, disbelief threading through his words. "This is so absurd—"

Before he could finish, Avra roared, "Shut up and listen!"

Her shout boomed across the room as she cocked her gun, the click echoing like a death ring.

"Our father pulled each of you from the gutter and transformed you into men of unimaginable wealth. Without him, where would you be? Still wallowing in the dirt. I guarantee you'd be nothing more than garbage collectors, janitors, or dishwashers! Do you honestly believe you'd be strutting around in tailored suits with bloated egos without his intervention? Hell no. You'd be begging for scraps on the cold, unforgiving streets!"

My sister's rage exploded, raw and fierce, sweeping the room like a volcanic eruption. In that electrifying moment, as I watched her become an unstoppable force, a shiver ran down my spine—a mix of fear and awe at the sheer power she exuded.

I steadied my breath, ready to match her strength, for that power, the potent legacy of the Vitalis name, was ours to wield without hesitation.

"I am the eldest Vitalis heir," Avra declared, her presence resonating with undeniable authority and the scars of past betrayals. "And if you complain about a woman wielding strength equal to any man's, remember this—you forced me into this role by callously ending my father's life. If you're looking for someone to blame, look no further than yourselves. Until you can scrape together even a shred of decency from your rotten souls and acknowledge our rightful place in this syndicate, I'll take out as many of you as necessary to show that traitors have no sanctuary here."

Moser hesitated, attempting to mutter, "There has never been a female—"

"Say 'female' again," I snapped, stepping forward, gun cocked, and ready to unload.

Each syllable was laced with bitterness as I moved forward, my steps hammering home the power shift. "We have no use for your antiquated justifications or backward beliefs. The era has shifted. It's our turn to lead. We won't be dictated to by those who pledged loyalty to a noble man and then fled at the first sign of adversity."

Franco's desperate protest hung in the air, his breath

shaky with rage and apprehension. "This isn't even about Juno—it's about women—"

"That's right," I cut in, my tone sharp. "And if we had dicks, you'd all be shaking in your fucking shoes."

Avra lifted her chin and continued for me. "But we don't. And if our actions aren't clear enough for you, we'll show you again and again that not having male anatomy doesn't lessen the explosive force behind our words. Never doubt that we inherited our father's unyielding, ruthless spirit."

A raw, bubbling fury surged within me as I stated, "We're just itching to blow your fucking balls off!"

Each word resonated with the promise of retribution and the unyielding spirit of our united resolve, leaving no doubt that we had finished adhering to their outdated rules.

Eighteen

Nikolas

My cock pulsed with an unquenchable raw desire as I drank in the sight of my formidable wife.

I felt her energy crackle in the air, an electric force hinting at a warrior who had triumphed in countless battles. She stood, shoulders back and chin up, radiating assurance like a guiding light.

Her eyes sparkled with fierce determination that challenged anyone to approach her. She was an unstoppable force, wild and formidable.

In that instant, I was entranced, admiring her majestic presence as she and Avra advanced into the syndicate's core, exuding undeniable authority.

With every step, the sound of her heels resonated through the dim room, piercing the silence like a resolute drumbeat. I felt the intensity of their gaze, sharply observing me as I navigated through the crowd, focusing on the godfathers whose scarred faces revealed stories of violence. An undeniable aura of power cloaked them, commanding respect from men who thrived on cruelty.

Tension filled the air. The women stood strong, their steadfast gazes reflecting the confidence built through years of hardship.

They held their heads high, their eyes piercing through the facade around them, each symbolizing the battles fought against a world that often overlooked them. They embodied the avengers of a legacy tainted by sexism, and their powerful presence compelled the cruel, misogynistic men to retreat into the shadows, unable to withstand the force of their united strength.

Even with the barrel of cold, unyielding metal aimed at them, these men maintained their defiance. Their gritted teeth and sneering expressions couldn't hide their deep-seated anger and resentment.

I couldn't help but wonder if Juno Vitalis, the epitome of unrestrained power, were to walk into the room, whether those cowards would immediately collapse, dropping to their knees as if drawn to worship the very symbol of authority he represented.

Their pathetic refusal to accept the Vitalis sisters on their own formidable merits, simply because of their gender, was about to be met with a ruthless, unforgiving lesson in the brutal realities of the modern world.

Still, the idiot men refused to yield even with the cold steel forced up against their faces.

In that charged moment, Franco's taunt cut through the gathering like a finely honed blade, exuding a smug, malicious intent. "Avra, you know your husband was present when your mother died, don't you? How can you ever forgive Elias for this?"

Until that fateful moment, Avra had maintained an icy, unyielding disposition of stoic rage, her expression as impenetrable as a fortress. However, Franco's feeble attempt to unsettle her provoked something fierce and deadly, like a tempest gathering force, ready to erupt.

"You dare attempt to drive a wedge between me and my husband?" Her temper unfurled like a coiled serpent thirsty for retribution. "You're nothing more than a weak underling trying to cover his tracks."

Franco's jaw clenched. "You are—"

"Go on," Avra interrupted him. "Continue distorting the past, rewriting history with your lies, because everyone in this room knows the unassailable truth. Elias had nothing to do with my mother's death. However, what you did to my parents is unforgivable, no matter how much you twist it now."

I glanced over at Elias and noticed the same awe and admiration in his eyes as he looked at his wife, mirroring the silent reverence I felt for Layana.

Elias and Avra exchanged a silent nod, a mutual understanding forged from their shared experiences of standing strong and honorable in the face of immense betrayal.

Avra's eyes narrowed to icy slits, her gaze slicing through the dimly lit room as she lifted her pistol, the metal glinting ominously in her steady grip.

She fixed Franco with a glare that could freeze the deepest pits of hell, her lips curling slightly in a smirk of pure derision. Her head moved side to side in a slow, deliberate motion, each shift of her neck a silent dismissal of every vile syllable that had spilled from Franco's lips.

"When I look at you, Franco Dimitri," she began, her eyes narrowing into slits, "I see nothing but deceit and betrayal. Were you ever truly loyal to my father? You stand here, a figure cloaked in lies, staining his memory and tarnishing his name with every breath. And now, you dare to confront me directly? Tell me, what vile rumors have you been weaving behind my back? Have you been perpetuating that disgusting lie, claiming Elias was involved in my mother's death? At what point, I wonder, when will your deceit finally end?"

For a brief, charged moment, time seemed to freeze as she scrutinized the weight of guilt etched into the lines of his face, her lips curling in a disgust palpable in the air. Franco stood across from her, his brow slightly furrowed, meeting her unwavering gaze with confused innocence. His eyes, dark and deep, revealed not even the smallest flicker of regret, remaining still and unreflective like a calm, muddied pond.

In a quiet yet unsettling tone that carried a sense of

inevitability, she stated, "I believe there's unfortunately only one thing that can stop you."

Without hesitation or a warning, she squeezed the cold, metallic trigger of the pistol. The quiet of the dimly lit room shattered as the sharp crack of the gunshot reverberated off the walls.

The bullet flew through the air with pinpoint accuracy, striking Franco Dimitri squarely between his eyes. His expression shifted from shock to emptiness as his body, once rigid with defiance, slumped forward from the high-backed chair. The weight of inevitability dragged him down, and he collapsed onto the polished wooden floor with a final thud. The impact reverberated through the room, shattering the silence and leaving the onlookers immobilized in shock.

Moser took a step back, his eyes wide open as he tried to grasp the chaos unfolding around him. Faces contorted with rage pushed through the haze, leaving him dazed and unsure of what was meant to come.

Avra's intense gaze cut through the confusion, her head tilting, daring him to react.

"Do I need to clarify my point?" she inquired, with a nonchalance starkly contrasting the turmoil surrounding them.

Moser shook, his body sinking under the burden of defeat. He lifted his hands in a gesture of surrender, yet it felt feeble against her steadfast gaze.

"No, no..." he stammered, fear evident in the quiver of his lips.

A brief, humorless laugh slipped from her lips, a sudden, cutting sound that pierced the tension. She slowly shook her head, her gaze sweeping over the room filled with people. Every face exhibited a blend of awe and muted fear, eyes wide and breaths held, as if blinking might provoke her formidable presence. The air was electric, vibrant with the unspoken acknowledgment of her authority.

"You can call me a ruthless, violent elliniki godmother if you want," she declared, her gaze steady and filled with fierce conviction. "Let history refer to me as a merciless figure. I am undisturbed by judgment. My mission is clear: to restore my family's rightful place at the heart of this region's power dynamics. With my sisters' support, I will pursue this goal. If anyone has doubts or questions, now is the time to voice them—fate's inevitable progress will soon render them speechless."

Moser's hands trembled as he stuttered, "What do you mean by that? Isn't each region governed independently?"

His confusion and bewilderment brought a smirk to Avra's lips.

"Tsk, tsk." Avra shook her head. "That's how things are now, but it was never supposed to be this way. I'm surprised you haven't figured it out yet, Moser. Perhaps your outdated thinking is making you slow." She fixed him with a sharp look. "I want it all back—every bit of power my family lost after Papa's assassination, and everything that rightfully belongs to us. I plan to take control of the entire region, and no obstacle or enemy will stop me. It's not just ambition. It's our birthright."

In that suspended moment of charged confrontation, Moser's eyes widened, pupils dilating as they darted toward me. His brow furrowed, and his lips parted as if to ask a question, silently pleading for an explanation of the sudden turmoil erupting around us.

Elias stepped up beside Avra, his resolute expression echoing off the walls as he said, "She's right."

His conviction was a palpable force that filled the room, prompting everyone to pause.

I moved deliberately toward Layana, and with Elias, we formed an unbreakable, living shield against the impending threat of betrayal.

"Yes, she is," I asserted, steady in my conviction.

Vik stepped forward, anchoring himself behind us, a powerful presence reinforcing our united front.

Leon Boscos sat at the polished oak table, his fingers tracing the intricate patterns of the wood as if searching for answers. Suddenly, as if compelled by an unseen force, he slid his chair back, the faint sound breaking the silence, and rose. Shoulders squared, he fixed his gaze ahead, striding toward us with determination, each footfall resonating on the marble floor. He lifted his chin, a silent defiance against the weight of expectations looming above.

When he arrived by our side, he declared, "I stand with them."

A radiant smile spread across Layana's face, enhancing her beauty and highlighting her inherent strength. In that instant, I yearned to wrap her in my arms and whisper that she was truly magnificent. Yet I restrained myself, knowing this was not a time for tender whispers but for the resounding celebration of her indomitable, unyielding power.

NINETEEN

LAYANA

As I settled into the soft leather of the car seat, a sigh escaped my lips. I watched Vik's sleek black SUV pull away, heading toward the outskirts of our territories. The rest of us prepared to return to the estate, flanked by our security teams. At the same time, a few of our most trusted and experienced soldiers stayed behind in Athens to oversee the meticulous clean-up of deceased godfathers and their associates.

Following Avra's ruthless elimination of Franco, we had no option but to triple our defenses, aware that our enemies were increasingly threatened by the shifting power dynamics favoring the Vitalis Family.

Elias and Avra had decided to stay at Niko's and my

estate for now, adding another layer of security. Vik mentioned that keeping all three sisters in one central location, surrounded by three strong support systems, would alleviate the stress we continually seemed to place on him.

The meeting concluded swiftly after Leon Boscos spoke on our behalf. Everyone else held back their comments prudently and accepted Avra's terms to prevent further provoking her and risking the same predicament as Franco.

My body continued to hum with excitement from the day. And from the gleam in Avra's emerald eyes, it was clear she was riding high as well.

The pride I felt for my big sister exceeded anything I could ever convey to her. She was nothing less than a superhero.

In my mind, she was fearless, a warrior overflowing with courage that surpassed anything I could ever imagine. Simultaneously, she was protective and loving toward Cali and me. Avra was the ideal godmother to guide the Vitalis family into the future.

The image of her composed, nearly tranquil face in the moment before her bullet shattered the silence and struck Franco right between the eyes would forever be a cherished memory of her unapologetic power.

"You were incredible, Avra," I declared, unable to hide my admiration.

With a mischievous glint in her eyes, she shot back, "Who said only men know how to handle things?" accompanied by a wink.

"Not me." I laughed, the tension momentarily dissolving between us.

"Although," she added, shrugging as if to dismiss any lingering consequences, "I realize I just fanned the flames a bit higher. We'll have to deal with what comes next."

Sitting beside me, Niko exuded quiet intensity. He hadn't said much since our departure from the meeting, yet his silence was as loud as a roar. I longed to pull him aside and explore the tumult of thoughts swirling in his mind.

I understood my presence could ignite his simmering temper, yet I willingly embraced that risk. If he wanted to be angry with me, so be it; I was determined to conduct business on my own terms. The sooner he realized this, the smoother our journey would be.

The words I had overheard earlier still echoed in my mind. I felt a flicker of pride in his passionate defense of our family's honor, but a nagging thought persisted: if he was so earnest, why had he concealed the details of the meeting from me? It made me question whether he doubted my abilities. I held onto the hope that this wasn't the case and silently prayed our bold actions today would dispel any lingering doubts for good.

"I've said it before, but men lash out when their egos are bruised," I remarked, somewhat lost in thought.

"Hey," Elias interjected with theatrical mock outrage.

Avra shrugged her shoulders. "Don't deny it—you know deep down it's true."

"Come on." Niko finally broke his silence, rolling his eyes.

"What?" I asked, daring him to respond. "You know it's true," I added confidently, expecting him to concede my point.

Niko's eyes gleamed with seriousness that belied the banter as he continued, "Perhaps you two don't care what anyone thinks, but I assure you that Moser is on the phone with everyone else, plotting to escalate his scheme to destroy us. Just because we're seen as soft, he feels so threatened by our power that he resorts to desperate measures."

Then, shifting the conversation, he added with genuine conviction, "A confident man who is secure in his place in the world naturally appreciates a powerful and strong woman. Wouldn't you agree, Elias?"

"Absolutely," Elias affirmed without hesitation, nodding with steadfast conviction.

Niko's eyes then met mine, shining with deep sincerity that conveyed more than he could ever say. "I'm not intimidated by your power, Laya, or Avra's. Having both of you by our side means we're unstoppable together. Why should I feel threatened by that?"

"You speak the truth, Niko," Elias added.

Avra smiled brightly as she looked at the two of them.

"I'm grateful we have both of you," she said.

Apparently, he shared the same sentiment. As soon as we arrived at our estate and stepped inside the house, Niko excused himself and pulled me aside.

"I need to speak with my wife alone. We'll be back shortly," he said, his firm stance inviting no further debate.

He guided me through a long, shadowy hallway and

down a steep stairway that led to the cool, damp cellars. My mind raced with intrigue and expectation.

"Niko, what are you doing?" I inquired, feeling a whirlwind of surprise and eagerness swirling inside me.

His reply was a curt, "I need privacy," that echoed in the dim corridor.

With careful steps, he guided me deeper into the shadows until we reached the end of the hall. He opened a heavy wooden door to a small, seldom-used tasting room, gesturing for me to enter.

Inside, the room revealed its long-forgotten history, showcasing stacks of ancient, dust-covered barrels and rows of empty, brittle wine bottles, testifying to years of neglect. The scents of aged wood and lingering must filled the air.

I turned back to Niko, feeling a bit confused.

"What are—" I began to ask, but before I could form another word, his hand shot up to grasp the column of my neck.

He pressed me firmly against the heavy wooden door, and in that charged moment, before any protest could slip from my lips, his own captured mine.

The kiss burst into a fiery, passionate blaze that stole every breath and thought, leaving me dizzy and yearning for more.

Twenty

L AYANA

In the cellar's oppressive darkness, Niko yanked his mouth away from mine with a force that had me gasping for breath.

His eyes deepened like smoldering coals, revealing an almost predatory hunger.

He reached out and grasped a fistful of my hair, yanking my head. "Layana, do you know what you do to me?"

The raw emotion sent a flood of arousal through my core.

"Niko, I—" I started, but he silenced any protest with another searing kiss that was both fierce and quick, igniting a whirlwind of need and uncertainty within me.

I found myself adrift in a torrent of confusion, caught

between the terrors of fatal violence and the irresistible pull of lust. Amid this swirling ambiguity, a powerful surge of desire emanated from deep within me, leaving me fervently hoping that his intentions were nothing short of carnal delight.

"You," he hissed, his head swaying, eyes wild and dilated. "Watching you today made me as hard as a rock."

With possessive urgency, he seized my hand and pressed it against his tense groin, the undeniable firmness, and instinctively, I curved my fingers to cup him.

"That's what you do to me, Laya! You drive me fucking crazy with the heat of your presence, with the burning lust in your gaze, with an insatiable hunger that I can't contain!"

His eyes searched mine for a heartbeat, the silent exchange brimming with a fierce, unspoken promise, before he claimed my mouth again.

He spread my lips open like unveiling a hidden treasure, thrusting his tongue inside in a collision of desperate need and reciprocal desire. I responded to his fervor with a moan of surrender, my body arching into his embrace as I pressed my breasts against his chest.

Then, as abruptly as before, he tore his mouth away, leaving behind an aching need only he could quench.

"All I could think about, Laya," he declared, his rumbling confession, "was fucking you, from the moment you stormed through that door and pinned that bastard down with the point of your gun as if you ruled the damn world with fearless fury. If it weren't for your family being there, I would have claimed you on that table."

"I am fearless," I spat back, lifting my chin defiantly against the whirlwind of passion and power swirling around us.

A wry smirk played on his lips as his eyes danced with dark amusement and raw desire. "My darling, you are the most enticing, breathtakingly sexy woman I have ever laid eyes on."

In that charged moment, I squeezed his rigid shaft, marveling at the low, rumbling growl that vibrated deep within him, while the pulse of desire sent spasms of ecstasy coursing through me.

Niko was a force of feral passion, a blend of dark, unrelenting, violent yearning, and ruthless power. And beneath all that ferocity lay a core of unyielding loyalty. Today, he had deliberately taken a step back, allowing Avra and me to navigate the perilous situation on our own without a single disapproving utterance escaping his lips.

As the realization slowly dawned on me, it became clear that his silence was not a sign of doubt. Instead, it was a deliberate effort to shield me, as Vik had hinted before, until I was ready to uncover the truth.

Once Avra and I had stepped into chaos, he trusted us to take control. That unwavering loyalty, unique among traits I had encountered, only heightened my desire for him, binding us in a moment that was as terrifying as it was intoxicating.

I was already captivated by Niko. In truth, my affection for him had grown deeply. There was much to admire about him.

It wasn't just his name, rich with legacy, his wealth

symbolizing power and influence, or his expansive estate showcasing his achievements. What truly caught my eye during our first encounter was his commanding presence and that incredible body.

He truly captured my soul when he offered his unwavering support. He stood by me when I needed him most, displaying the utmost confidence in the Vitalis family as it existed today. Supporting me didn't make him weak. It simply showed he trusted my judgment and regarded me as a partner.

His wife.

Those words resonated with thrilling clarity. While my courage excited him, his loyalty to me had an equally strong effect.

This time, I ripped my mouth from his and reached up, cupping his chiseled cheek, and gazed up at him.

"Thank you for standing by me and not intervening today." My gratitude overflowed. "I can't express how much that means to me."

"I trust you completely," he said. "You're smart, Laya. You are fearlessly intuitive, and I do not doubt that together, we will make an unstoppable team, no matter our goals."

"Thank you for saying that," I replied, my heart swelling with emotion.

"I'm sorry for not telling you about the meeting; I was only—"

"—trying to protect me, I know," I interjected.

"Yes," he admitted, like a tender confession.

His lips found mine again, insistent and possessive. He

kissed me with intense passion and urgency, and I mirrored his fervor. His hand wove through my hair again, his eyes wild and untamed as they locked onto mine.

He stepped closer, the space between us shrinking until I could feel the heat of his body radiating off him. His eyes locked onto mine, deep and hypnotic, capturing every ounce of my attention.

"Now that we're alone, you're mine, do you understand?" His quiet command wrapped around me and made my heart race.

His possessiveness fed the arousal burning inside me.

I tried to resist them, to deny the emotions they stirred in me. Yet, he was right—when we were alone, I belonged to him. In those private moments, I craved his touch, his control, to be marked as his and his alone.

"You're no longer in charge, Laya," he murmured, his lingering kisses tracing along the sensitive skin of my neck.

I leaned back, surrendering to his quiet command as his lips traced a fiery journey across my skin. The heat of his mouth sent shivers through me, awakening every nerve. Light kisses transformed into firm presses as he explored my collarbone, trailing lower and igniting a craving that consumed me and left me breathless.

His fingers traced the edge of my skirt, sliding beneath the fabric with a deft movement. Each inch he bared sent a thrill coursing through me, making the room seem to shrink and the air thicken with an undeniable tension.

His breath coasted over my exposed skin, heightening every sensation as he explored.

"Again?" he asked, laden with yearning, authority, and oozing a delightful blend of dominance and raw lust. "You sexy little whore!"

His fingers, both searching and assured, found the slick desire between my thighs, plunging viciously into my aching pussy.

A sharp cry escaped me, equal parts plea for escape and command for more. My knees trembled under the intensity of his whispers and caresses.

"No," he said abruptly, withdrawing his hand with a calculated gleam.

I whimpered in protest, my body desperate for the pleasure that only he could evoke.

He brought his lips close to my ear and vowed in a tone barely above a whisper yet laden with unyielding authority, "You aren't going to come. You're mine, remember? I say where. I say how. I say when."

I gaped at him, filled with both apprehension and arousal, as his declarations etched themselves into my consciousness. I bit my lip in silent submission.

He reached up once more, grasping my hair and twisting it, his fingers tangling in the soft strands as he pulled me closer. His grip was firm and insistent.

He leaned closer, his eyes heated and radiating dominance. "Do you understand me?"

I nodded, my breath coming in quick, uneven gasps, the air thick with anticipation.

"Say it," he commanded.

"Y—you say when," I replied, my lips trembling.

My body hummed with unquenched arousal, and I was so ready to beg for relief.

"That's right, good girl," he praised, and I couldn't help but shiver.

His approval and revealed desire served as a provocative seduction for my senses.

He rested his other hand on my shoulder, decisively guiding me downward. "Now, get on your knees, darling."

I eased myself down onto the cool floor, feeling the chill seep into my skin. My eyes locked onto him, heart racing as a wave of anticipation surged within me, each breath heavy with need.

My heart pounded in an erratic rhythm, and goosebumps pricked my skin as his fingers moved to the belt of his trousers.

In an instant, his pants dropped, exposing his throbbing cock—heavy, magnificently thick, hard, and so fucking beautiful. Without a moment's hesitation, he held my face, directing his swollen shaft toward my eager mouth.

"I want to feel those pretty lips wrap around my dick, Laya," he whispered.

I pressed my back against the coolness of the wall, my head tilted back as if inviting his gaze. My heart raced, every nerve ending tingling as I met his eyes, vulnerability washing over me like a wave, unmanageable and overwhelming.

His dark eyes burned with desire. "Open up, Laya. Let me fuck your mouth."

In that charged moment, I completely surrendered to his

desires, a surge of longing igniting within me as I sensed his arousal.

Darting my tongue out, I licked up the bead of precum on his cockhead.

Niko released an animalistic groan, tightening his grip on my hair. The throbbing between my legs grew, and I followed his unspoken command and took him deep.

His hips moved with a slow, intentional rhythm, each thrust creating ripples of pleasure within me. My eager and nimble tongue danced along the firm, thick length of his velvety, engorged dick, exploring every ridge and contour.

"Yes," he growled, deep and full of satisfaction. "That's it, baby—keep doing that thing I enjoy."

I moved my tongue skillfully around the tip, my determined actions echoing his fervent need. His deep, rhythmic moans resonated like a passionate symphony in the air. As I sensed him tense, an increasing pressure built up, telling me he was near. I increased my pace, twirling my tongue faster and sucking him with ever-growing hunger.

"Fuck," he grunted, giving me wicked hints of his imminent climax.

Abruptly, he withdrew, the sudden shift in rhythm making my head spin as he lifted me to my feet with surprising force.

"Niko..." I whispered, the sound mingling with our ragged breaths.

"Shhh, walk to the table," he ordered, taking charge as he guided me to a small dining table tucked into a shadowy corner.

With a skillful maneuver, he turned me face down onto the table's smooth surface. In a single, seamless action, he pulled my skirt up around my hips, exposing my bare lower body to the air.

"God, look at you," he murmured in a husky and deep voice. "The most beautiful pussy in the world, all spread open and aching for me. Tell me you're mine, Laya! Say it again!"

It was both a command and a caress, and I felt the insistent nudge of his cock against the entrance of my pussy.

Without hesitation, I parted my legs, offering myself with complete desire. As soon as he entered, the closeness of our connection was marked by a breathless cry.

"I'm yours, Niko! Every part of me, every heartbeat, every desire is yours," I declared, surrendering completely.

"That's right," he responded with an air of satisfaction, pushing forward decisively.

A cry of pure bliss escaped me; the sensation of him filling me sent thrilling waves of pleasure coursing through me. I instinctively raised my hips, craving his deeper, more commanding presence.

"Laya," he all but growled as he began to withdraw, the silky, sensuous shaft of his cock trailing through the slick inner walls of my pussy. "It's so good, you're so fucking good!"

Each word dripped with raw intensity and unwavering desire, leaving me trembling in the wake of our shared, limitless passion.

He rammed himself inside again, and again, and again,

until we were rocking against each other, both of us trying to get him into my pussy as hard and deep as possible.

His thrusts were rough and forceful, his hips slamming into me, impaling me on his cock as he fucked me with abandon.

"This pussy is mine, Laya!" he declared with a possessive, commanding edge.

Lost in a haze of ecstasy as the fullness of his throbbing cock claimed me, I could only moan in response, to the cascade of sensation.

Every fiber of my being fixated on Niko, his sculpted body, the heat of his powerful cock, and his sultry, seductive words that danced along my skin. My wet, inviting core convulsed and pulsed around his engorged shaft as every deep, delicious thrust sent waves of pleasure crashing through me.

"Yes," I finally cried out, trembling with urgency. "Please don't stop! I'm about to come. Niko! Niko! Niko!"

His reply dripped with raw desire. "Yeah, you love it, don't you, babe? You love my cock, don't you?"

I could only exhale a fervent "Yes," pleading silently as my body shuddered with the unstoppable tide of sensation.

"Are you that close?" he hissed, the rolling pleasure inside me building into a fierce, consuming storm.

Abruptly, Niko pulled out completely. His firm hands seized my hips as he turned me to face him, giving me barely a chance to take a breath before he thrust back inside me with renewed determination.

I couldn't help but gasp at the pleasure-filled pain of the invasion.

"I'll let you come, darling, but first I want something."

"You have all of me. What more could you want?" I cried out, desperate for an even fiercer intensity, fast, hard, raw, and unyielding. "Fuck me, Niko!"

A wicked grin spread slowly across his face as he slowed his pace.

"Niko!" I cried, frustrated and needing relief. Then he withdrew completely once more, and I whimpered as he deftly traced the head of his insistent cock along the sensitive rim of my quivering clit. My nerve endings sizzled under his teasing touch, each delicate caress leaving my body pleading for even more.

"What do you want?" I demanded, frustration mingling with excruciating arousal.

He hovered over me, his breath ghosting near my lips, his dark, lust-filled gaze full of raw emotion.

"I want to hear it again," he demanded, rolling his hips so that his pulsating cock grazed the brink of my entrance once more, teasing me with relentless precision.

His every movement was an exquisite torment, and I could tell he relished every moment.

He cupped my throat and tugged my head back, making me look up at him.

"Say what? I told you I'm yours," I protested, a mixture of exasperation and need in my tone.

His fingers flexed on my skin, and he leaned in. "Tell me you love me again, Laya."

He had never expressed those words to me before, yet he expected them from me again. If he only looked close enough, my feelings for him were clear, leaving no room for doubt.

Suddenly, an overwhelming cascade of emotions bombarded me, making it hard to think, only feel.

Before I realized what I was doing, I said, "I love you, Nikolas."

This time, there was no regret, just happiness in revealing my truth, fully accepting what lay in my heart and soul.

Niko was mine, and I loved him. He turned me, lifting me onto the table, and threaded his fingers into my hair. The intensity with which he stared at me was beyond anything I expected.

Then, he aligned his throbbing cock, sank deep into me, and whispered, "I love you too, Laya."

My eyes grew wide, tears pricking at the backs of them. I wrapped my arms around him, pulling him closer. Our mouths met, and I widened my thighs, inviting him not only deeper into my body but also opening the gates of my heart to him completely.

"Mine. You're everything, Laya. My world. Never forget that," Niko said.

I nodded. "Yours."

Those were the last words we spoke as our bodies took control, urging us to lose ourselves to one another and our desires.

Twenty-One

N IKOLAS

For the past week, it felt as though the entire city was holding its breath. Late-night patrols revealed empty streets beneath flickering neon signs, with not even the hum of distant engines breaking the silence.

I sat in my study, staring at the rain-streaked window, feeling my nerves tingle with the sense that the quiet concealed something ominous.

My men had searched every narrow alley and broad boulevard, keeping their eyes peeled as they scanned dark doorways and parked cars for any sign of trouble.

Yet they returned with nothing but quiet nods—no suspicious chatter or furtive glances. It was almost as if

Moser, with his gruff build and intimidating glare, had retreated from the chaos. Perhaps he was biding his time, carefully plotting his next move, with only his closest lieutenants aware of his whispered plans.

Deep down, I knew that danger was approaching—a reckoning that always followed the seizure of new territories. You couldn't shift power without a cost, and shaking godfathers from their comfortable seats nearly always ended in violent retribution.

This was even riskier now, especially with women involved, particularly my woman, my wife, my partner—a symbol of defiant strength in a society that still viewed her as fragile.

In our ruthless world, that kind of vulnerability was a mistake that could not be forgiven.

Every whispered conversation among my men echoed the same names, the air thick with rumors. Even Laya, with her sharp eyes, and Avra, whose calm presence commanded respect, were caught in the same tension that gripped Elias.

At night, we gathered in small, shadowy rooms, our voices lowered as we checked every sensor, every camera, and every patrol route around our properties. Avra and Elias spent long hours reinforcing barricades and locking gates, their faces set in grim determination.

Every passing minute only heightened the tension, stretching it like a drawn bow, each silent second marking the approach of an inevitable storm. The quiet around us seemed to convey one message: some of the old family heads still hadn't realized that the Vitalis family was reclaiming its territory. Even if the new leadership arose from the brothers rather than the sisters, any initial anger would soon yield to a true power struggle.

In our harsh, patriarchal world, the sisters were consistently marginalized and excluded from the brutal contests where men flaunted their weapons and boasted about their exploits. Their exclusion of females wasn't merely for traditional reasons. Rather, it served as a cruel method to suppress even the faintest hint of ambition.

But those old-school men had a fatal blind spot: they underestimated their female counterparts' cool precision, relentless determination, and lightning-fast strategic minds. These women were trained in the ruthless lessons of our underworld by their steely father and further honed under Vik's brutal regime until every move they made became deadly efficient.

Avra's swift retribution on multiple occasions and her hand striking out like a viper to silence a traitor proved that the sisters wielded a power capable of making even the most hardened patriarchs tremble.

Amidst the immediate dangers, another concern troubled me late into the night—the eerie silence from my brothers. Typically, their requests for money would echo through the office, each issue a blend of legal complications and financial crises that I needed to address with urgent calls to our lawyers and accountants.

Their silence now was as loud as any shouted demand. I recalled the day they crossed the line and confronted my wife;

the shock and disbelief on their faces were etched in my memory.

That moment, full of adrenaline and a dangerous mix of admiration and desire, made my heart race. Laya's barely concealed savagery brought out a darker part of me, something fierce, like a blend of love and raw lust that consumed an untamed beast because she was mine.

I was fascinated by the duality of her nature. She was a relentless warrior in combat, each move calculated and deadly.

However, in private, she transformed into a gentle vulnerability, a striking contrast to her fierce power. In moments of calm introspection, I even confessed that I secretly hoped my idiot brothers had already faced her wrath.

To me, they were nothing more than persistent, annoying obstacles—reminders of familial obligations that only seemed to stir up chaos wherever they went. Rumors began to spread like wildfire in local pubs, carried on the heavy, smoky air of dim, boozy corners where hardened men, usually secretive about syndicate matters, could be heard grumbling about disruptions in our world with every shot of whiskey.

The sound of clinking glasses intertwined with the whispers of discontent in the back rooms of these taverns. Names such as Avra, Cali, and Laya were mentioned with both respect and trepidation. The uneven cadence of these discussions and the cautious looks exchanged over scarred wooden tables signaled that something significant was imminent. More than anyone else, I felt the brewing storm beneath their calm demeanor, poised to unleash chaos on those who dared to underestimate the power of the Vitalis family.

The Vitalis sisters had to confront more than just the stubborn old godfathers clinging to outdated rules. They faced a centuries-old mindset ingrained in nearly every man, a toxic, patriarchal ideology that could not be eradicated with a single move.

You might eliminate every Franco Dimitri you encountered, but another would always rise from the ashes, carrying the same inherited curse of misogyny. Changing that was not something that could be accomplished overnight.

This battle would be long and exhausting, with each grueling day chipping away at entrenched beliefs. Yet, if anyone could succeed, it was Laya and her fearless sisters. Still, I couldn't help but feel a sting of bitter disappointment whenever I heard my brothers showing signs of resistance. I was determined to shoulder that burden as best I could, stationing my most trusted men around them at every turn, ready to alert me at the slightest deviation. The constant worry about them gnawed at my nerves, compounding an already overwhelming list of challenges.

My anger simmered as I flipped through the morning reports from my accounting team. Every figure and line of profit testified to the success of the estate my father had built, now mine to run. My father had once seemed almost mythical, effortlessly commanding an empire with daily strategic brilliance.

In the past, I questioned if I could ever measure up to such big shoes. However, reflecting on the difficult choices he made had shown me that, although the path was challenging, it was manageable. I successfully kept the empire thriving, and I believed he would feel proud and impressed by my achievements.

Leaving the stack of reports behind, I strolled down the polished marble corridors in search of my fiercely devoted warrior bride. The rhythmic clicking of my steps blended with the ambient sounds of the building, guiding me toward the kitchen, where lively voices spilled out through the doorway.

"He's only nodding his agreement because he doesn't want a bullet in his head," Cali said, her words echoing down the hall and sending a jolt of anxiety through me.

As I rounded the corner, I found Cali and her sisters gathered around a long wooden table, their expressions serious and etched with worry. I walked over to the coffee maker, poured myself a steaming cup, and let the rich aroma blend with the tension in the air.

"We received a call from one of the regional godfathers," Avra explained.

I drifted over to Laya. Her presence always grounded me amid the chaos. Leaning in, I kissed the top of her head, inhaling the familiar scent of her lavender shampoo, uniquely hers. Sitting down next to her, I intertwined my fingers with hers.

"Which region did they call from?" I asked.

"Thrace," Laya replied, a slight crease forming between her brows as if the name carried extra weight.

"That's one of the largest regions," I noted, feeling the

gravity of the situation settle in. "So what's with all the talk about bullets?"

Cali clenched her jaw. "Regional godfathers are covertly pursuing their own agendas behind closed doors to gain more power. And, frankly, this call came from the one asshole who dares to think differently."

"I agree." Avra smoothed away a crease of concern on her brow. "But we need to handle this with skillful precision—keep everything at a diplomatic level."

I leaned forward, both eager and cautious. "What exactly did they say on the call?"

"They want to forge an alliance with the Vitalis family." Avra paused as she carefully chose what to say. "The plan is to prevent any fallout in that region by strategically aligning with us."

"Smart thinking, though I understand Cali's point about the bullet," I remarked.

Cali nodded emphatically. "Tell him everything, Avra."

Avra continued, "He mentioned wanting to change how the others manage their territories."

"Really?" I raised an eyebrow. "It might sound clever, but I can't just buy into their true motives without investigating further."

"I was thinking the same," Laya murmured, her hand tightening around mine.

Her touch always reassured me, even in uncertain times.

Curious, I asked, "And who exactly made the call?"

"Anastasios Balaska," came the reply.

"Balaska may be smart enough to outmaneuver his peers, but he always looks out for himself. The moment he tries to fit in, it's less about loyalty and more about self-preservation."

"I trust no one in that circle," Avra stated flatly.

"Neither do I," Laya added

Then Cali cut in with raw intensity, "Absolutely not. We're not trusting any of them. Our guard is up after everything those pompous godfathers did to Papa."

Avra's tone hardened with determination. "So here's the plan: we give each godfather just enough freedom to eventually get tangled in their own excess—a slow collapse of their control."

Laya nodded in agreement, a playful smirk revealing her excitement.

Avra continued, "We'll accept his offer while keeping a close watch on his moves. If he's truly smart, he'll soon realize that his best long-term bet is with us, and he'll maneuver to help us extend our influence into his region."

"I've been cooking up a plan to make that happen."

Avra's eyes softened as she turned to me. "Niko, ever since you joined our cause, your loyalty has been crystal clear. And seeing how well you treat my sister warms my heart—I've rarely seen her so happy."

Laya's cheeks turned a shade of crimson as she lightly reprimanded her sister. "Avra! Stop it!"

"Am I not being sincere?" Avra responded with a smile.

Laya paused for a moment and then continued, "You know..."

Cali added, "Her expression is so unmistakable, it could wake the sheep in the distant fields."

A rich sound of amusement escaped Laya, mixed with a touch of exasperation that filled the space around us. I soon found myself caught up in the waves of ecstasy.

With a confident gesture, I proclaimed, "Let everyone hear it. I take great pride in what I possess."

Half-embarrassed, Laya muttered, "This is so awkward. Anyway, Niko, share your brilliant plan so we can finally stop discussing our sex lives."

I kissed her cheek and said, "As you wish, dear wife."

The room filled with low, knowing chuckles, and a surge of happiness rushed through me. Yes, we were plotting hostile takeovers of entrenched mafia territories, and the weight of our mission hung heavily in the air. But at that moment, the teasing banter, sly smiles, and casual camaraderie created a sense of belonging—a family bond I hadn't felt since my parents and Cora.

In just a few weeks, we had grown so comfortable with one another that it felt like a cherished secret.

Then, I laid out my proposal with urgency and hope. "We need to stay ahead by being proactive. If we can accelerate the process, our influence will spread more quickly. I have a wide network. My cousins eagerly stir up some carefully orchestrated chaos in those rival territories. Their kind of trouble can be devastating."

"Can you break that down for me?" Cali's eyes sparkled as she raised an eyebrow. "All this roundabout talk is making my head spin! So, who exactly are we planning to take out this time?"

Laughter rippled through the room at her bluntness.

"You know me too well," I said with a grin. "I'm not referring to playing executioner. Instead, if my cousins disrupt our enemy's supply lines, their entire operation unravels. Their cash flow diminishes, leaving them confused and cornered. Once a few key players falter, the rest will see the writing on the wall."

Cali's eyes narrowed. "So you're planning to undermine their drug shipments and essentially cut off their illegal revenue?"

"Exactly," I agreed. "Not just drugs, but anything they trade illegally. Things they're too scared or too corrupt to report. And believe me, when you start digging, you'll be amazed at how much is off the books."

Avra stepped in. "We've left no stone unturned. Vik and I thoroughly checked every syndicate operation before we returned. No shady corner was overlooked."

I appreciated her thoroughness. "I expected nothing less from you. Your reputation for leaving nothing to chance is well-deserved."

She thought for a moment and added, "That means I'm fully behind your plan. Please let me know if you need any extra support in the future."

"Thank you, I'll certainly keep that in mind," I responded, meeting her steady gaze.

She grinned again, and for a moment, it felt like time stood still as she remarked, "Thank you, Niko. I truly believe the Vitalis, Xenos, and Galanis families will become unstoppable."

In that moment, Laya's radiant smile brightened the dimly lit room, filling every corner with a glow. She reached out and squeezed my hand, her touch sending a jolt of energy through me. I was mesmerized by the depth of emotion in her piercing emerald gaze, a look that made my heart race. This intense connection sparked a familiar awakening of feelings deep within my soul, reminding me of our unspoken bond.

TWENTY-TWO

L AYANA

The midday sun warmed our faces as Cali and I walked down the bustling sidewalk, our arms casually linked as if nothing could interrupt our easy pace.

We passed the main shopping center, where a stream of colorful shoppers flowed in and out of glass-fronted stores, their laughter and lively chatter blending with the distant sounds of street musicians.

Every step brought a fresh sense of delight—a freedom born from wandering without the worry of prying eyes or whispered judgments.

This uncomplicated pleasure and unburdened walk felt like reclaiming a piece of my soul. It reminded me of the thrill I experienced earlier while handling my weapon—a quieter yet equally authentic expression of who I was. I was a Vitalis, and that truth shone as brightly as the golden light showering us.

Looking at Cali, I noticed how much the overall energy around her had changed. The timid spark from her past had been replaced by a determined glimmer and a wisdom earned through hardship. While the memories of her former self still lingered in her gaze, each day she grew a little stronger, a little more defined. I knew that if danger ever set her nerves on edge again, the vengeance she'd unleash on her enemies would be formidable, and I planned to stand by her side without hesitation.

For now, the joy of simply drifting between the shops filled me with contentment. Cali's genuine smile illuminated my heart more than any sunbeam ever could. Around us, our security detail moved with practiced efficiency. They meticulously scanned every passerby in a silent, coordinated dance. Down the street, I envisioned Niko unwinding in his favorite barbershop, the crisp clatter of scissors providing him a rare moment of calm in his relentless schedule.

Yet amid the brightness of our day, a subtle tension nagged at the back of my mind. Like a dark cloud that refused to dissipate, the threat posed by our enemies lingered even in our brightest moments. Only within the secure walls of the estate did we truly feel at ease. Even then, we were always ready to act in case a breach occurred.

We were always prepared for anything.

This was why I couldn't help but grumble as Cali and I left a charming ice cream shop.

"Does he think his team is better than ours?" I murmured while trying to balance towering, intricately swirled kaimaki ice cream cones and not scowl at Niko's extra security team lingering among the Vitalis men. "As if I wouldn't notice the Galanis men hanging around."

"I spotted them hours ago but kept quiet, knowing it would annoy you." Cali grinned. "Niko's just overprotective, Laya. You might as well get used to it. I don't see that changing anytime soon. God, imagine if you had children! Those poor kids wouldn't be able to breathe without Niko hooking them up to an oxygen tank to make sure they have enough."

I shook my head. "That's absurd."

"But you know what I mean," she said with a light shrug, diffusing any real tension.

With a sigh, I joined her on a nearby park bench, where the steady flow of passersby provided a pleasant backdrop for enjoying our chilly treats.

The hum of conversation and the rustle of the crowds created a sense of normalcy, even as a trace of guilt gnawed at me. Niko's concern was genuine; his constant alertness came from a desire to keep us safe.

"So, how did he take your protest?" Cali asked, curiosity softening her tone. "Because from where I'm sitting, he ignored you."

I frowned and shook my head, a grin creeping onto my face. "After he went on about trusting his gut, I insisted that our security was more than enough. Thanks to all the planning Vik put into it, I figured we'd reached a consensus."

"Figured is the key term here." Cali's giggles echoed as she licked her ice cream cone. "You two make quite the pair."

I leaned back with a sigh as I unlocked my phone.

"I suppose a little extra security never hurt," I admitted, then typed out a brief message to Niko.

Laya: Thank you for sending your men, even though I never agreed to have them join the Vitalis security team. It's better to be overprepared than underprepared.

Niko: I believe you misunderstood something, darling. They were going to be there whether you agreed or not. I protect what's mine. I apologize if you thought my offer of protection was a request for permission. You are mine. Therefore, Galanis soldiers will accompany you wherever you go. See you soon, my love.

The absurdity of it all lifted my mood, and I smirked as I relayed, "Apparently, I misunderstood, and they would have been around whether I wanted them here or not."

Cali's eyes twinkled as she added, "I like him. He's got guts."

Instead of being exasperated with my baby sister, I reveled in the unabashed images of Niko's naked body dancing through my mind.

I quickly pushed those intoxicating thoughts aside. Now wasn't the time for distractions, even though my skin still craved his touch, his intense thrusts, his vicious demands, and his unrestrained lust.

Goosebumps pricked my skin as arousal surged in my body.

Our passion and need for each other seemed to have consumed us recently. It was like an insatiable, unstoppable tidal wave that overshadowed everything else.

To everyone's annoyance, we found every opportunity to be alone and tended to lose track of time as our lust and desire overtook logical thought.

And when it came to sleep, that was a faded memory, replaced by nights consumed by need and unquenched raw sex.

I wasn't sure if this was normal for marriages, but it was my marriage.

Being with Niko was less a dream and more an awakening.

He devoted himself to fulfilling my every desire, prioritizing my pleasure over his own, leaving me quivering and each encounter more intense than the last.

"Oh, God, I said the wrong thing." Cali rolled her eyes. "Stop thinking about your naked husband."

"Ugh," I groaned, attempting to shake off the lingering memory.

"Isn't there more to your marriage than just always fucking like rabbits?"

Her humor caught me a bit off guard.

"Is that really how it appears?" I asked.

She shrugged. "Not at all...I'm just teasing. But seriously, how do you feel? It's clear that Niko adores you. He shouts it from the rooftops."

"I adore him too," I confessed, a hint of vulnerability in my admission. "Honestly, Cali, I had no idea what I was getting into. I chose Niko as if I were selecting a candidate for a job position. I never expected an arranged marriage to blossom into something resembling romantic love. I wasn't searching for this kind of bond. My only hope was that he was a good man and that our union would fortify the Vitalis empire."

I paused as I recalled the first day I met him.

The day we rescued Cali, I suspected he was a good man, his undeniable strength and quiet kindness shining through. Over time, it became clear that he was more than just someone useful to our cause. He was a man of deep passion and extraordinary character, claiming my heart in ways I'd never imagined.

"What I discovered was far more intense," I began. "Niko and I are friends and have an undeniable connection. We often lose track of time while talking, becoming fully engrossed in our own little world."

A mischievous glint sparkled in her eyes as she reclined. "That's not the only thing you two do for hours."

"Hush!" I urged with a conspiratorial wink. "We just can't help it. It's like we're magnetically drawn to each other, our hands finding one another whenever possible."

Cali finished the last bite of her ice cream and said, "I'm happy for you, I really am, Laya."

"Thank you, Cali," I replied. "Let's head to that cozy bookstore we discussed last week."

"Sure," she said, rising to her feet with enthusiasm.

We tossed aside our ice cream wrappers and walked down the sunlit sidewalk, the murmur of the city intertwining with the cadence of our footsteps.

Our companions followed behind us in a protective formation, creating a silent barrier around us as we ventured forward together, enjoying the moment.

"You know, sis, there's something I've wanted to discuss," I said, daring to approach this sensitive subject now.

But Cali seemed unusually open today, and I wanted to ensure she understood my thoughts.

"Remember how we all agreed on our plan together when it was first laid out? I want you to know—nobody expects anything from you now. You don't have to marry into one of the other syndicates if you don't want to. That part of our plan is off the table."

Cali's thoughtful nod gave me the impression that the tension in the air was easing.

"Thank you for saying that." The relief on her face made me want to sigh.

I continued, wanting her to understand what lay deep in my heart. "You've endured so much, sweetheart. We would never force you into an unhappy marriage merely to bolster our power. All we've ever wanted is for you to marry for love, if that's your choice. It's your life, after all. You may be a Vitalis, but you have the freedom to decide what your future looks like."

"You and Avra have shown me love and patience," she expressed. "Truly, I cannot imagine how I would have managed without either of you."

I reached out and gave her hand a reassuring squeeze.

"We love you, Cali, endlessly," I insisted, my resolve firm and unwavering.

Then, with a steady, reflective air, she added, "I appreciate you clarifying any expectations, Laya. I feel better now—slowly healing, yet always aware that my past is a part of me. I'm coming to terms with it, even if it pains me. I know this will remain part of my life forever, and I could never be with someone who doesn't understand why it is so significant."

Her confession hit me like a tidal wave, and tears pricked my eyes. Her raw honesty tore at my heart, and I silently wished for the power to manipulate time. If only I could shield her from this relentless anguish, I'd endure any hardship for her sake.

After a lingering silence, she took a deep breath and said, "I've given this a lot of thought, you know? About our old plan. I agreed to it once, but now I see that carrying it out would mean surrendering to those who caused us so much grief. I refuse to allow them to dictate our future and our family's destiny. They haven't broken or defeated me."

I admired her steadfast resolve and tenacity. My little sister was a warrior like no other.

"I admire your strength, Cali," I said, filled with pride and a touch of awe.

"I won't give them another ounce of my soul," she declared, embodying a storm of determination.

I returned her smile with one of pure encouragement.

"Of course," I murmured, silently hoping she could feel the full weight of my supportive approval.

My heart brimmed with the simple truth that if anyone deserved genuine love and happiness, it was my little sister.

With that, she nodded firmly.

"So," she declared, "I plan to marry, but only on my terms. I want a man who truly comprehends my journey and is willing to navigate the tough times with me." She continued, "I'm not looking for a partner who only appears impressive on paper. Laya, you and Avra must understand that I will meet each option first. If there's chemistry, then we'll proceed to the next step. I want to move at a pace that ensures I'm completely certain."

I couldn't help but grin widely. "That sounds like a perfect plan to me."

With that, we stepped into the inviting atmosphere of the bookstore. As we wandered among the creaking shelves and the murmurs of pages turning, I felt hope soar in my heart. Cali was healing, truly setting her life on her own course. Hearing her assert her desires, establish her boundaries, and build a life she genuinely wanted was a victory.

We, as Vitalises, were born into paths predetermined by family tradition, with destinies written in our very veins.

I watched her gracefully enter the bookstore, following closely and taking in every detail of her elegant movements. She carried herself with ease and confidence, her head held high, exuding an inner pride that clearly reflected her self-awareness.

Despite what those men had attempted, they couldn't

break her spirit. Her resilience was far too strong to be crushed by anything they did.

"Look at this book," Cali called, as she reached for a volume on the shelf and presented it to me as if it were a hidden treasure.

Curious, I asked, "What is it?"

"It's a book about plants," she explained with a wink, "but not just any plants—these are the ones that might be the key to achieving one's goals."

I tilted my head, examining the title with curiosity. "Wicked weeds? A collection of poisonous botanicals?"

She responded with a mix of humor and sincerity. "Hey, you never know when you might require a specific piece of knowledge to shield yourself."

I nodded in agreement. "That's true. Fortunately, thanks to Vik, we have acquired the necessary skills for effective protection."

Her smile grew reflective as she admitted, "I used to despise those endless hours of training he forced on us, but now I'm truly grateful for the skills I've gained."

"Me too," I replied. "Cali, I can't express how thrilled I am to see that spark returning in your eyes."

"Thanks, I feel good. I think I'm ready, Laya," she confided.

A thrill of anticipation ignited my voice as I suggested, "Once we get back home, we should call Avra and share the news."

"Yes," she affirmed, taking the book from my hand and

tucking it under her arm like a treasured secret. "I'm getting this. It's all for research."

"Research, of course." I nodded in agreement. "What else would you call it?"

I linked my arm with hers as we strolled through the labyrinth of shelves, where the aroma of old paper and ink enveloped us, creating an ambiance perfect for curiosity and exploration.

As we approached the section dedicated to romance and desire, she stopped before a display and took another book from the shelf.

"Perhaps you need this?" she held up a volume on the Kama Sutra while wagging her brows and pursing her lips.

"Seriously?" I rolled my eyes and pointed to the shelf. "I believe I'm managing just fine. Put that back."

"If you say so," she replied, carefully setting the book down while flashing an adorable smirk. "I hope that one day I find someone with as much passion for me as Niko has for you."

"Cali, you're an incredible woman." I smiled. "Any man would count his blessings to have you by his side. I honestly don't think you have anything to worry about in that area."

"You and Avra make it look almost effortless," she mused.

"What? Marriage?" I asked, half-amused, half-incredulous.

"Yeah." She shrugged, but it was evident she worried about her future. "Everyone says marriage is a daily effort—if you don't give it constant attention, the spark fades away."

"That's true," I conceded, "but when you find someone who is genuinely compatible and equally invested in the relationship, it hardly feels like work. That's why it seems so natural between us. It really is that easy."

"You two made the right choice," she remarked.

"We did," I replied with a contented sigh. "I wasn't sure we would, but everything turned out better than we ever expected."

"I want that too," she murmured, and I pulled her into a tight hug.

"You'll find exactly what you're looking for, Cali. I promise," I murmured in her ear.

She drew back and nodded in acknowledgment. "I know."

"Hey, let's head over to the poetry section. I want to pick something out for Niko," I suggested.

"So romantic," she cooed into the quiet, book-lined corridor. "I believe it's just around the corner."

But as we turned that corner, our lighthearted conversation abruptly ceased. Standing before us, shrouded in an ominous shadow, were Stefano and Markos, Niko's brothers. Their faces, twisted into sneers, made it clear they hadn't come to browse the shelves at all.

"Well, well, well, if it isn't the Vitalis sisters," Markos drawled.

"Markos. Stefano. Hello," I replied coolly, though I refused to hide my utter disdain for them. "I'd say it's a pleasure to see you both, but we both know that wouldn't be the truth."

I sensed Cali's anxiety and fear growing, a palpable energy radiating from her, so I instinctively stepped to her side, positioning myself as her shield.

She had come so far in her journey. I refused to let these bastards take an ounce of her newfound joy.

My words seemed only to enrage them further, and they advanced, their very presence meant to menace and threaten. Adrenaline surged through my veins, and my heartbeat quickened.

This situation was on the brink of becoming very complicated.

Behind me, my security team moved in, creating a protective circle, their eyes sharp and attentive.

In an instant, Stefano and Markos unsheathed their weapons almost simultaneously, provoking a similar response from my own team.

A cold, calculating rage spread through me as I met their gazes. "I don't know why I ever assumed you two had any semblance of intelligence. Clearly, I was mistaken."

"Insult us all you want. It doesn't affect us," Markos declared, lifting his chin and pointing his gun in our direction.

I raised my hand, halting any action from my men, knowing all too well that they would spring into action the moment I gave the signal or if either of these idiots came any closer.

"What exactly do you want? Why have you so rudely disturbed my peaceful afternoon with my sister? Weren't you humiliated enough during our last encounter?" I demanded.

"We're here to remind you of what we discussed last time," Stefano replied coldly.

"Gentlemen, this song and dance is getting boring," I countered. "How many times will we repeat this ridiculous discussion?"

"Until you leave," Markos said flatly.

I laughed, shaking my head. "That day will never happen."

"Oh, but it will," Stefano growled, stepping closer. "Willingly or not."

"Is that a threat?"

"No," he replied, shaking his head dismissively. "It's a fact."

"Is that so?" I arched a brow, curiosity battling defiance. "You seem so certain. I wonder what gives you such confidence?"

"You'll see," Markos retorted ominously.

I narrowed my gaze. "Please, do enlighten me, gentlemen. You've piqued my curiosity."

"The Vitalis name is worthless!" Stefano suddenly shouted. "How dare you return expecting respect? Our family has never, and will never, honor your name. It has long been associated with weakness and failure. And now, you have the nerve to control our brother?"

"Control? No one controls Niko. He makes his own decisions." I exploded, disbelief mingling with fury. "We're married, you fucking idiots!"

"We won't stand idly by while you tarnish the Galanis bloodline with your venomous, corrupted lineage," Stefano snarled. "We won't allow you to destroy the legacy our family has built."

"That's comical." I laughed bitterly. "Pray tell, how do you enrich your family's legacy? Is it anything beyond nothing? Or do you merely squander money like a pair of reckless party boys, wasting every legitimate heirloom your family has ever earned?"

My questions hung in the air, wrapping around us like a living entity.

Markos's eyes raged with fury as the bookstore's otherwise peaceful ambiance contorted under the weight of the confrontation.

"You know it's true," I said, disdain dripping from my lips. "Everyone knows it's true."

He sneered. "No, that sounds like something my brother fed you. You lead him around by his cock, and he lets you! It's pathetic."

He could insult me all he wanted, but Niko was off-limits.

An all-consuming urge made my hand twitch, desperate to draw the hidden pistol tucked into the holster at my ankle and fire a clean shot between his eyes.

Instead of discharging my weapon, I drawled words like finely sharpened daggers. "Oh, Markos, I assure you, I make it worth his while. It turns out, a well-handled dick is a very satisfied dick."

I let my eyes roam over his body in exaggerated disgust.

"But I suppose you wouldn't know anything about that, would you?"

For just a heartbeat, his eyes flickered with seething rage before plunging into blind fury. Without a moment's hesitation, he squeezed the trigger of his gun. The deafening crack sent a forceful jet hurling me violently against a wall lined with shelves.

A searing heat coursed through my veins, each heartbeat echoing the pain.

Lying on the cold floor, I gradually lifted my gaze to the ceiling, my mind a foggy jumble of confusion.

"Layana!" came a desperate cry as Cali rushed to my side. Chaos erupted around us in an instant, filled with frantic voices and clattering sounds.

I blinked up at her, still dazed, shaking my head as her trembling hands pressed against my chest, a gesture that broke my heart.

"No," I insisted through gritted teeth, pushing her frantic hands away. "I'm fine."

With every ounce of strength, I fought against the pain pulsating through my body as I struggled to sit up.

"Layana, be still!" Cali ordered with an unhidden edge of worry.

"No, let me up," I rasped, trying to push myself to my feet. I managed to get onto my knees before the room spun wildly, forcing me back down onto my bruised backside, clutching the cold wall for support.

"Stay down!" Cali barked, shifting from sisterly concern to authoritative firmness.

In that moment, she wasn't my little sister anymore. She was a commanding force, a grown woman managing the chaos, and the sight of her fierce determination was somehow endearing.

"Somebody help!" she shrieked over her shoulder, her head turning wildly as she called for assistance.

"That fucker, Markos," I growled, anger flooding every nerve as I gritted my teeth. "Where the hell did he go?"

"I don't know, just be still, Layana. Please, don't move," she pleaded as tears brimmed in her eyes.

I muttered through clenched teeth, "I hate that asshole so much, and his horrid brother too."

Cali's wide, wild eyes mirrored her deep worry, and I longed desperately to erase every trace of that terror.

"Just be still, Layana, be still," she whispered, tears streaming down her cheeks as she pressed harder against my wound.

"God, Cali, that hurts. Can you please stop?" I managed to say, my breath ragged as the noise throbbed in my head, drowning out everything else around me. My chest tightened, and urgency spilled over the edges of my plea as I struggled to keep my composure, hoping for some relief from the relentless pounding within me.

Before I could continue, the shattering sound of glass ripped through the tension. I tried to push myself upward again, but Cali's determined grip forced me back down.

"No!" Cali snapped. "If you try to get up one more time, I swear to God, I'll knock you unconscious, Layana. I love you, and I fucking mean it."

"Jesus," I muttered. Blinding pain burned through my body, making it hard to think and forcing me to tilt my head to the side in a futile attempt to focus. "Why are you being so damn bossy? I just want to kick that little slimy asshole's teeth in."

"Because it's my turn to step up," she hissed with frustration. "Look at you...you're dripping in blood, you idiot! Shot and still mouthing off?"

Her outrage hit me like icy water, making it painfully clear that I hadn't fully grasped the gravity of my injuries until now.

I gazed down at the dark crimson blotches spreading across the material of my dress, each pulse of pain sending the room into dizzying spins at a faster pace.

That motherfucker Markos had shot me. Shot me!

A low, trembling growl escaped my lips as I vowed, "I'm going to kill him."

My vision blurred, and my mind clouded. The energy in my body seemed to seep away with every breath.

"I believe Niko will surely take care of that for you," Cali interjected, leaving little room for debate. "If he doesn't, I certainly damn well will."

The fire in her eyes was unmistakable, reflecting the defiant spark I had seen in Avra's and my own reflection. No one escaped unharmed when a Vitalis was involved, regardless of family or name.

Then, voices began to rise in the background as if on cue. I craned my neck, straining through blurred vision to catch a glimpse behind Cali.

The shattered window of the bookstore revealed a scene of utter chaos. Stefano and Markos lay sprawled on the sidewalk outside, my men holding them down with guns drawn, while the two brothers engaged in a chaotic, heated argument.

"You stupid motherfucker, what were you thinking?" Stefano roared, trying to keep his face from digging into the broken glass.

"She pissed me off!" Markos insisted, with a mix of anger and panic. "They can't prove it was me!"

"Everything pisses you off! Didn't you think, for once? We were supposed to take her somewhere safe, not shoot her in fucking public, in plain view of every goddamned camera in that shop! You're such a fucking dumb idiot! I can't believe I'm related to you!" Stefano's outrage cut through the air like a whip.

"Fuck the cameras!" Markos barked back, desperate. "We can wipe the evidence clean. The cops, if you think about it, are already on the Galanis payroll."

"God, you're even stupider than I thought!" Stefano bellowed back. "They're not on our payroll; they're on Niko's! They owe us nothing. Are you insane? How many more disasters will you cause, Markos? Wasn't your last mistake enough to teach you a lesson?"

"Don't you dare bring that up!" Markos shouted, his anguish evident as rage twisted his speech into incoherent fury.

"I'll say whatever I want, you asshole! Because of you, we lost Mama and Cora. The target was Niko, not them. They were innocent, Markos! I forgave you once, but that was a mistake. You're never going to learn!" Stefano spat out as if his mouth was filled with something heavy and bitter. "You're the reason I don't have a mother and sister."

"You bastard! You know that was a mistake, and now you're blaming me? How was I supposed to know that Niko would change his routines that morning? This wasn't my fault! It simply wasn't!" Markos's bravado faltered, shifting from anger to despair, but I felt no compassion for him.

As he broke down, all I could think about was the consequences of his actions. The weight of the moment hung heavily in the air between us, an unbridgeable gap of misunderstanding and resentment. I stood firm, unmoved by his turmoil, aware that he needed to confront the reality of his choices.

That man was responsible for shattering so many lives.

"Mama and Cora were the only good things this family ever had," Stefano seethed through gritted teeth.

"All you needed to do was make a call and confirm. If you had done that, they would still be alive. Their deaths are on you, Markos. There's nothing you or anyone else can do to change that. I hope the memory of what happened haunts you every single day for the rest of your life."

My eyes flicked over to Cali, who absorbed everything said with grim concentration.

In a low, almost inaudible whisper, I murmured, "Oh, poor Niko," even as the room began to swirl again, darkness crept in, and the world faded to black.

Twenty-Three

N IKOLAS

A deafening gunshot shattered the calm of the afternoon, reverberating off brick walls and sending a jolt of terror racing through every fiber of my being. In that split second of chaos, my gut screamed that Laya was in mortal danger.

Without hesitation, my men and I sprinted toward the source of the desperate screams, skillfully dodging a tidal wave of panicked pedestrians flowing in the opposite direction.

Each pounding step on the cracked pavement matched the frantic racing of my thoughts, as fleeting, brutal images of what lay ahead flashed before my eyes.

I saw fragments of my past: my mother's gentle smile, my sister's comforting embrace, even my father's steady hand.

All of them were gone.

The thought of losing Layana gripped me like an iron fist. She had become the center of my universe.

I knew, without a doubt, I'd never be able to survive the loss of Layana.

I needed her. She was the most important person in my life.

My phone buzzed in my pocket, but I ignored it.

I shoved past surprised onlookers to quicken my pace. In the distance, I spotted a crowd gathered like ants around the local bookstore, and a sharp, sinking feeling settled in my chest.

Laya and Cali had specifically mentioned visiting that exact place.

I charged forward, but my legs felt like they were wading through thick, heavy mud. It was like being trapped in a recurring nightmare, where every movement forward involved a struggle against an unseen, draining force.

Wrath and rage coiled within me like a tightening snake with each labored step.

"Fuck!" I snarled under my breath.

The unfolding chaos was unmistakable, a public spectacle that guaranteed a messy aftermath. Scores of witnesses were present, and soon enough, a multitude of names would need to be silenced by whatever means necessary.

My phone vibrated again, cutting through the cacophony

of panic, so I yanked it free from my pocket as I maneuvered past the scattered, fleeing bodies.

"What!" I barked harshly into the line.

"Laya has been shot," came Pavlos's urgent, strained voice. "The women have barricaded themselves inside the bookstore. We need to get her to the hospital fast, boss."

A furious mix of rage and dread momentarily froze me. I staggered over my own feet but quickly regained my balance, charging with renewed, wild determination toward the bookstore.

"Who did it?"

There was a brief, tense silence before Pavlos replied, "Your brothers."

Anger exploded inside me, turning the world a vivid, furious red. "Where are our men?"

"I'm with the women now," he answered. "The others have your brothers outside."

I hung up the phone and quickened my pace.

When I finally arrived at the bookstore, a dense crowd had gathered around the entrance. Pushing and shoving my way through, I broke into the center of the commotion and was instantly met with a scene that left me frozen in place.

There, on the concrete of the sidewalk, my men had forced both of my brothers to lie face down, their heads pressed against the cold ground with the unforgiving barrels of their guns.

The metallic scent of fear and blood mingled in the air as the siblings locked eyes and hurled bitter accusations at one another. Shards of glass, remnants of the broken storefront window, gleamed in the streetlight, likely the work of a security team desperate to control the situation.

For a fleeting moment, I absorbed every grim detail, the shattered glass, the tense silence broken only by the ragged breaths of the onlookers, and the raw, seething betrayal reflected in my brothers' postures.

No explanations were needed. Pavlos had told me precisely what I needed to know.

The time had come to reclaim control, and I was determined to deliver justice with my own hands.

I stepped forward, gripping the pistol I'd drawn during the run, and stood poised at the perfect angle right between them.

"Look at me!" I demanded.

Both brothers slowly turned toward me, their eyes widening in a mix of shock and fear as they saw my gun pointed at them.

"Niko!" Stefano gasped, an amalgam of disbelief and fear.

"Shut up!" I snapped, silencing him with the weight of my anger. "I just want you to look at me clearly as I end this. You thought you could hurt my wife and live? You're both more foolish than I ever imagined."

With that, I pulled the trigger. The eruption of metal and sound was quick and brutal.

One shot for Stefano.

One for Markos.

In that moment, the frightened crowd dispersed like leaves caught in a whirlwind. I barely registered the shock or the disapproving stares that ensued. The only thing that mattered was Laya.

"Where is she?" I shouted, spinning around.

Not far off, I spotted Pavlos behind the jagged shards of the storefront glass.

"Inside," he said firmly as soon as he saw me.

He quickly moved aside, and I jumped through the broken window. The chilling air mixed with the scent of shattered glass and despair as I rushed into the shop. My eyes immediately found Cali and Laya on the floor amid a heap of toppled poetry books. What had once been a serene space was now marked with crimson, resembling a tragic poem written in blood.

I sank to my knees beside Laya, my heart pounding as I reached out to her lifeless body.

"Laya," I cried, taking in her condition.

Her skin was stained with blood, and every shallow breath she took seemed labored.

"Oh, my God!" I exclaimed.

Pavlos's gravelly interruption cut through the tension. "The ambulance is on its way, Niko. Don't move her."

Cali's face blurred with tears as she spoke through her sorrow. "She's okay... I think so. She was talking just a few minutes ago. She's so fucking stubborn!"

Her desperate hope clashed with the grim scene before us.

I could only manage a weak, "I know..." The pain inside me felt like it was eating away at every part of me. Gently, I leaned closer and brushed strands of blood-soaked hair from her cheek while whispering, "Laya, baby, hold on, sweetheart."

I couldn't hide my fear and desperation as I gripped her hand and clutched the ring I had lovingly chosen for her, trying to offer her some of my hope.

"I love you, Laya. Please stay with us."

Cali placed her hand on my arm, her features awash with despair as she shook her head.

"We need to get her to the hospital," she pleaded, just as the distant wail of a siren cut through the heavy air.

I pulled Cali close, my face buried in her tear-streaked hair.

"She's going to be okay, Cali, don't cry," I said, even as I lied to myself.

A mix of dread and helpless anger churned in my stomach as I glanced at Pavlos.

The pain in his eyes spoke volumes. With a resigned shake of his head, he rushed off to meet the approaching ambulance.

Twenty agonizing minutes later, I watched numbly as paramedics hurried my wife through the familiar hospital corridors. This place, where I had often made donations and exchanged quiet words of loyalty, now felt like a battleground of hope. Every bump and jolt in the ambulance felt like another stab of fear as I saw Laya drift further into unconsciousness.

Inside the ambulance, paramedics worked meticulously around her still form while monitors beeped persistently. I stood frozen, praying to any god who might listen that my wife would hold on, even if it meant taking my fate along with hers.

Once we arrived, they whisked her away into the sterile chaos of the operating room, leaving Cali and me to sink into the cold waiting area, accompanied by Pavlos and several security personnel whose somber efficiency deepened our despair.

I began to pace, each step echoing like a restless heartbeat in a quiet room. The anger that had fueled me when I confronted those responsible still burned within me, but now there was no outlet—only a tide of emptiness and profound grief. It felt as though I were reliving the loss of my mother and sister all over again—the sting of guilt and regret that nothing could bring them back.

I silently cursed myself. I should've been there to stop it. I should've protected them. I should've been the one to prevent this nightmare. Every memory of that unbearable loss seared through me, fueling both self-loathing and despair.

I yearned to burst into that operating room and alleviate the pain myself, regaining even a portion of the power I felt I had lost. But deep down, I knew that her life was now in the hands of professionals.

"Fuck all this waiting!" My anger and panic grew with every passing moment. "I'm going back there if we don't hear anything in the next fifteen minutes."

"Niko," Cali whispered, tugging at my sleeve with trembling urgency. "Please, come sit beside me."

The thought of holding back felt like a betrayal to her.

How could I possibly sit by and do nothing while she fought for her life behind those sterile doors? Yet the sorrow in Cali's eyes mirrored my own and silently begged for comfort.

Reluctantly, I sat beside her, wrapping my arm around her trembling shoulders in a tight embrace. Her soft sobs blended with the ticking of the clock on the wall, each beat echoing our shared fear.

"Avra and Vik will be here soon," I informed her. "Pavlos called them."

Cali nodded, her shoulders still trembling as another wave of sobs wracked her body. "I know," she managed between gasps.

"She's going to be okay, Cali," I repeated, trying to reassure her, but everything I said sounded hollow to my own ears. "I promise."

We sat in a heavy silence that stretched on, caught between hope and despair. Every second felt eternal as the uncertainty of her fate gripped me. Despite my inner turmoil, I clung fiercely to the belief that she would pull through.

Across the room, Pavlos met my gaze with a weary expression, creating a fleeting moment of shared understanding amid our sorrow.

It felt like hours passed in that oppressive waiting room before a doctor finally emerged. He moved slowly, his bright blue eyes dark with worry and unreadable thoughts. Cali and I instantly stood up, hope battling the desperation within us.

"Mr. Galanis?" he asked, extending a hand that trembled slightly as I shook it.

Without waiting for more, I managed a tight nod.

"Is my wife, okay?" I demanded, the weight of every unsaid prayer and silent tear pressing down on me as I searched his face for any sign of hope.

He gave me a firm nod, his eyes steady as he spoke. "She survived the surgery. She's asking for you. Follow me, and I'll take you to see her."

"Can I come too?" Cali asked. "She's my sister."

She was coming with us, whether the doctor liked it or not.

He glanced in my direction, met my scowl, and then turned to Cali.

"Sure," he replied with a curt nod, then turned on his heel.

We fell into step behind him, my heart hammering in my chest with a mix of dread and hope.

Layana was alive—she was okay! I closed my eyes for a brief moment, whispering a silent prayer of gratitude to the very god I had nearly condemned only moments earlier.

Cali squeezed my hand, her gaze tentative yet reassuring.

"It's okay," I murmured to her.

The doctor guided us down what seemed like an endless series of immaculate white hallways. Our shoes clicked rhythmically on the shiny linoleum floor, each step echoing against the sterile walls. The corridor was lit by fluorescent bulbs reflecting off every polished surface, while the scent of antiseptic mixed with an unidentifiable clinical aroma. Upon reaching a door on our right, the doctor opened it and motioned for us to enter.

"I'll be right back," he assured me in a calm, measured tone before stepping away. "I just need a minute, then I'll return to discuss your wife's condition."

"Her condition?" My entire body froze like a shockwave, immediately tightening the grip of worry in my gut.

I had only heard that she had made it through the surgery. Was there something else that had gone horribly wrong?

I rushed through the door. My eyes immediately fell upon Layana's fragile form lying in the sterile room.

I stood frozen, unable to do anything but stare at her, entangled in a maze of wires connected to beeping machines. Her exposed shoulders revealed bruises and bandaged areas that sharply contrasted with her pallid skin.

A fresh surge of anger welled up inside me, nearly boiling over as I silently cursed my brothers under my breath while I advanced as fast as possible in her direction without running.

She lifted her head as I reached out to take her hand.

When my fingers brushed against it, I resisted the instinct to draw back. Needles jutted from her fragile skin like unwelcome thorns.

"Sorry," I whispered, shock mingling with concern. "Laya, are you okay?"

Before I could collect my thoughts, Cali rushed to the other side of her sister, tears streaming down her face as she saw her sibling's fragile state.

"Shhh, I'm fine," Laya reassured us. "It looks worse than it is. Cali, please stop crying. I'm okay."

My eyes scanned her frame, absorbing every visible inch of her.

"What did the doctor say?" I asked.

"Nothing much, actually," she replied softly, the mystery still lingering in the air. "I caught him whispering with the nurses, but I couldn't make out what was said. He only mentioned that he would come for you when I asked for you again."

"He said he'd be right back," I replied. "I'm sure everything is fine."

She offered me a crooked, tired smile, her eyes reflecting both sleepiness and hope.

In that moment, my heart brimmed with gratitude, surpassing my body's exhaustion. The tension that had knotted inside me slowly unraveled until I felt as weak and vulnerable as a puppy.

"I'm so glad you're okay, my love," I whispered, tucking a stray strand of hair from her forehead.

"Me too," she replied, then asked, "What happened to your brothers?"

I shook my head, determined to keep the moment free from further worries. "Shh, we can discuss all of that later. You're safe now. I promise you that. Nobody will ever hurt you again, Laya."

"Niko, it wasn't your fault," she insisted, but I knew the truth, and nothing would persuade me otherwise.

"Hush," I said, placing my finger on her lips. "We have all the time in the world to discuss this later. Let's focus on getting you completely healed, all right?"

Glancing over my shoulder, I scanned the hallway for the doctor, my impatience growing with each passing second. I exchanged a worried glance with Cali before quickly looking away.

I wouldn't stop worrying until I knew Layana was out of the woods.

"I'll be right back," I announced, leaving Laya and Cali to their quiet conversation as I set off to find the doctor.

I left the door ajar, a fragile lifeline connecting me to her side, resolute in my determination to return as swiftly as possible.

My heart pounded louder as I approached the nurses' station, anxiety swirling with each heartbeat.

"I'd like to speak with my wife's doctor. He said he would return shortly. Where is he?"

The nurse looked up at me with calm efficiency. "Oh, yes, of course. You're Mr. Galanis, aren't you?"

"Yes," I confirmed with a tight nod.

"Dr. Moros will be back shortly. I'm sure he'll find you as soon as he can."

"His name is Dr. Moros?"

A chill of dread ran down my spine. In the labyrinth of Greek mythology, Moros personified impending doom and death.

"Yes, Mr. Galanis," she confirmed.

"You have to be kidding me," I couldn't help but shout. "I want another doctor! Immediately!"

Over my dead body would anyone associated with dying treat my wife.

Every instinct in me screamed to grab her and leave.

"There is nothing to worry about, Mr. Galanis. I assure you." The nurse's lips curved into a grin, and she shook her head as if my outburst was amusing. "I know it sounds odd, but believe it or not, many consider it good luck to have Dr. Moros as their physician."

"Is that so?" I questioned, bitterness mingling with relief at her attempt to soothe my fears.

"He's a brilliant doctor—meticulous, compassionate, the very first I'd trust with my own family," she assured warmly.

"A little reassurance," I grumbled, though the tension in my jaw softened slightly. "Perhaps he should have a less foreboding name that doesn't scare patients half to death."

Her laughter was like a gentle melody in the clinical glare of the ward.

"He won't be long," she promised.

I nodded and returned to Laya's room. Inside, surrounded by the sterile brightness and the hum of medical devices, I found Laya and Cali engaged in a silly conversation that had them giggling intermittently between whatever outrageous things Cali was discussing.

I paused to watch them, the sound of their joy providing a balm for my tormented soul. Just hours earlier, I feared I would never hear my wife laugh again, but now that worry dissolved in the melody of that sound.

"The doctor is taking his sweet time," I remarked wryly.

"Well, he is the doctor of death or something," Cali teased, her humor a splash against our shared anxieties. "Maybe that's a good omen."

"I see you were informed of his name too," I said, half-smiling.

"I told her," Laya responded, intertwining her fingers with mine. "Niko, relax, babe. I'm okay. I promise."

I couldn't help but offer a sardonic retort. "I'll relax once I hear that reassurance from someone other than the person who, despite being shot, was trying to get up and fight back."

I shot her a pointed look, and in response, she glanced at Cali as if to share a secret rebuke.

"What? Why are you looking at me like that? I simply told the truth." Cali shrugged defensively. "We had time to talk while we were waiting."

"I craved vengeance," Laya admitted, clearly annoyed with her predicament.

"I understand."

She nodded slowly at me, a silent promise passing between us. What else was there to say? I understood her urge, and luckily, I'd dealt with it.

"Thank you," she whispered, and I leaned down to kiss her forehead with a tenderness that belied the storm raging inside me.

"The pleasure was all mine, but you're welcome," I said, turning back toward the door. "Where is this blasted doctor?"

With that, I rose and resumed pacing, each step echoing my inner turbulence—a blend of hope, fury, and an undying commitment to shield the woman I cherished more than life itself.

"Niko, seriously." Laya's exasperated interjection almost

had me smiling. "I am fine. Let the doctor tend to the patients who require his immediate care."

I turned to face her, shaking my head slowly to dispel the turbulent emotions swirling inside.

"Must I remind you, my dearest wife, that it was my reckless brother who shot you? A jagged bullet tore into your flesh, forcing you into surgery. As much as I long to assert that you are the very embodiment of perfect health and beauty, I cannot deny the harsh reality. You are far from okay, Laya!"

"Stop being so dramatic," she retorted, rolling her eyes.

A wry smile tugged at my lips as I replied, "I suppose I should have been even more dramatic."

Her brow furrowed in confusion. "What are you talking about?"

"You should always have an army by your side, my love. If I had sent even more guards to protect you, none of this would have happened. But rest assured, this will never happen again. Not only will you be surrounded by a battalion of well-trained fighters, but you will never leave my sight. I promise to protect you to the very end if I have to."

"Oh my God," she said, shaking her head and sighing as if to dispel the intensity of the statement. "Good luck with that, Niko. Need I remind you that I am a grown woman, perfectly capable of caring for myself?"

I frowned and countered, "Then why are you lying there with a gunshot wound and a head injury?"

A flash of anger crossed her features, and I instantly regretted my reaction.

What was wrong with me?

"I'm so sorry, Layana," I blurted, rushing to her side with desperate urgency. "I'm incredibly frustrated. I can't believe this has happened, and all I want is to take you home, lay you in our bed, and keep you safe forever."

Slowly, the flames in her gaze softened, replaced by a forgiving smile illuminating the dim room like the first rays of dawn. As I cupped her cheek tenderly, I leaned in and brushed my lips against hers, a kiss filled with both apology and promise.

"Are you always going to be so overprotective, darling?" she teased, despite the lingering shadows of the day.

I nodded, fully aware of my nature.

"Yes, absolutely," I affirmed. "It comes hand in hand with my love—a complete package deal."

Her gaze locked with mine, deep and earnest.

"I understand that, my love," she murmured, her irises sparkling with both affection and fierce resolve. "But please, believe me when I say that if you ever try to keep me confined like a caged bird, you'll unleash the wild tiger within me."

My eyes widened in startled surprise at her fierce declaration.

"I hope you know that's not what I—" I began, wanting desperately to defuse the charged air around us.

"Hello!" the doctor cheerfully announced as he entered the room, his presence slicing through our quiet conversation like a sudden gust of wind.

I slowly turned to face him, bracing myself for the weight of his impending news. My heart raced in anticipation, and my muscles tensed as I prepared for a stern lecture or some grave revelation.

Instead of any preamble directed at me, he moved purposefully toward Laya. His eyes scanned every detail as he examined the neatly wrapped bandages covering her wounds. At the same time, his skilled fingers explored the array of tubes accompanying the rhythmic beeps from the machine connected to her frail body.

I took a sharp breath, praying for calm. This harbinger of dread tested every ounce of my patience. He reached the end of the bed, grabbed her chart with methodical efficiency, and quickly scribbled a few notes before finally lifting his gaze to meet Laya's eyes.

"Mrs. Galanis, may I have your permission to discuss your medical condition openly in front of your husband and sister?" he asked, maintaining a professional demeanor that conveyed the seriousness of the subject.

Laya's eyes widened as she gave a timid nod before saying, "O-of course, yes."

"Excellent, thank you," he replied, his attention once again focused solely on her as though we were mere spectators of an intimate, life-altering conversation.

Cali and I exchanged nervous glances, our unspoken understanding suggesting the seriousness of the matter about to be revealed.

"We conduct a complete blood screening on all of our patients before preparing them for surgery," he began, each word measured and deliberate.

Laya furrowed her brows in confusion as she nodded, her eyes reflecting a mix of worry and perplexity.

"Your results revealed something unexpected that we need to discuss. Fortunately, the bullet only pierced your shoulder. We conducted precise, localized imaging on that area, ensuring the necessary surgical intervention was targeted and successful. We're confident that we've eliminated all imminent threats, so further surgery isn't necessary."

Every sentence out of his mouth added to the already palpable tension in the room. Each of us held our breath in quiet suspense as we awaited his next revelation.

Time seemed to stretch endlessly as this gloomy harbinger of fate savored each prolonged moment.

Was my wife teetering on the brink of death? What was the astonishing secret that had been uncovered? I felt an uncontrollable urge to shake him, to jolt him into revealing the truth more quickly.

Internally, my fists clenched as I urged my agitated body and the enigmatic Dr. Doom to end the delay and reveal the truth without hesitation.

"Mrs. Galanis, were you aware that you're pregnant?" he finally asked, his tone matter-of-fact yet holding an undercurrent of genuine astonishment.

In an instant, the room fell silent. My heart skipped a beat and then seemed to stop entirely. It was as if the deep, unyielding void of this revelation consumed time.

"Pregnant?" Laya's surprise was as evident as mine.

"I take it from your reaction that the news is as unexpected for you as it is for your husband?" he pressed.

I shook my head, struggling to draw in life-giving breath.

"We-uh-we weren't planning on conceiving," Laya stammered, her face growing pale.

"Oh, you were using birth control?" the doctor pressed further, his curiosity unwavering. "May I ask what method?"

I almost laughed out loud. The absurdity of it all overwhelmed me. We had never once discussed any plan or precaution regarding birth control. My mind spun, realizing we resembled a couple of reckless, passionate teenagers, indulging in wild abandon as if invincible and untouchable.

I shook my head slowly. "We weren't trying to avoid it, any more than we were trying to make it happen."

"I see," he replied with a knowing nod. "Now that you know, I'll schedule an appointment with our best obstetrician immediately. Rest assured, everything appears very healthy so far—the baby is unharmed."

"Thank you." The relief and wonder on her face were beyond beautiful.

As the doctor departed, I recalled the nurse's remark about his ironic luck—a bearer of fortuitous tidings amidst despair.

When my gaze met Laya's, an unspoken connection sparked a wave of unexpected joy within me.

"Are we really going to have a baby?" I breathed, my thoughts swirling with a mix of disbelief and affection.

"I suppose we are," she breathed, tears of fear and elation welling in her eyes. "How do you feel about it?"

"How do I feel?" I echoed, my heart overflowing with both fierce love and spine-tingling terror.

The idea of having a tiny being to nurture and protect with every ounce of passion alongside my beautiful wife terrified and thrilled me beyond measure.

"I'm utterly shocked but overjoyed," I confessed, a bittersweet smile tugging at my lips.

"Me too," she sobbed, her tears mapping the story of our lives on her cheeks.

"Why are you so shocked by this? I'm not." Cali threw her hands up in the air, her exasperation comical. "It's like living with rabbits that mate day and night. I'm amazed it took this long for it to happen."

I shrugged my shoulders, glancing in Laya's direction, and smirked. "She's not wrong."

The door swung open at that moment, and the mood immediately shifted. Avra and Vik rushed into the room, worry etched on their faces. They suddenly stopped as they took in the scene of our happiness.

"I'm all right!" Laya declared briskly, a spark of reassurance. "And I'm pregnant!"

Avra's eyes lit up with delight while Vik's jaw dropped.

Avra rushed forward and hugged Laya, conveying volumes of sisterly love and shared happiness.

As I watched them revel in the joy of our discovery, a deep happiness surged through me, a feeling I hadn't experienced since Mama and Cora passed away. We hadn't expected our family to expand so quickly. Yet, in that electrifying moment, I vowed to dedicate my life to protecting everyone we loved—Laya, our unborn child, and all those who were part of our unconventional world.

In the embrace of shadow and passion, I'd found my sanctuary. This was no ordinary love—our union was forged in darkness and tempered by desire. As the night deepened, I resolved to be the steadfast guardian of our fierce and tempestuous bond. This love illuminated even the bleakest corners of our twisted, beautiful existence.

Are you ready to see Calista regain her strength and meet the man who heals her heart as he seeks vengeance against those who have hurt her?

Grab POWER, the conclusion of the Sisters of Wrath Series.
The Vitalis Sisters will claim it all and serve their enemies on a platter for all to enjoy.

https://geni.us/PowerSiennaSnow

Calista Vitalis vowed never to let anyone control her again.

But in a world where loyalty and power are everything,
she has no choice but to marry Leon Boscos,
a man as ruthless as he is captivating.

Forged by loss and driven by vengeance, Leon has become an
unrivaled force determined to protect what's his. Yet, their
union isn't about love—it's a strategic alliance, a dangerous
game where passion is a weapon.

With every stolen touch and heated glance, the lines between
revenge and desire blur,

igniting an intensity neither anticipated.
As past enemies resurface, bringing deadly threats, Calista and Leon must confront their own dark secrets.

Will their fiery bond consume them, or will their mutual vengeance forge a strength no enemy can break?

In this explosive conclusion to the Sisters of Wrath series, desire is deadly, and love could be the ultimate weapon.

Perfect for readers who crave fierce heroines, ruthless antiheroes, and passion so dangerous it could destroy them both, fans of JT Geissinger, Sophie Lark, and Rina Kent will be captivated by ***Power***.

Dangerous King

Vicious Prince

Deceptive Knight

Ruthless Heir

Violent Delights

Claim

Defy

Own

Sin and Lies

Sin and Betrayal

Sin and Deception

Sister of Wrath

Legacy

Power

Sinful Gods

Forbidden Empire (Oct 8, 2025)

Dark Alliance (2026)

Broken Crown (2026)

Collections

Reckless Romeo

Take Me To Bed (2019)

Meet Me Under The Mistletoe (2021)

Nightingale (A charity anthology in support of Ukraine) - (2022)

Darkly Ever After (An Organized Crime Anthology) (2022)

RARE Melbourne Anthology (2023)

About the Author

USA Today bestselling author Sienna Snow loves to craft dark and extremely sexy stories centered on anti-heroes and the strong, unapologetic women who bring them to their knees. Her books immerse you in a world of indulgence, suspense, and undeniable steam.

Her heroines are vibrant and self-assured, often discovering love and romance under unconventional circumstances. Sienna offers her readers enticing glimpses of steamy romance filled with empowerment and indulgent satisfaction.

Sienna loves a life filled with travel and adventure. She plans to explore even the farthest corners of the world and revel in experiencing the diverse cultures along the way. When she isn't writing or traveling, Sienna is focused on her "happily ever after" with her husband and children.

Sign up for her newsletter for notifications of releases, book sales, events, and so much more.
http://www.siennasnow.com/newsletter
contact@siennasnow.com

* 9 7 9 8 8 8 5 3 5 0 4 2 6 *